3

in series

Dear Daphne

Home, Hearth, and the Holidays

Home,
Hearth,
and the
Holidays

MELODY CARLSON

This is a work of fiction. All characters and events portrayed in this novel are either fictitious or used fictitiously.

HOME, HEARTH, AND THE HOLIDAYS

WhiteFire Publishing
13607 Bedford Rd NE
Cumberland, MD 21502

ISBN: 978-1-939023-71-1 (print)
          978-1-939023-72-8 (digital)

Chapter 1

With Thanksgiving behind her, Daphne Ballinger was *almost* ready to start thinking about Christmas. However, she was not as ready as her neighbor across the street. Sabrina Fontaine had started putting up colorful lights two days *before* Thanksgiving. Daphne's new charge, seven-year-old Mabel, thought it was wonderful, but Daphne felt it was a tad premature.

She decided on Friday afternoon, though, that it wasn't too soon to start baking Christmas cookies. Her Aunt Dee had always made cutout cookies right after Thanksgiving. It was a tradition she and Daphne had enjoyed for years while Daphne was growing up. They would bake dozens of them. Then they would layer them between wax paper and freeze them unfrosted. About week before Christmas they'd get them out and have a cookie decorating party.

After Daphne explained the process to Mabel, they both donned aprons and went to work. To be honest, part of Daphne's motivation was to distract Mabel from the fact that Daniel had relocated down the street that morning, back to his mother's slightly dilapidated house.

"I don't see why Uncle Daniel didn't want to stay here with us," Mabel said as Daphne poured sugar into the measuring cup.

"Maybe he needs more space." Daphne watched as Mabel dumped it into the bowl, then handed her the butter to put in. She didn't want Mabel to know that she'd been secretly relieved when Daniel announced he was going to stay at his mother's house. Not because Daniel Myers wasn't a nice guy and well-mannered houseguest, but simply because it had started to feel a bit awkward. For one thing, he was so good looking. That in itself was a bit disconcerting. She just wasn't used to having a tall, dark, and handsome marine pop around a corner in her house, greeting her with a hearty *good morning!* Especially when she was still blurry eyed, in her bathrobe, with her red hair suffering from severe bed-head. Like this morning.

"Okay." Daphne handed Mabel a brown egg. "Try to get it into the bowl."

Mabel cracked it so hard that it split in half, sending gooey egg down both sides of the bowl. "Oops."

Daphne grabbed a paper towel to sop up the mess. "It's okay." She got out another egg.

"I liked having Uncle Daniel in our house," Mabel said as Daphne picked up the egg carton. "And I don't even care that he wakes me up sometimes."

"*What?*" Daphne stopped from getting the next egg, staring at Mabel with concern. "Uh, why does he wake you up, sweetie?"

"I forgot." Mabel covered her mouth with her hand. "It's a secret."

Daphne set down the egg carton, watching Mabel closely.

"Well, it's a secret I need to hear, Mabel. Especially since Uncle Daniel has been staying in my house. Please, tell me why he woke you."

"It's not his fault, Aunt Daphne. He just has really bad dreams. I heard him yelling the first night. It was *weird.*"

"I can imagine." Daphne was surprised—why hadn't she woken up too? "Did it frighten you?"

"At first. I went to see what was wrong, but it looked like he was asleep. I told him about it in the morning."

"And what did Uncle Daniel say?" Daphne wondered if the ex-marine might be struggling with a little PTSD.

"He told me he had a bad dream. He said not to worry about it. And he asked me not to tell anyone." Mabel looked concerned. "You won't, will you?"

"The secret is safe with me." Daphne handed Mabel another egg. "Try it again. More gently this time."

With an intense expression, Mabel gave the egg a careful crack before she dumped the contents—as well as some shell shards—into the confines of the mixing bowl.

"Perfect." Daphne extracted the eggshell pieces from the sugar and butter and handed her another egg, watching as she cracked this one neatly into the bowl. "Nicely done."

Mabel wiped her fingers on the paper towel. "Is Uncle Daniel going to stay in Appleton *forever?*" Her question sounded hesitant. Was she perhaps fishing for information?

Daphne handed her a teaspoon. "I don't think he knows for sure yet." She suspected Mabel had overheard the adults' conversation this morning. Daphne had been surprised to hear that Daniel was interested in returning to the Marines and being based in North Carolina—about a thousand miles from Appleton.

"He showed me his fancy Marine uniform. He's going to wear it to Grandma's memorial next week. It's really nice."

"Uh huh." Daphne poured vanilla into the teaspoon, then watched as Mabel slowly poured it into the bowl.

"Is Uncle Daniel still a marine?"

"Not exactly. He's kind of on a break, but he could go back to the Marines if he wanted to."

"Does he want to?"

"I don't know. I don't think he knows for sure either. I'm sure it'll take a while for him to figure everything out."

"You mean about *me*?" Mabel tipped her head to one side with a quizzical look in her dark brown eyes. In many ways this little girl was much older than seven. "Does he have to figure out if he wants to keep me?"

"Well, yes...that's a very big part of it. As you know, your grandmother planned for your uncle to care for you. I already explained about her will making him your guardian."

Mabel bit her lip as she set the teaspoon on the table.

"And, really, sweetie, it's not for you to worry about these things. Everything is going to work out just fine." Daphne smiled as she handed her the big wooden spoon, hoping to convey more confidence than she felt. This wasn't easy for any of them.

"I really do love Uncle Daniel." Mabel struggled to stir the stiff ingredients. "But I love you too, Aunt Daphne."

Daphne gave Mabel a squeeze. "And I love you too, Mabel. But just like your grandma, I want what's best for you." She took the wooden spoon from her. "How about I get this softened up a little, then you can really stir it up." Daphne put her whole arm into it, stirring vigorously in an attempt to distract herself from this uncomfortable conversation...that she had known was coming.

As they sifted dry ingredients into a separate bowl, Mabel grew very quiet. Daphne wasn't sure if it was because she was concentrating on the measurements or something more. But by the time they had rolled out the cookie dough, cut a couple dozen Christmas shapes, and put the first batch into the oven, Mabel finally spoke up again.

"I want to be here with *you*, Aunt Daphne," she declared as she reached for the rolling pin.

Daphne made a stiff smile. "You *are* here with me."

"I mean for always." She looked up with misty eyes. "I do love Uncle Daniel...but I want to stay *here.*"

Daphne pursed her lips, trying to think of an appropriate response. "I want you to stay here with me too, Mabel. But it's not really our decision."

"Why?"

"It's a grownup thing." Daphne tried to think of a simple explanation for child custody laws and came up empty. "But I have been praying about it, Mabel. A lot. I've been asking God to make sure you get to live in the place that's the very best for you. But we don't really know where that is...yet."

"I know the best place." Mabel reached for the angel cookie cutter. "Appleton is best."

"I have to agree with you on that." Daphne picked up the tree-shaped cutter, sinking it into the dough.

"Your house is the best too. And my school is the best. I didn't used to like it, but now that I have friends I like it a lot. And I like my teacher too. Miss Simmons is really nice." Mabel reached for a star shape now. "And I *love* my BFF Lola." She pointed to a lopsided angel on the cookie sheet. "That cookie is for Lola. See, I put an L on it."

"I'm sure she'll like that."

"And I love you, Aunt Daphne." She pointed at the cats sitting in the sunshine by the window. "And I love Ethel and Lucy. And I love Sabrina and Tootsie. And I love going to church. And I love this house. And—"

"And you are just so full of love." Daphne laughed as she wiped a smudge of flower from Mabel's nose. "Isn't it wonderful to have so much love to share? You're a blessed girl, Mabel Myers."

Mabel sighed happily as she peeled the star off the dough board, setting it onto the cookie sheet. Daphne wasn't sure these shapes would be very recognizable when they came out of the oven, but at least they were having fun. And it was good to see Mabel happy—despite the uncertainty of her situation. Although, from what Daphne knew, Mabel's situation had been fairly uncertain since birth.

As she removed a sheet of cookies from the oven, Daphne recalled the first time she'd met Mabel. Back in early October, she'd spotted the scraggly little girl attempting to abduct one of the cats. When questioned, Mabel had claimed it was because she was lonely and "wanted a friend." And so Daphne had offered her friendship—and pumpkins. It was a perfect arrangement. But as they wheeled the wagon of pumpkins down the street, Daphne had begun to understand what a poor lost waif this child was. With a dad in prison, a mother who'd died of an overdose, and a grandmother with terminal cancer...Mabel's sad little life had seemed almost hopeless.

"I'm going to pray for God to let me stay here forever," Mabel declared as Daphne placed the hot cookies on a cooling rack. "Because this is the best place in the whole world."

Daphne suppressed a feeling of guilty sadness as she put the next cookie sheet into the oven. Perhaps she'd been mistaken to create such a comfy haven for Mabel. Turning the guest room into a little girl's dream room, getting her a whole new wardrobe, new toys and activities. She'd only done these things out of love, trying to make up for the abundant losses in the child's life. But perhaps she'd set Mabel up for heartache. Especially if Daniel decided to relocate the little girl to North Carolina.

"There's the doorbell," Mabel called out. "Can I get it?"

"Sure." Daphne peered out the window to see Lola on the front porch. Wearing a zebra-striped helmet, she tugged on one of her blonde pigtails with a hopeful expression as her pink scooter leaned expectantly against the porch steps. As Daphne set cooled cookies on a plate, she could hear Mabel's happy shrieks reverberating through the big old house. She imagined the girls hugging, like they always did, acting as if they hadn't seen each other for weeks instead of a couple of days.

"Can I ride my scooter with Lola?" Mabel asked with excitement.

"Put on your jacket and helmet." Daphne held out the plate of unfrosted cookies. "Maybe you girls should take some cookies along in case you get hungry while you're scooting about."

They gratefully agreed, and Daphne used paper napkins to make two little bundles, helping them to tuck them into their jacket pockets. As the girls hurried outside, Daphne followed.

From the front porch, she reminded Mabel of the scooter rules that they'd established after Sabrina had presented Mabel with the flashy purple scooter and matching helmet a week ago. "To help her get past losing her grandmother," Sabrina had said apologetically to Daphne. "I hope you don't mind." Of course, she didn't.

"And you can go all the way around the block since Lola is with you. But no crossing any streets. And make sure you watch for cars backing out of driveways." She always felt like a "real mother" when she said things like this—and that felt nice. So nice, in fact, that it troubled her. After all, she was not a mother. She wasn't even an aunt.

As the girls took off down the sidewalk, Daphne remained on the porch, just watching...and thinking about what Mabel had confided to her. She wasn't too surprised that Daniel had nightmares. It seemed like many servicemen who'd seen active duty suffered from some sort of PTSD. Hopefully Daniel was getting help to deal with it. And it was a relief that he'd been honest with Mabel about it. Another good sign that he was up for the task of parenting. It should've been reassuring to her.

Daphne could hear the girls shriek as they reached the corner. Feeling concerned, she leaned over the railing, peering down the street to see if someone had fallen, but it turned out to be a happy shriek, and now they were tearing around the corner. She glanced across the street at Sabrina's elaborate Christmas decorations. "I'm pulling out all the stops," she'd happily told Daphne yesterday. "For Mabel and me—it's our first Christmas in Appleton."

Daphne sighed to think it might also be Mabel's last Christmas here. Not that she planned to let Mabel in on this.

But Daphne wondered which of them would be hurting more if Daniel swooped Mabel off to North Carolina. Mabel would get a new home, a new school, a new teacher, and before long she'd probably find a new BFF as well. But Daphne would never get another Mabel.

She swallowed hard against the lump growing in her throat. It was too easy to get in over your head when a child was involved. She'd only been trying to be a good neighbor, to help a child in need—and look where it had gotten her. Sometimes, like now, it just didn't seem fair.

Chapter 2

"**H**ey neighbor!" Sabrina waved from the sidewalk.

Daphne greeted her from the porch, watching as her petite blonde friend scurried up with her little dog scampering at her heels. The brown Chihuahua was sporting a hot pink jacket with white fur trim. Never mind that Tootsie was a male dog—just one reason his name was fitting. But Sabrina, being Sabrina, dressed Tootsie however she liked. Often to match her own colorful outfits, although she was wearing an aqua velour jogging suit today. The rhinestone bedazzles down the front of her jacket sparkled in the sunlight as she came onto the porch. Daphne chuckled to remember how Sabrina considered outfits like this *casual* wear.

"How are you two doing?" Daphne smiled brightly, hoping to cover her melancholy thoughts.

"We just had our little walk. And Tootsie got three compliments from three different ladies." She grinned. "He's the talk of the town."

"I'm surprised you aren't hitting the mall today." Daphne

knew how Sabrina loved to shop. Even burdened downed with multiple shopping bags and four-inch heels, this fashionista could outlast Daphne by hours. She was like the Energizer bunny on triple shot espressos.

"Oh, I *never* shop on Black Friday," Sabrina said in her honey-coated Southern accent. "Goodness—can you imagine little ol' me grubbing around with a bunch of greedy bargain hunters? Or camping in a parking lot just to get a big screen TV?" She wrinkled her nose. "That is not my style, thank you very much."

Daphne nodded as she bent down to pat Tootsie. "Nor mine."

"Although I must admit I found a couple of great deals on HSN." Sabrina winked. "Wait until you see the Christmas dress I just ordered for Mabel. Her favorite shade of lavender too. It's velvety velour with lots of lacey trim. She'll look like an angel in it."

"It sounds perfect. Mabel just took off with Lola—on their scooters."

"I saw them." Sabrina nodded.

"They look so cute together. I'll have to snag some pictures when they come back." Daphne frowned to realize that she should be gathering lots of photos of Mabel...that might be all she'd have before long.

"I also observed that hunky marine of yours a couple hours ago. He was toting his big duffle bag down the street." Sabrina's brow creased. "Don't tell me you gave him the old heave-ho?"

"Not exactly." Daphne shrugged. "I'd only meant to invite him to stay with us for his first night here. And that was because Mabel insisted—and the next day was Thanksgiving. But after three days and two nights, I think it was time."

"If it were me, I'd be thinking of excuses to keep that boy around." Sabrina giggled.

Daphne glanced at her watch. "Yikes. I need to run before our cookies are toast." She whipped open the door. "Time for tea?"

"Tea and cookies?" she asked hopefully.

"Sure."

"Let me go put Tootsie in the house and I'll be right back."

Relieved that Sabrina wasn't bringing Tootsie inside, which always sent the two cats into a dither, Daphne made a beeline for the kitchen where the timer was dinging impatiently. She was just putting the darkened cookies on the cooling rack when Sabrina returned.

"I'll clear this off." Sabrina started gathering up the baking supplies, setting them on the counter. She paused to examine the cookies. "Interesting." She pointed to a dark misshapen one. "That one looks like a gorilla."

"It's supposed to be an angel." Daphne chuckled. "I guess it's a gorilla angel."

"Seems a little early for Christmas cookies. Unlike decorations, they go stale." Sabrina rinsed the washrag and started wiping flour from the table.

"We're going to freeze most of them to decorate later. That's what my Aunt Dee always used to do with me."

"Good idea." Sabrina sat down.

"It makes the decorating day more fun because you're not worn out from making so many cookies. We used to get pretty creative with our frosting."

"For a single girl you're really quite domestic," Sabrina told Daphne.

"Thanks...I guess."

"And I must say, Thanksgiving dinner was fabulous," Sabrina said. "I'm so grateful you included me. Which reminds me, I have a thank-you card to bring over to you."

"But you just said thank you. You don't need to give me a card."

"It's how we Southern women are trained. *Mannerly-ness is next to godliness.*"

"I thought that was supposed to be cleanliness."

"Trust me, etiquette supersedes hygiene—at least where I was raised." Sabrina laughed. "Anyway, that's how it is in my family."

"Well, Thanksgiving was fun for me too." Daphne put the teakettle on. "It was the first time I've ever really done it myself. I mean cooking everything and having a traditional sit-down dinner. It was a challenge, but fun too."

"Everyone had a great time."

"I actually thought I'd made too much food. I figured we'd be eating leftovers for days. But there's hardly anything left."

"That's because it was all so delicious." Sabrina patted her midsection. "I have you to blame for the fact that I'm wearing sweatpants today. I needed the expandable waistband."

Daphne laughed.

"So, I'm dying to know, Daphne. What do you really think of Daniel?" Sabrina asked with unveiled curiosity. "You've had plenty of time to get acquainted now."

"I think he's a nice guy. And I can tell he's quite fond of Mabel. They really hit it off." Once again, Daphne considered how she'd feel if he took Mabel to North Carolina.

"*But...?*"

"But what?" Daphne turned away, focusing on putting a spoonful of Earl Gray tea leaves into the teapot.

"Something is troubling you. I can tell. What is it?"

"I'm fine," Daphne said lightly as she dipped the spoon in the tea canister again.

"You can't fool me. I saw you standing on the porch, looking like you'd lost your best friend. What's going on?"

Daphne took in a deep breath. "Oh, I suppose I was just wondering how it would be if Daniel took Mabel away."

"*Took Mabel away?*" Sabrina sounded truly alarmed. "What on earth are you talking about, Daphne Ballenger?"

"Well, despite his early discharge, Daniel's not sure he's ready to give up the Marines yet. And, really, you can't blame him. He hadn't finished his twenty years, and it sounds like the benefits get significantly better the longer you stay. Anyway, there's a Marine base in North Carolina and he was talking about taking Mabel there with—"

"He cannot do that," Sabrina exclaimed. "We won't let him take our little girl away from us."

"She's not *our* little girl." Daphne placed a pair of cups on the table with a grim expression.

"But we rescued her. And Vera was truly grateful for our little intervention. I bet if you'd asked Vera—before she passed on—she probably would've given you custody of Mabel. She really liked you, Daphne. She trusted you with Mabel."

"Maybe...but I don't know that she would've handed over Mabel like that. Family is family, Sabrina. And as dysfunctional as Vera's family might've been, she probably wanted Mabel to be with blood relatives—like her only son. Besides, as you can see, Daniel is really a great guy. And Mabel loves him. And like he was telling me, a Marine base isn't such a bad place for kids to grow up."

"But Mabel needs a mom. She needs a woman's touch. Remember what a mess she was when you first found her, Daphne. Good grief, I couldn't even get a brush through that tangled up mess of brown hair on her little head. That's why I had to cut it all off, although I must say she's adorable in the pixie cut. Still, my point is—*Mabel needs a mother's touch.*"

"I know. But it's not up to us to—"

"Call your lawyer," Sabrina commanded. "See if Jake can fix things for you. Didn't he get you temporary guardianship? Maybe you could prove that—"

"*Sabrina,*" Daphne said firmly but gently. "I appreciate your concern, but really there's nothing we can do. We need to let it play out. It's possible that Daniel will realize that a single man in the military doesn't make for the best parent." She sighed. "At least that's what I'm hoping."

"I was hoping that you and Daniel would hit it off," Sabrina confessed. "He's *so* good looking, Daphne. I can't believe you let him get away like that."

Daphne couldn't help but laugh as she poured hot water into the teapot. "I did not *let him get away.* He simply went to stay at his mother's house."

"But that place is such a dump. Well, other than the room we fixed up for Mabel, and I can't imagine him staying there—sleeping in the little princess bed." She chuckled.

"He's going to start cleaning it up," Daphne explained. "To get it ready to sell. He hopes to get it listed next week, and to sell it before the New Year."

"Who buys a home during the holidays?"

"I don't know, but that's his plan. I've already given him names of some of the guys who helped around here. He said he'll call Tommy Troutman today. Wants to get the whole place painted, starting with the exterior before the winter weather sets in. According to the weather forecast, it's going to get really cold next week. We might even see snow."

"Maybe while he's fixing his little old house up, he'll discover that Appleton is a delightful town. Maybe good sense will kick in and he'll decide to stick around," she made a mischievous grin, "and maybe he'll fall in love with you and the three of you will all live happily ever after—*right here.*"

"You sound just like Mabel."

"Aha." Sabrina pointed a pink polished nail in the air. "So that's what Mabel wants too."

"But like I told Mabel, I've been praying for what's best. What's best for everyone. Only God knows what that is. We have to be patient."

"So are you saying you don't like Daniel at all? There's no attraction? You don't think you could be romantically interested in him?"

Daphne let out an exasperated sigh as she filled their cups with steaming amber tea, inhaling the soothing sweet scent. It reminded her of lavender.

"It's not like you can afford to be real picky," Sabrina continued. "I mean, if you haven't noticed, the clock is ticking. And, from what I can see, you're determined to let all the available bachelors just slip through your fingers. And I hate to say it, honey, but you're not getting any younger either."

"Thanks so much." Daphne rolled her eyes as she sat down across from Sabrina.

"Seriously, girlfriend. Your Aunt Dee's generous offer to leave you everything will expire in *less than six months*."

As she sipped her tea, Daphne regretted having spilt the beans to Sabrina. To be fair, Sabrina had pretty much figured it out on her own. And, really, it was a bit of a relief to have someone else in the know about her deceased aunt's strange will. Someone besides Aunt Dee's attorney, that is. Although Jake McPheeters was fairly laid back about it. But sometimes she wished Sabrina would get a mild case of amnesia—at least about this.

"I'm surprised you're not giving me the day, hour, and minute count," Daphne said wryly. "Maybe while you're decorating your house for Christmas, you could put up a gigantic illuminated time-clock to remind me of my fate every time I look out my kitchen window."

"You know, I've considered putting a special app on my phone to track it for you," Sabrina said in all seriousness.

"Oh, puleeze." Daphne rolled her eyes.

"You need someone to encourage you, Daphne. Honestly, you could lose it all. This beautiful Victorian house that you've worked so hard to fix up. And think about the fabulous garden Mick helped you to create. And that gorgeous old Corvette in the garage. What about your adorable cats? Not to mention your sweet little ol' neighbor who loves you like a sister. You could lose *everything*! In less than six months too!"

"Thanks for the news flash." Daphne grimaced.

"Well, time's a wasting." Sabrina made a dramatic shudder. "Honestly, with the holidays upon us, you couldn't even start planning a wedding until after New Year's. And four months is not enough time to plan a decent wedding."

"I'm not planning any kind of wedding, decent or indecent, Sabrina."

"But if you want to keep Mabel—and I know you do—maybe you should start planning a wedding—a wedding with a certain good looking marine. Before it's too late."

"I'm so glad you came over to lift my spirits," Daphne said drolly. "Whatever would I do without you?"

"Well, somebody's got to give you a reality kick in the behind from time to time. What're friends for, anyway?"

"Here's to reality." Daphne attempted a brave smile as she held up her cup of tea.

"To reality." Sabrina clinked her cup against Daphne's. "Just don't let it slap you in the caboose on your way out."

Chapter 3

Sabrina was still there when Mabel and Lola burst into the house. "*Aunt Daphne!*" Mabel cried out.

"I'm *here.*" Daphne sprang to her feet, worried that Mabel was hurt. "What's wrong?" She met the flush-faced girls in the dining room.

"Lola asked me to be in the Christmas parade with her!" Mabel's eyes were big and brown. "I've *always* dreamed of being in a real parade. Please, please, can I do it?"

"I don't understand." Daphne peered at Lola. "How are you going to be in the parade?"

"Miss Kristy's Dance School is in the parade," Lola explained. "The big girls are gonna dance on the street and the younger girls, like me, getta ride on the float."

"But you're not in Miss Kristy's Dance School yet," Daphne reminded Mabel.

"Yeah, but you signed me up for ballet—you said I start after Christmas—*remember?*"

"Yes, but I'm not sure that means—"

"It's okay," Lola reassured her. "Miss Kristy is Mommy's best friend. She'll let Mabel come."

"But the parade's tomorrow," Daphne pointed out. "Mabel wouldn't know what to do, or where to go."

"Mommy can tell you all that stuff."

"Please, Aunt Daphne," Mabel begged. "I want to be in a parade more than anything in the world. *Please!*"

"Maybe we should call Miss Kristy," Daphne said with uncertainty. "Or if your mom's such good friends, maybe I should call her."

"Yeah," Lola agreed. "Call Mommy."

Daphne reached for her phone. "I've got her number. Why don't I just give her a call?" When Becca answered, Daphne quickly explained the girls' idea. "I hate to disappoint Mabel," she said quietly. "But I don't want to assume it's okay either."

"Oh, Kristy won't mind. Especially since Mabel is signed up for dance in January. But I'll call her if you want."

Daphne thanked her for her help, and Becca promised to get back with an answer. "Well, it sounds like it might be okay," Daphne told Mabel. "But Becca's checking to be sure."

"How do y'all plan to dress for the parade?" Sabrina asked with interest.

"I'm wearing my pink tutu over my leotard," Lola told her. "But Mabel can wear whatever she wants."

"What's a *tutu*?" Mabel asked.

"You know," Lola said, "a fluffy skirt. It's what ballerinas wear."

"Oh, yeah, I know what you mean, but I don't have a tutu." Mabel sighed.

"Oh...?" Lola looked concerned. "It's okay."

"But I have the dress I wore to your dad's wedding," Mabel told Daphne. "It's a very pretty dress."

"Well, if you are going to take ballet lessons and be a real ballerina, you should have a real tutu," Sabrina declared. "And Auntie Sabrina would be happy to help. In fact, I remember seeing a cute little dance shop at a mall recently. If it's okay with Aunt Daphne, we'll shop for one today."

"You've already been very generous," Daphne told her. "You don't need to—"

"I *want* to," Sabrina declared. "And if you're worried I'm spoiling her, we can just call it an early birthday present, because I happen to know this little girl turns eight in about ten days." She grinned at Mabel. "Right?"

Mabel nodded.

"So if Aunt Daphne agrees, I want to take you shopping today."

"I thought you *never* shopped on Black Friday," Daphne teased as her phone signaled for a text message.

"I make exceptions for exceptional girls." Sabrina patted Mabel's head.

"This message says that Mabel is officially invited to be in the parade," Daphne announced, smiling at Mabel. "Looks like your dream is about to come true."

Mabel grabbed Lola's hands, and the two did a happy jig together.

"Well, you girls can keep playing for a while," Sabrina told Mabel, "but if you want to get a tutu today, I think we should leave in about an hour." She looked at Daphne. "If that's okay with you."

"It's just fine." Daphne smiled as the girls ran off.

"You can come too," Sabrina offered. "Although I'm well aware you don't much enjoy shopping."

"I've got some catching up to do around here," Daphne told her.

"Working on your novel?" Sabrina said with interest.

"Something like that." Daphne made a mysterious smile as she went into the kitchen. Sabrina didn't know everything about Daphne's life. And that was for the best.

"Well, instead of using your free time to work on your novel, I would suggest you spend some time thinking about poor Daniel."

"*Poor Daniel?*" Daphne frowned as she cleared the tea things from the table.

"Yes." Sabrina nodded firmly. "The good man has been serving his country all these years. He's lost a sister and a mother and now he's down the street probably feeling quite blue. Imagine...sifting through all those things...dealing with those memories. I'm sure he would love some company."

Daphne could see right through Sabrina but decided to play along. "And you're suggesting that, as a good neighbor, I should go down there and offer my help?"

"What a lovely idea." Sabrina smiled.

"Right..." Daphne put their cups into the dishwasher.

"I saw him watching you closely yesterday, Daphne. It was obvious that he likes you. And he complimented you on everything. He was very appreciative. For all we know, he could be smitten with you and just too shy to show it."

"Or you could simply be letting your imagination run wild with you." Daphne rinsed out the teapot.

"But think about it—how wonderful would it be for Mabel

if it turns out that you two really were meant for each other? Why, it would be just like a fairytale come to life."

"Uh huh." Daphne closed the dishwasher.

"Promise me that you'll at least think about what I'm saying," Sabrina insisted. "For Mabel's sake."

"And for yours too?" Daphne teased.

"I'll admit that it would be awfully nice to keep all three of you in the neighborhood. I certainly wouldn't complain about that."

Daphne patted Sabrina's back. "No, I wouldn't either."

It was around three by the time Sabrina and Mabel left to go tutu shopping. Daphne went directly to her office and sat down to work on the nationally syndicated advice column that she'd inherited from her aunt—the original *Dear Daphne* that had been going since the 1950s.

It was amazing how easy it was for Daphne to give love advice to perfect strangers regarding the various intricacies of their romantic lives. In less than an hour, she had whipped out three good-sized response letters, enough to fill a column. And as she went over her work, tweaking and editing, she had to admit these weren't only insightful letters, they were rather witty as well.

She'd been writing this anonymous column for six months now, and she still sometimes imagined Aunt Dee standing behind her, gazing fondly over her shoulder as she whispered fitting and pithy answers into her ear. Oh, she knew that wasn't really happening. It wasn't as if she believed in ghosts or anything like that. But sometimes it was uncanny how on-the-nose Daphne's responses seemed. And she even received thank-you letters from the people she'd helped.

And so it felt rather ironic, not to mention downright frustrating, that Daphne was usually at odds when it came to her own romantic challenges. So much so that she sometimes wrote her own letters to "Dear Daphne" in the hopes that her response (a product of Aunt Dee's legacy) might somehow enlighten her. Strangely enough, that was often the case. Naturally, she never published these letters, although she had accidentally let one slip through to Jake back when he was helping her to get comfortable with the column. Anyway, feeling confused about a lot of things—and with no interest in working on her novel—she decided to write a letter.

> *Dear Daphne,*
>
> *I find myself in an awkward position and don't know what to do. There are circumstances in my life that compel me to get married within a fairly short period of time. One of my primary motivations is a child who has become very dear to me. In order to keep this little girl in my life, I am tempted to enter into a romantic relationship with her uncle, who has legal custody. I barely know this man, but he appears to be honest and hardworking and, I must admit, handsome. Also, he seems to love this child—and she loves him. It all sounds rather picture perfect, somewhat fairytale-like...and yet I'm uncertain. Would it be disingenuous to pursue a romantic relationship in order to preserve a lifestyle that I've become accustomed to?*
>
> *Awkward in Appleton*

Dear Awkward,

Several questions come to mind. First of all, you don't mention how this man feels about you. Does he even love you and want to marry? Second of all, and more importantly, you never mention that you love him. That in itself is a huge flag. Perhaps you should ask yourself if you're willing to settle for a loveless marriage in order to keep a child. And don't forget that a child is only in your home for a few years, but a marriage should last the rest of your life. At least I'm sure you would want it to.

Daphne

Daphne stared at the computer screen. Once again *Dear Daphne* was right. Except that she wasn't sure she could dismiss the possibility of love between Daniel and herself just yet. After all, they'd only known each other for three days. Oh, she'd heard that most people usually fell in love instantly—or within a few minutes—but she suspected that wasn't always true. And to be honest, she'd had a love-at-first-sight experience before. And that hadn't turned out too well. What if what some people assumed was "love" was actually infatuation or simply a chemical reaction? A girl couldn't be too careful. Except that Daphne wasn't exactly a girl. In fact, she was thirty-four and, until Mabel had come into her life, she'd been living with two cats.

As she turned off her computer, she knew that Sabrina would not want her to give up so easily. So, seeing that she still had some time before Sabrina and Mabel should be home, she left them a note and walked down to check on Daniel. *Just being neighborly,* she told herself as she rang the doorbell.

"Hey there." He greeted her with a warm smile. "What's up?"

"Just checking on you," she told him. "Sabrina was worried that it might be a little depressing for you down here. I mean... after losing your mom. And it wasn't that long ago your sister died. I guess I hadn't really thought of it like that."

His smile faded. "Yeah, seems like it's been a pretty rough year over here on the home front. I think I prefer active duty compared to what my family's been through. At least you know what to expect over there." He looked around behind her. "Where's Mabel?"

She explained about Sabrina's trip to the mall with his niece and then asked him if he needed any help. "You know we started to sort some things out. We put a lot of boxes of what seemed like junk out in the garage, but we never threw anything away. Well, except for garbage." She smiled. "Your mom was a sweet lady, but she was a bit of a packrat."

"Tell me about it." He shook his head. "I called for a Dumpster to be delivered, but it won't get here until Monday morning. In the meantime, I'm just throwing stuff out into the garage. I don't want to throw away anything important, but there's not a whole lot to salvage."

"Well, I'm happy to help if you like."

"Mostly it's just taking out the trash." He shrugged.

"Maybe I could sort through to see if there's anything Mabel might appreciate. You know, someday when she's older." Daphne shared about how much her aunt's old letters and things had meant to her. "I probably wouldn't have cared as a child. But as an adult, I'm thankful to have them."

"Feel free to take anything you want. It's all going into the Dumpster come Monday."

"Great. I'll go dig around."

"I appreciate how much you've helped Mabel already. You went way beyond the call of duty." He looked intensely into her eyes. "I'm really grateful."

"Well, Mabel is a joy. It's been my pleasure having her around." Daphne felt close to tears again. "And I will miss her dearly if you decide to go to North Carolina."

"Yeah...I kinda figured you would." He put a hand on her shoulder. "Believe me, I'm giving this a lot of thought, Daphne. And I'd really like the chance to discuss the whole thing with you. I mean, privately."

She nodded. "Yes. I don't think it's fair to talk about this in front of Mabel. She's already getting pretty concerned."

"Do you think Mabel could stay with Sabrina tonight? And maybe you and me could go to dinner or something?"

"I'm sure Sabrina would be happy to have her."

"And you'd want to go out with me?" His dark eyes, so similar to Mabel's, lit up.

"Sure." Daphne smiled. "I'd love to."

He seemed genuinely happy. "Great. There's been so much going on, so much to figure out. It would be a huge relief to have a good long chat with you."

"I'm looking forward to it."

He glanced at his watch. "Is seven okay? I think I could almost get the rest of the house cleared out by then. Tommy is coming tomorrow to start painting the exterior, but I thought I could start on the inside too."

"Seven is perfect."

"Alright then." He made an uneasy smile. "I just remembered I don't have a car."

She laughed. "How about if we use mine?"

"Great. I'll come by at seven."

As Daphne sifted and sorted through the musty piles of junk, she could see that it really was, for the most part, trash. But she did find a box of mementos and trinkets that must've belonged to Mabel's mother back when she was a teen. Judging by the era, Mabel's mother must've been just a couple years younger than Daphne. Her name was Denise, and like Mabel and Daniel, she had soulful brown eyes and dark brown hair. Although it looked like she bleached her hair in her later teens. Seeing Denise's paperback books, CDs, and photos suddenly made her seem more real. Realizing how Mabel's mother's life was so senselessly snuffed out made Daphne unbearably sad. Part of her was tempted to just drop the box and let it get buried with the rest of this family's past.

And yet she knew that someday Mabel would be a teen. Someday she'd ask the hard questions. And someone—whether it was Daniel or Daphne—would need to have some answers. This box might help.

After she stowed the box safely in the attic, Daphne considered Daniel's gratitude toward her today. And his eagerness to spend some time with her—just the two of them. Perhaps her Dear Daphne response letter had been wrong. Or just premature. Because who could tell what was brewing here? Wouldn't it be amazing if Sabrina's high hopes for the three of them remaining happily ever after in Appleton was more than just a fairytale?

Chapter 4

Sabrina and Mabel got home shortly after Daphne and, judging by their bags, bought more than just a tutu. But when Daphne saw Mabel's happy face, she didn't have the heart to question Sabrina about her generosity.

"Looks like you girls had fun." Daphne gave Sabrina a knowing look as they dumped their bags onto the couch in the living room. "So much for your anti Black Friday rule, eh?"

"You have to see this, Aunt Daphne." Mabel opened the biggest bag, extracting a lavender tutu with a satin bodice. Sparkling sequins and glitter adorned the entire outfit, and, in Daphne's opinion, were a bit over the top.

"Oh, my." Daphne glanced at Sabrina.

"Isn't it the most beautiful thing you've ever seen?" Mabel held it up with a dreamy expression.

Daphne slowly nodded. "And sparkly too. But I'm not sure it will be appropriate for dance class, Mabel. According to the brochure Miss Kristy gave me, you're supposed to wear a black or pale pink leotard and you can have a pale pink tutu skirt if you like, but you're not—"

"Oh, this one's just for fun," Sabrina assured her. "We found it on the markdown rack. It was so cheap it was practically free. How could we resist?"

"Oh." Daphne looked at what Sabrina was pulling out of another bag.

"This is for class." She produced a black leotard and a pale pink tutu made of fluffy net. Then she pulled out another wrap around skirt made of stretchy satin, as well as a couple pairs of tights.

"Wow." Daphne gave Sabrina a curious look. "Auntie Sabrina has been very generous."

"It's an early birthday present," Sabrina reminded her.

"And she got me ballet slippers too." Mabel produced a slender shoebox.

"Well, you are all set." Daphne smiled at Sabrina. "Thank you very much."

"Yes, Auntie Sabrina, thank you very much." Mabel beamed at her.

"I thoroughly enjoyed it."

"She got Tootsie a new tutu too," Mabel told Daphne.

"Well, of course you did." Daphne laughed.

"Can I go try on the fancy tutu again?" Mabel asked Daphne. "So you can see it?"

"Why not." Daphne chuckled as Mabel, still hugging the lavender tutu, headed for the stairs.

"Don't forget these." Sabrina held up a package of tights and the ballet slippers. "To complete the outfit. And remember the tights go *under* the tutu." She laughed as Mabel scurried up the stairs with her arms full.

Daphne turned to Sabrina. "So how does it feel to play fairy godmother?"

"It feels perfectly delightful. Thank you for sharing your little princess with me." Sabrina frowned. "But I have to say that the whole time we were shopping, I kept thinking we cannot let Daniel take her away from us." She grabbed Daphne by the hand. "You have got to do something!"

"As a matter of fact..." Daphne made a sheepish grin as she quickly explained her visit to Daniel.

"I am dumbfounded," Sabrina exclaimed. "You actually took my advice?"

"Well, I got to thinking...maybe he could use a friend. Turns out you were right, he was feeling a little overwhelmed. He asked me to go to dinner with him tonight."

Sabrina's eyes lit up. "That's fantastic!"

"But I need someone to stay with Mabel."

"She can come home with me," Sabrina offered. "We'll have a sleepover with popcorn and Disney movies and the works."

"She'll love that."

Sabrina pointed to Daphne. "What are you wearing?"

Daphne looked down at her jeans and plaid shirt which was still smudged with traces of baking ingredients. "Well, not this, of course."

"You got that right." Sabrina's brow creased. "We need to fix you up."

Daphne held up her hands. "That's all right, I think I can handle this."

Sabrina grimly shook her head. "No, you definitely need help, girlfriend. Let's go check out your closet."

"But I—"

"Come on, Daph. Just show me what you plan to wear, and I'll give you my opinion."

Imagining herself decked out in a sparkly tutu sort of outfit, Daphne decided the quickest way to handle this would be to just give in—for now anyway. She would do as she pleased after Sabrina went home. She led her into her bedroom. "Well, my closet is kind of a mess. I dragged my stuff down here right before Thanksgiving so that Daniel could have my old room upstairs, to be close to Mabel. I haven't had time to organize anything yet."

"You aren't kidding." Sabrina frowned into the closet. "My word!"

"I warned you." Daphne stood back, watching as Sabrina attempted to dig through the piles heaped on the floor. She looked like a bargain hunter going through Macy's markdown basement.

"This!" Sabrina held up a wrap dress in a paisley print. "And where are those brown suede boots you wore last week?"

Daphne went over to a small pile of shoes, dredging out the boots.

Sabrina tugged Daphne over to the full length mirror on the closet door, holding up the dress. "We'll need to steam those wrinkles out, but I think this looks pretty good."

Daphne studied her image. "Yeah, it's not bad."

"Those teal shades really bring out the green in your eyes," Sabrina observed. "And set off your auburn hair." She nodded in satisfaction. "You can be very beautiful when you try, Daphne."

Daphne just laughed.

"And I really do think you resemble Lucille Ball—when she was younger. I just watched an old movie with Desi Arnaz. I can't remember what it was called, but they had this enormous trailer—"

"*The Long, Long Trailer*," Daphne told her.

Sabrina nodded. "So where's your steamer?"

"Steamer?" Daphne frowned.

"Never mind, I'll run home and get mine."

Mabel struck a pose in the doorway. "Here I am!"

"You look beautiful," Daphne told her.

"Adorable," Sabrina declared.

Mabel did a wobbly pirouette followed by a clumsy bow.

"And guess what?" Sabrina said to Mabel. "You get to spend the night with me."

Mabel gave Daphne a concerned look. "*Why?*"

"Because your Aunt Daphne is going to dinner with your Uncle Daniel." Sabrina winked at Mabel.

"Oh...?" Mabel's face lit up.

"And you and I are having a slumber party," Sabrina told her. "So go get your jammies and toothbrush together while I run home to get something. And I need to let Tootsie out too."

As Daphne helped Mabel pack an overnight bag, Mabel questioned her about Daniel. "Are you going out on a *date* with him?" she asked.

Daphne wanted to question whether Mabel even really knew what a date was, but supposed that she probably did. "No, it's not really a date. At least I don't think so."

"Oh." Mabel looked disappointed.

"But maybe it is. I mean, he did invite me to dinner. I suppose that means it's a date." Daphne picked up the jeans and sweatshirt that Mabel had discarded for the tutu outfit. "Do you want to change back into your clothes now or just take these to Sabrina's?"

"Take them to Sabrina's."

"Well, you might want to take care of this." Daphne pointed to the sparkly tutu. "You won't want to spill food on it before the parade tomorrow. I doubt it washes up too easily." She zipped the overnight bag closed.

"Will you marry Uncle Daniel?" Mabel asked with earnest eyes.

"Oh, honey, I don't know. I barely know him. We just want to talk and get to know each other better."

"But if he likes you and you like him, will you marry him?"

"I suppose if we both fell in love...I *might* marry him. I mean, if he wanted to get married. But that's a long, long ways down the road, sweetie. Right now we're just friends, okay?"

"Okay." Mabel's mouth twisted to one side. "But I hope you do fall in love."

"I have an idea," Daphne said suddenly. "Let me take a photo of you on my phone and I'll show it to Uncle Daniel tonight. I'm sure he'd like to see you looking so gorgeous."

"Okay!"

As they went downstairs, Mabel asked if they could send the picture to Lola too. "I mean on her mom's phone."

"Sure." Daphne pointed to the fireplace as she got out her phone. "You stand there like a ballerina."

They were just finishing the photo session when Sabrina returned with the steamer. "Just fill it with water and plug it in." She pointed to Mabel's bag. "Looks like you're ready to go."

"Uh huh."

"And Tootsie is eagerly waiting."

Daphne helped her into her parka. "The Christmas parade

starts at ten o'clock tomorrow. Lola's mom offered to pick you up here. You need to be all ready to go by nine." She kissed Mabel's cheek. "And make sure you go to bed early enough to be bright-eyed and bushy-tailed in the morning."

Mabel and Sabrina both promised they would and then they left, and the house was quiet. As Daphne stood there by herself, she realized how empty the house suddenly felt. But before she had a chance to get too lonely, Ethel and Lucy showed up, meowing in the way that announced they were ready for dinner.

By the time Daphne's wrinkled dress billowed with steam, nerves fluttered in her stomach. Oh, it wasn't about the "date." Dating wasn't so intimidating anymore. Even dating men she barely knew wasn't such a big deal. The problem with tonight's date was that it felt like so much was at stake. In essence, *three lives.* Daniel had a big decision ahead. Actually, he had a couple. Would he become a fulltime civilian or return to the Marines? If he did return to the Marines, would he take Mabel with him?

"Just stop it," she told herself. And instead of obsessing over all the what-ifs, she decided to put her attention on her hair and makeup. Sabrina would definitely approve. As usual, Daphne preferred a lighter touch. In her world, less really was more. A touch of coral lipstick. A smoothing of her natural curly hair. And she even put on a pair of small gold hoop earrings and a bangle. For Daphne, this was dressed up.

At exactly seven o'clock, the doorbell rang. As Daphne went for the door, she wondered how Daniel would be dressed. Certainly not in uniform, although she knew he looked handsome in it. But how would she feel if he showed up in a t-shirt and jeans like he'd had on yesterday? To her relief, he had on a dark sports coat and gray trousers.

"You look pretty."

"Thanks." She felt her cheeks warm. "You do too. I mean, not pretty. You look nice." She handed him the car keys. "If you want to get it out of the garage, I'll get my coat and lock up."

"Wow, I didn't know folks locked their doors in Appleton. Times must be changing."

She laughed. "Well, to be honest, that was an old New York habit that I had nearly kicked. But when Mabel came to live with me, I returned to it. I suppose I feel protective, you know?"

"Yeah. I get that."

"Anyway, the garage is unlocked."

As he went for the car, she pulled on her trench coat, tightening the belt snugly around her waist. It felt nice to be dressed up for a change. Something she had been doing less and less of since leaving New York last May.

Seeing Aunt Dee's copper Corvette parked out front, Daphne locked up and hurried over to it. But before she got there, Daniel was out, politely opening the passenger door for her. "This is quite a car, Daphne. A fifty-five or fifty-six?"

"Fifty-five. Her name's Bonnie."

"Gorgeous color."

"Yeah, they only made fifteen in copper."

"It goes with your hair."

Daphne laughed. "Aunt Dee was a redhead too."

"So I thought we could go to The Zeppelin, if that's okay with you."

"Sounds good." She leaned back, trying to relax, although she was secretly concerned—what if Daniel wasn't a good driver? Was she nuts to allow him to drive this car? But, to her relief, he seemed to be driving very cautiously. "We don't have a whole lot of restaurant choices here in Appleton," she said as he cruised down Main Street.

"More than there used to be when I was in school."

"So, I know you went to Appleton High, but I'm not sure which year you graduated. How old are you?"

"I just turned thirty-seven."

"So you were a few years ahead of me."

"Probably more than a few years. Are you even thirty?"

She laughed. "I'm thirty-four, but thank you."

"Well, even if we were in school together, you probably wouldn't remember me. I kept a pretty low profile. Rode my motorcycle to school, left as soon as it was done. And I went straight into the Marines out of high school. That's where I really grew up." He chuckled as he turned into the restaurant parking lot. "The Marines gave me the parenting I never really had at home."

"Interesting." Daphne had suspected that Daniel's upbringing hadn't been ideal. "Well, I think the Marines must've done a fine job."

"Thanks." He parked over on the side in an open area. "Do you mind walking a bit? I didn't want anyone swinging their doors open and dinging this little beauty."

"Good thinking. Thanks."

As he hurried over to the passenger side, she felt appreciative of his thoughtfulness, but as he opened her door, she noticed a familiar SUV pulling up a few spaces away. Jake McPheeters sat behind the wheel.

"Isn't that Jake?" Daniel asked as he helped her out of the car.

"Yes. With his daughter Jenna."

"Oh, yeah, he told me about his daughter. I didn't realize she was that old."

"She's fifteen."

"Hey, Daniel and Daphne," Jake called out. "Fancy meeting you guys here. I'm surprised you're not home eating leftovers."

She smiled. "There wasn't much left over."

"And I figured after all the cooking Daphne did for Thanksgiving, she could use a night out," Daniel said as the two guys shook hands.

"Hi, Jenna," Daphne said cheerfully as they all headed inside. "Are you enjoying some time off from school?"

"I guess. But I can't go anywhere because I got roped into helping carry the marching band banner in the parade tomorrow."

"Mabel's going to be in the parade too." Daphne pulled out her phone to show them the picture, explaining how Mabel had "dreamed" of being in a parade and Sabrina's early birthday present.

"We made reservations," Jake said as they approached the maître d' counter. "But you guys are welcome to join us if you like."

"I made reservations too," Daniel told him. "But thanks."

Jake peered curiously at Daphne, almost as if he expected her to accept his invitation. "Sounds like fun," she told him. "But we sort of need to talk in private." Of course, when Jake's brows arched at the word *private*, she instantly regretted it. She hadn't meant to sound like that. But Jake turned to talk to the maître d' and there was no point in trying to take it back. And maybe it didn't matter.

As they waited to be seated, Daphne tried to examine her feelings toward Jake. At the moment she felt confused and conflicted. On one hand, she really liked him and appreciated his friendship. On the other hand, she sometimes resented that he was the only one—besides her—who fully understood the implications of all the stipulations in Aunt Dee's will. Sometimes it felt like that gave him the upper hand. And yet, he had always been supportive and helpful and understanding. So why did she feel a tinge of irritation to run into him like this tonight?

Chapter 5

As fate would have it, Daniel and Daphne were seated directly across from Jake and Jenna. If Daphne looked over Daniel's right shoulder, there was Jake. She considered asking to switch seats, but the waiter was already filling their water glasses. Instead, she adjusted her chair, moving it slightly to her right so that Daniel's head blocked her view of Jake.

"Thanks for coming out with me tonight." Daniel set his napkin in his lap. "I really do need someone to talk to. So much to sort out."

"Which reminds me, how's the planning for your mother's memorial service going?"

"Your friend, Pastor Andrew, has been very helpful. It's really nice of him to handle the service—especially considering Mom never went to his church. But, to be honest, she hadn't attended church anywhere. Not since I was a kid anyway. Back before my parents divorced. Pastor Andrew asked if Mom was a believer, and I told him I think she must've been since she always told me she was praying for me in her letters."

"It's hard to pray if you're not a believer."

He made a relieved smile. "That's what Pastor Andrew said."

"So it's all set for Monday afternoon then?"

"Yes. Two o'clock." He paused for the waiter to set down a basket of bread and take their orders. Daniel went for the New York steak dinner, and she asked for the seafood pasta special.

"You mentioned Tommy's coming to paint tomorrow," she said after the waiter left. "Do you think you'll be able to attend the Christmas parade in the morning? I know Mabel would appreciate it."

"I wouldn't miss it. That was real sweet of Sabrina to get her that ballerina costume. Mabel must've been over the moon."

"Oh, she was. She still had it on when she went over to Sabrina's tonight."

He chuckled. "She's really something, isn't she? I never realized I could fall so hard for a little girl. If anyone had ever told me anything good would come out of Nissie's life, I never would've believed it."

"Nissie?"

"Short for Denise. My sister. Mabel's mom."

"Oh. Vera never really spoke of her. Mabel doesn't either."

"Well, she and Trent were a mess. Mabel is lucky to be free of them."

Daphne didn't know what to say.

"I don't mean to sound like I'm glad my sister is dead," he said grimly. "I'm not. But I am glad Trent's locked up."

"Mabel's dad?"

"Yeah. He and Denise never got married, but he's the loser that got her into drugs. He got put away for dealing and several other fairly serious convictions."

"Do you know when he'll get out?" Daphne wasn't even sure she wanted to know the answer. The idea of sweet Mabel having a criminal dad was hard to absorb.

"He must have about fifteen years left."

"So, unless he got paroled, he'd never have custody of Mabel."

"Even if he got paroled, it's not likely. At least not if I have anything to say about it."

"That's good."

They paused while the waiter set down their salads. As they started to eat, Daphne brought up the topic of North Carolina. "I think Mabel heard us talking about it this morning. She was pretty concerned."

"Concerned?"

"You might as well know that she's in love with Appleton. She loves her school and her teacher and her best friend Lola and—"

"You."

Daphne nodded. "That little girl has a heart full of love."

"I know." He sighed deeply.

"She loves you too, Daniel. Very much."

"Yeah, and that makes my decision even tougher."

"And no one expects you to make a decision today," Daphne said quickly. "But I just want you to know that Mabel is so happy here. And, as you know, I'd be more than willing to keep her." Daphne took in a deep breath. "I mean, if you need to go back into the Marines until you're ready to retire. I could gladly take care of Mabel until you were ready to settle down."

"You'd really do that?" Daniel looked truly surprised.

"Of course. I'd love to. And Sabrina would love to be an

auntie too. We adore Mabel."

"Well, that's good to hear." He buttered a piece of bread. "But my mom's dying wish was for me to have Mabel. She believed that I could somehow make up for all the mistakes of our family." He made a sad smile. "As if that's possible. Poor Mabel really got dealt a bad hand."

"Well, no family is perfect. And, if you ask me, she's a pretty well-adjusted kid, all things considered."

"I have to agree with you."

"Although if I was to keep her, I had planned to set her up with some counseling sessions. Just in case she's dealing with some baggage related to her, uh, parents. As well as the death of her grandmother."

"That might be a good idea. I should keep that in mind too." He paused as the waiter set down their entrées. "Looks good," he told the waiter. "Thanks."

As they ate their dinner, Daphne tried to keep the conversation light, telling him stories about funny things Mabel had said or done. And then he asked her about her own childhood. "I'm guessing you grew up in a normal family."

"Not exactly." She described how hard it was when her mother died. "I had my Aunt Dee to help, and I would stay with her after school and on weekends and summers and whatnot. She was like a second mother. And I recently discovered that she was actually my dad's mother, but that's a long story and just one more way my family wasn't exactly what you'd call 'normal'—if that even exists. But as a little girl, I took all the household chores on as my personal responsibility. I'm afraid that made me grow up too fast. I was a very somber child, and I didn't have a lot of friends. Even my best friend would complain that I was too serious. She still accuses me of being a workaholic sometimes. Although I think I've proven her wrong." Daphne chuckled. "Sometimes several days go by, and I don't even turn on my computer."

"I've been accused of overcompensating," Daniel admitted.

"I would think that would be welcome in the military."

"They like us to be balanced and healthy."

"Yes, of course." She was tempted to ask him about her PTSD suspicions but remembered her promise to Mabel.

"I thought I was ready for a break," he said quietly. "I thought I'd welcome returning to stateside life. Even if it was a little earlier than expected."

"But...?"

"But I'm not sure I like it so much."

"Well, you've only been here a few days."

"That's true. But I've been projecting what it might be like as a permanent lifestyle." He slowly shook his head. "I'm not sure I can handle it. Not sure I want to."

"Maybe it's not right for you." Daphne felt a flash of hope. Perhaps it would be for the best if Daniel realized he wasn't cut out for civilian life. Especially if she could convince him that Mabel would be better off with her. "But I'm curious. How do you really think Mabel would fare on a Marine base?"

His brow creased. "Honestly?"

"Of course."

"Well, the base is a family-friendly place. No doubt about that. But not so much for single parents."

She nodded. "Yes, I had wondered about that."

He looked directly into her eyes. "But if I had someone... someone who loved Mabel as much as I did...well, it could be really good." Now he started talking about friends of his with families, and how great it was for the kids living on the base. "It's like being part of this huge extended family. Everyone knows and cares about each other."

"Kind of like living in Appleton," she suggested.

"Yeah, I guess so. But to be honest, that was never my experience. Not Mom's either. Well, until you and your friends stepped in for her." He made a sad smile. "I'm grateful for that."

"I just wish I'd known she needed help sooner. But I hadn't been in Appleton that long. I only relocated here last May. There wasn't much time."

"And Mom was pretty private about her troubles. Plus, she only got custody of Mabel a few months ago...when Denise died."

"I'm curious, Daniel. Have you been married before?" She made a shy smile. "Frankly it's hard to believe a good looking, nice guy like you is still single."

He rewarded her with his own bright smile. "Thanks. The truth is, I've been married to my job."

"So no romances or anything?"

"I was with a girl for about six years. Trisha wanted to get married. She literally begged me to get married. But I just couldn't do it. It didn't seem fair to either of us—I was away so much, being on active duty. So she cut me loose. Since then I've gone out a few times, been set up a few times, but I just haven't seen anything out there that made me want to give up my freedom."

"But Mabel would make you want to give up your freedom?"

"I think maybe I could. For her."

"That's very honorable, Daniel. But I wonder if it would

really be the best for her. I mean, it might be like it was with Trisha—it might not be fair to either of you."

He laid down his knife and fork, pushing his nearly emptied plate to the side. "You could be right. But you'd have to admit that it would be different if I was married. If Mabel had a mom... it could work, don't you think?"

"Well, of course." Daphne wondered if he was thinking about Trisha...or perhaps he was thinking about her.

"I've got a lot to think about." He shook his head. "And I'm not really used to dealing with personal problems. My world is usually pretty cut and dried, black and white. That's one of the luxuries of being unattached. And now it seems like I have to consider all this personal stuff. I have to admit, I'm out of my comfort zone."

"Sometimes that's a good thing." Daphne told him about how it was when she moved to Appleton. "Even though I grew up in this town, I felt like I was out of my comfort zone too. At first."

"But you got used to it?"

"More than that, I realized how much I loved it. How I never wanted to go back to that fast-paced New York lifestyle." She considered Aunt Dee's will and how if she didn't get married, she might be forced back into a lifestyle like that again. As generous as Aunt Dee's will appeared at first glance, it also seemed unfair too. Or maybe just a really mean joke.

They were just finishing dessert when Daphne noticed that Jake and Jenna were getting up from their table. Daphne was about to give them a friendly wave goodbye when they came over to talk.

"Jenna has a good idea," Jake told them. "She wants to go

bowling and she wondered if you guys would like to join us. Might be more fun with four."

"Bowling?" Daphne tried not to look too disgusted, but something about the idea of putting on public shoes and throwing a heavy ball at pins did not appeal to her.

"I love to bowl," Daniel exclaimed.

"So you kids wanna join us?" Jake asked hopefully. "Can we challenge you to a little bowling match?"

"How about it?" Daniel asked Daphne. "You game?"

"Or do you need to get back to Mabel?" Jake asked.

"Mabel's spending the night at Sabrina's." And before she could tell them she'd only bowled one time in her life, it was all set. It was decided they would meet at The Big Apple bowling alley for the showdown.

"I don't even know how to bowl," Daphne admitted to Daniel as they walked inside.

"I'll help you. Pretty much you just roll the ball. It does the work."

It wasn't long until Daphne was exchanging her pretty suede boots for a pair of weird looking bowling shoes. At least she'd shaved her legs that morning. Still, she felt silly as she stood with a heavy ball attached to her thumb and two fingers. "What do I do?" she asked Daniel.

"Let's take a couple of practice shots," he said. "Let me help you. But let's try it without the ball first, okay?" And then he got behind her, sticking to her like a close shadow. Putting his arm around like he was holding the ball, he coached her, saying, "Step, step, step-slide and release." He pointed out the line she shouldn't go over, then took her back to do it again. "Step, step, step-slide and release." And then they did it with the ball, which went directly into the gutter. Then she tried it again—by herself—and this time it rolled into the other gutter. As Jake and Jenna clapped, she made a mock bow.

"This should be good," she told everyone.

"You'll get better," Daniel assured her.

Strangely enough, Daniel was right. Thanks to his coaching, which she tried to pay attention to, and probably a lot of beginner's luck, Daphne's aim steadily improved. She even bowled a couple of strikes. But Daniel shone, and by the time they were done with the first game, Jake and Jenna were the ones bowing to them.

The next game was pretty much the same. And Daphne had to admit that she was actually having fun. It was nice to see Daniel and Jake joking with each other as if they were old friends. Even Jenna seemed to be having a good time.

"You guys ought to go pro," Jake said as they turned in their shoes. "I'm glad we didn't bet on the game."

"It was Daniel," Daphne said with pride. "His score carried me."

"Your score was better than mine," Jenna pointed out.

"Maybe we can do this again." Daniel ushered them all through the parking lot.

"Jenna and I might need to sneak over here to practice first," Jake said.

"Maybe you should hire Daniel to give you lessons," Daphne teased.

Jake made a face. "Way to smash a guy's ego, Daph."

"I'll watch for you at the parade tomorrow," Daphne called to Jenna as they parted ways.

"That was fun," Daniel said as they got in the car. "I really like that Jake. For a lawyer, he's okay."

"So now that you're getting a new taste of Appleton, are you finding you like it a little better than you imagined you would?"

"I guess so. Maybe I need to give it a second chance."

"Maybe so." Daphne felt herself relaxing as Daniel drove them home. She wasn't sure where everything would land when it was all said and done, but it seemed like she had made progress with Daniel tonight. And she'd had a good time doing it.

At her house, he let her out before putting the car back in the garage, and then they met again on the porch. For one uneasy moment, she wondered if he was going to kiss her. She was not ready for that. Instead he took her hand. "Thank you for one of the best dates I think I have ever had," he said sincerely.

"Thank *you*," she replied. "I thoroughly enjoyed it too."

"Would you like to go to the Christmas parade together?" he asked hopefully.

"Sure," she answered. "I think Mabel would enjoy seeing us there to cheer her on."

"I figured we could just walk."

"Sounds perfect. If we go a little early, we could grab a coffee to keep our fingers warm."

"I like how you think." He saluted her. "Goodnight, Daphne."

"Goodnight, Daniel."

As Daphne went into the house, she tried to examine her feelings. It was true, she had thoroughly enjoyed herself tonight. Daniel was pleasant and thoughtful and easy to talk to. Plus he was a darn good bowler. Not to mention extremely handsome. But was it possible she was falling in love? And wouldn't it be convenient if she was!

Chapter 6

As Daphne was mentally calculating Daniel's numerous qualities the next morning, she had to add in *punctual*. Shortly after Lola and Becca picked up Mabel for the parade, Daniel arrived right on time. Dressed casually in jeans and a military-issue polar fleece jacket, as well as a Marines ball-cap, he still looked very handsome.

"It's kind of cold out there," he warned her. "Do you need a hat or anything?"

Daphne patted her thick, wavy hair. "With this mop?"

"*That* is not a mop," he told her. "You have a gorgeous head of hair, Daphne."

She blinked as she pulled on her gloves. "Well, thank you."

They chatted companionably as they walked to town. She told him about the little squabble she had with Mabel this morning. "It wasn't really anything much. She felt certain she wouldn't need her parka and I insisted she would." She chuckled. "Mabel finally confessed she was worried that no one would see her new tutu. So we compromised with a little purple hoodie that allows the tutu skirt to show. I told her if the sun came out she'd probably be able to take it off during the parade."

"Well, according to Tommy, who is getting the house ready to paint, it should get up to sixty by noon."

Before long, they had their coffees in hand and, spotting Sabrina with Tootsie dressed in a Santa suit standing in front of Midge's, they crossed over to join her. As they clustered together, a number of friends stopped by to say hello or chat, and she was conscientious to introduce them to Daniel, explaining how he'd been a career marine, originally from Appleton.

"This is my favorite landscaper," Daphne told Daniel as Mick joined them. "He also owns a gorgeous nursery just outside of town." She remembered the first time she'd visited the nursery—and her shock to discover it was actually her grandparents' old farm.

"Pleased to meet you," Mick told Daniel. "Any mate of Daphne's is a mate of mine."

"Are you from Australia?" Daniel asked.

"That's right." Mick poked Daphne. "I've been meaning to call you, Daph. You got your Christmas tree yet?"

"No, I've been so busy. I keep putting it off."

"Well, I got a bunch of them coming next week. They were supposed to be here by now, but the west coast weather slowed things down. If you like, I'll put you down for one and get it delivered to you as soon as they arrive."

"That'd be great." As Daphne thanked Mick, she silently questioned herself—*why hadn't it worked out with him?* He was such a great guy. But he was a great friend too.

"And I got holly and evergreens too. Nice looking stuff."

"I'd love some," she said eagerly.

"You got it." Mick grinned at Daniel. "Sorry to be so commercial, but a bloke's gotta make a living."

"No problem." Daniel just nodded.

Now Ricardo joined them, but before Daphne could begin an introduction or explain that Ricardo owned Midge's Diner and was the best chef in town, he grabbed Daniel's hand, heartily shaking it. "Good to see you, buddy," he exclaimed. "I heard you were in town."

"You guys know each other?" Daphne asked.

"Sure, we went to school together. We were both on the wrestling team during our sophomore year. But this guy quit." Ricardo poked Daniel in the arm. "Which never made sense because you were the best wrestler of the lot."

"That's not how I remember it," Daniel remarked.

Ricardo laughed. "I guess memories are like that. Different for everyone."

Now Jake crossed the street to join them. "This looks like the place to be," he said. "Room for one more?"

Daphne suppressed laughter over the irony of being surrounded by Appleton's most available bachelors. Maybe she should start up her own reality show? "Step right up," she told Jake as she moved to make a spot between her and Sabrina. "And we won't even tell Ricardo and Mick how badly we beat you at bowling last night."

"You guys went bowling?" Ricardo asked. "I love bowling. Next time, you better ask me along."

"Me too," Sabrina said. "That sounds like fun."

Just then the firehouse siren went off, signaling that the

parade was starting. First came the Color Guard. A small group of veterans of varying ages and military uniforms, including one paraplegic soldier in a wheelchair, presented the stars and stripes. Daphne glanced at Daniel as he respectfully removed his cap, holding it over his chest as they passed by.

"Thank you for your service to our country," Daphne quietly told him, feeling unexpectedly close to tears.

Daniel's chin barely dipped in a nod of acknowledgment, his eyes fixed on the flag bearers.

Next came a float of elves from the hardware store, followed by the Appaloosa Club complete with jingle bells, and then a flatbed truck with hay bales and a bunch of antsy preschoolers dressed like farm animals and singing "The Twelve Days of Christmas." Very cute.

"Here comes the marching band," Jake called out over the bass drums. "There's Jenna with the banner."

"That's Jenna's best friend, Mattie, with the clarinet." Daphne pointed her out to Daniel. "She's my cousin."

The next float was from a local church, featuring a nativity scene. Following that came the classic car club, roaring their engines and waving.

"You could be driving Bonnie with them," Daniel told Daphne.

"You're right, I could."

"And she'd be the best looking car of the bunch," he whispered.

She chuckled. "I must agree." She pointed beyond the cars to where some older girls were doing a dance number on the street. "That looks like the Miss Kristy's Dance School coming up next. Do you see Mabel?"

They spotted Mabel in her sparkly lavender tutu and, although her bare arms looked chilly, her smile was big and bright. She held hands with Lola, both of them waving energetically to both sides of the street.

"Hey Mabel and Lola," Daphne called out, holding out her phone to snap some pictures.

Mabel eagerly waved back, calling out to Daniel and Sabrina too. Even if Mabel never attended Miss Kristy's Dance School— if Daniel took her to North Carolina—Daphne felt certain the happy girl would remember this day.

"She looks adorable," Daphne said to Sabrina. "Thanks for taking her to get the tutu."

Sabrina looked slightly teary eyed as she nodded.

The parade continued with more groups and floats and animals and children, and finally Santa arrived in a farm wagon pulled by four handsome Clydesdales.

"Well, that was fun," Daphne declared as the boys and men with the manure shovels appeared to clean up the remnants of the parade.

"Now if anyone's interested in an early lunch, I've got my Hungarian Mushroom soup today." Ricardo opened the door to Midge's with a twinkle in his eye. "And some sourdough rolls that should be coming out of the oven about now."

"Mm, that sounds good," Sabrina said.

"Tempting." Daniel checked his watch. "But I need to get back to the house to help Tommy with the painting."

Daphne turned to Sabrina. "You save a table, and I'll run and get Mabel." She turned to Daniel. "Thanks for watching the parade with me. I know Mabel was thrilled to see you here today."

"Thanks for inviting me." He looked deeply into her eyes as he tipped his hat. "Have a great day, Daphne. Maybe I'll see you around later. I'd like to come visit with Mabel if it's all right."

"Of course it's all right. Come over as much as you like," she told him.

As she headed for the holding area on Oak Street where she'd been told to pick up Mabel, she wondered about Daniel. She was getting the strong feeling that he was really interested in her. And although a part of her was excited about this prospect, another part of her was uncertain.

"Aunt Daphne!" Mabel came running, her sweatshirt in hand.

"You were wonderful," Daphne told Mabel as she helped her into the sweatshirt. "But it's still pretty cold, you better put this on."

"Lola asked me to come play at her house," Mabel announced. "Can I?"

"What does Lola's mother say?" Daphne called out loud enough for Becca to hear since she and Lola were coming their way.

"That's fine with me," Becca assured her. "I'm home studying for my real estate license. As long as they keep the noise down to a loud roar, I should be okay."

"We'll play in the basement," Lola assured her. "And we'll be quiet."

"But you're still wearing your tutu," Daphne pointed out.

"She can borrow something of Lola's to change into," Becca offered.

And so it was settled. Mabel headed off with Lola and Daphne returned to Midge's to meet Sabrina. But when she got there, Sabrina was nowhere to be seen. Daphne was about to leave when she noticed Jake eagerly waving her over to his table. "Sabrina had to take Tootsie home," he explained. "She didn't have his carrying case."

"Oh." Daphne nodded.

"She told me to keep you here until she gets back." He waved to the seat across from him. "Then if you girls want to eat alone, I can go sit at the counter by myself." He made a mock frown.

"I don't mind if you join us." Daphne peeled off her jacket and gloves. "And I'm sure Sabrina would like it." Sabrina had already made it clear that she thought Jake would be a great catch—even if Daphne didn't want him. Not that Daphne had ever said as much. She'd only said that it was awkward since Jake was aware of her strange inheritance package.

Kellie ambled up to the table, setting a cup of coffee in front of Jake with a pleasant smile. Although Kellie was gorgeous and well liked amongst the male patrons, she wasn't Daphne's favorite. Not because Daphne hadn't tried to be congenial, but simply because Kellie resented any of Ricardo's female friends. And she didn't care who knew it either. "I'll just have a cup of your Earl Gray tea," Daphne told her.

Kellie rolled her eyes ever so slightly.

"I plan to order lunch when Sabrina gets back," Daphne informed her.

"Rightie-oh." Kellie made a smirk. "Tea coming right up."

Daphne watched as Kellie sauntered away. As far as Daphne could tell, that woman had more interest in the restaurant's owner than she did in waiting tables. Although she'd never say it aloud, Daphne felt that Ricardo was too good for Kellie. And she happened to know that Ricardo's mother felt the same way.

"So...it looks like you and Daniel have hit it off nicely," Jake said in a slightly stiff tone. Almost as if he didn't approve or somehow questioned it.

"Well, we've certainly had a lot to discuss and figure out," she said crisply. "Regarding Mabel."

"Seems like it's about more than just Mabel."

"What are you insinuating?" She looked directly into his eyes. Sometimes Jake was an open book to her, almost like a sweet big brother, and a lot of times she thought he could possibly be something more. But other times he was hard to read, opinionated and abrupt—like now.

"I'm not insinuating anything, Daphne. Just observing."

"Observing what?"

"Well, you two seemed pretty cozy at dinner last night. You seemed to be having a good time. And you really seemed to enjoy his bowling help. Then I see you two together again—at the parade just now. And it sounds as if he plans to come over to visit you later tonight and—"

"Don't you mean to visit *Mabel*?" she corrected.

Jake smiled. "Okay, so he said he wants to see Mabel. But his eyes looked like he wanted to see you. Don't kid yourself, Daphne. He's interested in you. I can tell."

"Oh..." She nodded, letting her guard down some. "To be honest, I was sort of wondering about that myself."

"So how do you feel?" Jake looked intently at her. "Are you interested in him?"

"He's a very nice man," she admitted. "And, as you can imagine, Sabrina has been really pushing me at him. She thinks that would solve *all* my problems."

"You wouldn't have to lose Mabel...and you could

simultaneously secure your inheritance." He sighed. "Nice package deal."

"You don't have to make me sound so mercenary."

"Sorry, I didn't mean it like that. And I can understand Sabrina's thinking. It seems rather perfect." He frowned. "But you know what they say, Daphne—when something looks too good to be true, there's usually a fly in the ointment somewhere."

Daphne made an amused smile. "Interesting way to put it."

"Excuse me for mixing my metaphors or whatever it was, but you get my drift."

"You're the skeptical realist who's looking for the down side."

He just shrugged, taking a slow sip of coffee with a creased brow.

"Daniel is talking about returning to the Marines," she said quickly. "He's talking about living on base in North Carolina. According to him it's a family-friendly place where some of his friends live. And he's talking about taking Mabel with him."

Jake's brows arched. "Oh, well, that does paint a different picture, doesn't it?"

"I never knew I could love a child as much as I love Mabel. Losing her sounds so painful I can hardly bare to think about it. I'd even considered asking you if there was some legal action you could take, like a custody battle, which seems ridiculous now. Plus the more I know Daniel, the more I know I could never do that. He's her uncle, and he loves her too. And she loves him. Besides, it was Vera's dying wish that her son have custody of Mabel." She sighed. "Even if it's not what Mabel wants."

"Can I assume that means Mabel has expressed she'd prefer to stay with you?"

Daphne just nodded.

"That's a quandary, all right." Jake sipped his coffee.

"I'm ba-ack," Sabrina announced in a lilting voice. "Did y'all order your soup yet?"

"We were waiting for you," Daphne said as Sabrina sat down.

"Sorry about that." Sabrina tugged off her fur trimmed parka. "Poor Tootsie, I felt bad leaving him home, but he seemed to have gotten a chill."

"In that warm looking Santa suit?" Daphne asked.

"Well, I probably should've had him in his traveling case. After all, he's a Chihuahua and he's always lived in Atlanta. And Chihuahuas don't much like cool temperatures."

"I heard this might be a cold winter," Jake said.

"I'll just have to keep poor little Tootsie inside more." Sabrina looked around. "Now where's that waitress? I was thinking about a warm bowl of soup all the way over here."

Jake waved to Kellie, and they quickly ordered. As Kellie was leaving, Sabrina turned to Jake. "So what do you think of Appleton's newest hottest couple?" she asked him.

"Who do you mean?"

"Daniel and Daphne, of course." Sabrina giggled. "Why, even their names sound almost musical together—*Daniel and Daphne.* I went online last night to research wedding napkins." She turned to Daphne. "Do you know that you only need to order a hundred napkins to get your initials embossed and printed? And I must say that *D and D* looked very classy."

"Oh, Sabrina."

"And I was thinking about your wedding flowers too, Daphne. If you have a spring wedding, I'll bet the daphnia will be in bloom. Y'all do have daphnia flowers around here, don't you? If you don't, I'll bet I could get my mama to ship us some from Georgia. Can you imagine how sweet that would smell? Mix in some peonies and roses and it would be lovely."

"You're getting carried away," Daphne told her. "Besides, if you want to talk wedding flowers, you'll have to get in line with Olivia. She's been planning my wedding flowers since last June."

"That's right. Olivia has the florist shop. I'll mention my daphnia idea with her. Say, when is her baby due, anyway?"

"February."

"Then you certainly wouldn't want to get married in February." Sabrina pursed her lips. "I actually think a May wedding sounds much better."

"Maybe you should plan a May wedding for yourself," Daphne teased. "Maybe Jake here would like to set you up on some blind dates."

"If the right man came along, I'd be happy to remarry." Sabrina looked at Jake. "Daphne doesn't want to admit that I was right about Daniel. She kept acting like he wasn't interested in her, but it's obvious to see she was wrong."

"So I've noticed." Jake made a stiff looking smile. "But I'm not convinced that Daphne is as interested in Daniel as he is in her. Maybe we shouldn't push her too much."

"She just needs to get used to the idea."

"Excuse me," Daphne said. "But please don't discuss me like I'm not even here. And if you two keep talking about Daniel like this, well, I'll just have to ask Kellie to serve my soup at the counter."

"Fine. If you insist." Sabrina wrinkled her nose. "Killjoy."

Daphne decided it was time to change the subject. "So I've been getting emails from your writer friend, Spencer," she told Jake.

"Wasn't he one of the blind dates Jake set you up with?" Sabrina asked.

"Yes." Daphne nodded grimly. "Jake's not exactly gifted at matchmaking."

"Yes, I'm aware." Sabrina gave Jake a dour look.

"Anyway, Spencer has been urging me to start a writer's critique group this winter. And I've decided it might be fun. We plan to meet on the second Tuesday of every month."

"What do you do in writer's critique group?" Sabrina asked.

"Writers just read what they've written aloud. It could be a chapter or an article or whatever. Then the others take turns offering helpful suggestions and advice."

"So you don't just brutally rip each other apart?" Jake teased.

"I doubt anyone would enjoy that much."

"I've always wanted to write," Sabrina said with a dreamy expression.

"Really?" Daphne was surprised. Sabrina had never mentioned this before.

"What would you write?" Jake asked.

"Romance." Sabrina sighed. "I've read about a million romance novels. Some that were pretty lame too. That's what got me to wondering if I could write one of my own. I actually took an online class a few years ago. But I've yet to really try my hand at it. I guess I'm afraid I'll fall on my face."

"You'll never know if you don't try," Daphne told her.

"That's true. And I've got some story ideas. One of them is about a lady pirate." Her blue eyes twinkled. "They call her Murdering Mary, although she never really killed anyone. They just think she did."

"Interesting." Daphne sipped her tea.

"Daphne and I used to know someone who was a very successful romance writer," Jake said in a mysterious tone.

"*Really?*" Sabrina's face lit up. "Is it a name I might recognize?"

Daphne shot Jake a warning look. What on earth was he doing?

He shrugged. "Sorry. I figured since you told Sabrina about Aunt Dee's will...well, you know...you must trust her."

"Of course she trusts me," Sabrina told him defensively. "Why wouldn't she trust me? Why, I would walk through hot coals for my dear friend Daphne."

Daphne patted Sabrina's hand. "Thanks."

"So are you going to tell me?" Sabrina looked hopeful.

Daphne still felt unsure.

"It's your call," Jake told her.

"I guess it doesn't really matter." Daphne exchanged looks with Jake.

"Come on," Sabrina urged. "I'm dying of curiosity now."

"You must promise not to repeat this," Daphne said in a serious tone. "Out of respect for someone I dearly love. Because it was her secret and that's how she wanted it kept while she was alive. Okay?"

"Of course." Sabrina's eyes lit up. "It's your Aunt Dee, isn't it? I mean your *grandmother.*"

Daphne simply nodded. Sometimes it confused her too. Growing up believing that Aunt Dee was her dad's older sister, only to discover Aunt Dee was actually Dad's birth-mother was still hard to grasp. Even her dad had difficulty with the surprising revelation, and he still thought of Dee as his sister. And Daphne still referred to her as "Aunt Dee."

Okay," she told Sabrina, "since you've kept my other secret, I know I can trust you to keep this one too. You're right."

Sabrina's brow creased. "But wasn't her name the same as yours? I don't recall seeing any romance novels by *Daphne Ballinger*. Although that does sound like a good name for an author. And I do look forward to seeing it on your book when you get published, Daphne."

"Dee used a pseudonym," Jake explained. "A pen name."

"And?" Sabrina looked hopeful.

Daphne grinned at Jake. "Should I tell her?"

Again he shrugged. "Up to you."

"Did you ever hear of Penelope Poindexter?"

Sabrina let out an excited shriek that made everyone in Midge's stop talking. "Sorry," she told the startled diners. "Please, excuse my outburst. I just heard some good news." As people turned back to their food, Sabrina's eyes grew wide and she grabbed Daphne's hand. "Get out of town," she said in a hushed tone. "Are you serious? *Penelope Poindexter is your grandmother?*"

"That's right."

Sabrina fanned her face with her hands. "I feel faint. I really, truly do. *Oh, my word!*"

Jake and Daphne both laughed in amusement.

"Penelope Poindexter is my all-time favorite romance

writer," Sabrina declared. "I have *all* her books. Some that I've read more than once." She slowly shook her head. "Oh, my goodness! I can't believe I bought a house directly across the street from where Miss Penelope Poindexter once lived. I feel like I need to pinch myself."

And even though Daphne had never meant to tell anyone of Aunt Dee's clandestine career as a romance writer, she did get a kick out of Sabrina's dramatic reaction. It was actually rather sweet that Sabrina was such a fan of Aunt Dee's work. And Daphne felt certain she could trust her with this secret. As different as she and Sabrina were from each other, she knew Sabrina was a true friend and she was grateful for her. Although she would be even more grateful if Sabrina would refrain from ordering embossed wedding napkins with D and D on them!

Chapter 7

After playing Old Maid, Go Fish, and a rousing game of Slap Jack, Daphne announced it was time for Mabel to get ready for bed. Judging by Mabel's lack of resistance, she was worn out. "And don't forget to brush your teeth," Daphne said as Mabel headed for the stairs.

"Give a holler when you're in bed," Daniel called out as he rubber-banded the cards together, "and I'll come up to read you a story and listen to your prayers." He glanced at Daphne. "If you don't mind."

"No, of course not." She stacked their ice cream dishes and stood.

"That little girl keeps surprising me." Daniel followed her into the kitchen.

"Surprising you how?" She set the bowls in the sink.

"She's smart as a whip." He grinned. "Did you see how clever she was at cards?"

"Your mom used to play cards with her." Daphne rinsed a bowl.

"Oh." He nodded as he put the rinsed bowl in the dishwasher for her. "Well, that makes sense. Mom always liked playing cards."

For a moment, neither of them spoke. She knew they were both thinking about Vera. And, really, Daphne could think of nothing to say. Nothing that hadn't been said already. "So, how's the painting coming along?"

"Tommy sprayed the whole exterior today. A nice soft shade of yellow." He set another bowl in the dishwasher. "I'll start on the trim tomorrow if this good weather holds up. Tommy suggested an off-white. But already it looks a hundred percent better."

"I'll have to stroll over tomorrow after church to take a peek."

"That's right. It's Sunday tomorrow."

"Would you like to go to church with us?"

He considered this. "I'd like to go, but I better get that trim painted. The weather forecast for next week sounds a little dismal."

Mabel called down that she was getting into bed. "That was quick." Daphne closed the dishwasher. "I hope she brushed her teeth."

"I'll ask," he said as he headed out.

Daphne leaned down to pet Ethel and Lucy. "You two already had your dinner," she told them. "Remember?" But she reached into the pantry for kitty treats anyway. She didn't mind spoiling them a bit. She knew that Aunt Dee used to do the very same thing. As she watched the cats nibbling on their treats, she wondered what Aunt Dee would think about the little girl upstairs. Although she felt pretty certain that she would approve. "But what about the man upstairs?" Daphne said aloud. What would Aunt Dee think about Daniel? She wished she knew the answer to that.

By the time Daniel came back down, Daphne was curled up in the big club chair with Lucy and Ethel in her lap.

Daniel pointed to the dark fireplace. "Do you want a fire? I wouldn't mind building you one before I go."

"That would be lovely. I was just thinking about it, but these cats were settled in so nicely, I hated to disturb them."

Before long, he had a nice fire crackling. He stood in front of it, just looking at her. "I guess I should get going."

"Unless you want to stay," she offered.

He looked slightly uncertain and she hoped that she hadn't made that invitation sound like more than she'd meant. "You know, to sit and enjoy the fire for a bit," she said quickly.

"Yeah, in fact, there's something I'd like to talk to you about." He sat on the sofa, leaning forward with his hands on his knees as if he had something on his mind.

Suddenly Daphne felt worried. All the silly things Sabrina had been saying about wedding napkins and flowers came rushing at her. Surely Daniel wasn't about to—

"Mabel reminded me that her birthday is next weekend."

Daphne was flooded with relief. "Yes. It's on Saturday."

"Did you know she wants to have a birthday party?"

"She mentioned that. I suggested that we might want to do something special with her and Lola."

"But did you know she wants to have a big birthday party?" He peered curiously at her.

"Yes." Daphne nodded. "She wants to invite her whole class."

"That seems like a nice idea. No one is left out. Is that a

problem? I mean, she could have the party somewhere else if you're worried about that many kids in your house."

"That's not the problem." She frowned. "I'm just worried that the kids won't want to come and Mabel will be hurt. Some of those kids were pretty mean to her when she first moved here. She got teased and bullied a lot."

"Why?" Daniel looked indignant. "Did the kids know about her mom and dad?"

"No, that wasn't it. I think it was because she looked rather odd. Not odd. Just unkempt. Your mother was sick. Mabel was sort of on her own. She went to school looking like a homeless waif, and some of the kids picked on her for it."

"Stupid kids."

"Yes. So how do you feel about inviting those same stupid kids to a birthday party? And what if they turned up their stupid noses and hurt her feelings?"

His jaw grew firm. "I see your point."

"Or if they did come, how would you feel if they were rude to Mabel?"

"If I was around, they wouldn't get a chance to be rude."

Daphne smiled. "Yes, I suppose you could put on your uniform...put the fear of the Marines into them."

"Not a bad idea." He chuckled. "I have another idea. What if we came up with a party that would be so fun that everyone in her class would want to come to it?"

"What kind of party would that be?"

"When we were at the bowling alley last night, I noticed they had what they call The Big Apple Fun Center. It looked like a place for kids."

"That's right," Daphne said suddenly. "I've heard ads for

that place. They have games and miniature golf and lots of fun things for kids. And I think you can reserve it for parties too. But I'll bet it's expensive."

"So." He shrugged. "This party is going to be on me. And unless you have some major objection, I'd like to do it."

"Do you think it's too over the top? I mean, do you ever worry that we could be spoiling her?"

"She doesn't seem spoiled to me, Daphne. She's sweet and kind and, as far as I can see, very appreciative."

"Well, it's a question I keep asking myself. I'd hate to give her too much. You know, trying to make up for everything. I want her to stay balanced."

"So do I. And it's not like she could have a party like this every birthday. We can make it clear this is a one-time thing. A little girl only turns eight once."

"But she only turns nine once. And ten once. And—"

"Yes, I get that. But I feel like I've missed out on so much with her. Maybe I could make it seem like I was doing this as much for me as for her."

Daphne smiled. "Well, I think it's a wonderful idea. And I know Mabel is going to love it."

Daniel sighed. "But I've got so much on my plate this week. Monday's Mom's memorial service. And then I'm trying to get the house fixed up. And I need a realtor—"

"My step-mom, Karen, is a good realtor," Daphne told him.

"Great. Can you give me her number?"

"Absolutely. And how about if I take care of the party planning for you."

"Would you mind?"

"I think it would be fun. I've never organized a kids' birthday party before. And I'm sure Sabrina will want to help."

"And don't forget, I'm footing the bill." He slowly stood up.

She chuckled. "Hopefully you won't be sorry when you see the bill."

"Don't worry. If anyone deserves a party like this, it's Mabel."

"Okay, as long as we both agree, we won't let it spoil her."

"Agreed." He extended his hand for a handshake, looking into her eyes as they shook. "I think we make a pretty great team, Daphne. I mean, when it comes to Mabel. It feels like we're on the same page."

She felt her cheeks growing warm as he released her hand. "I think we both love her very much."

He nodded. "Thanks for the cards and ice cream." He looked at the fire. "How about I toss another log on there before I go?"

"Thanks," she told him. She watched as she placed a log on top. He was so big and strong and good looking...what would it be like to be in love with a man like that?

"Don't get up," he told her as he turned around. "No need to upset the kitties. I'll see myself out. Goodnight, Daphne."

"Goodnight, Daniel." As he left, she continued to play with this idea. What would it really be like if they were married? She imagined the two of them in this house together. Helping to raise Mabel together. Fixing meals together. Working in the garden together. It was not a bad picture. Not at all. And she could think of nothing that would please Mabel more. Not to mention Sabrina.

"Sabrina said we should wear black to Grandma's memorial

service," Mabel said on Monday morning as they were having breakfast. "But I told her I don't have anything black." She looked down at her green and navy plaid dress. "Is this okay?"

"It's perfect," Daphne said. "And wearing black is sort of an old fashioned idea. Nowadays, it's acceptable to wear dark colors like your dress. And some people just dress as they please. I think the important thing is to dress in a respectful way. Something that you think your grandmother would appreciate. Like what you're wearing. I'm sure your grandmother would be proud to see you in that."

"Can she see me?"

Daphne shrugged. "I don't really know. There's a lot of things we won't know about heaven until we get there. But I used to get the feeling that my mom could see me sometimes. When I was little anyway."

"You don't feel like that anymore?"

Daphne considered this. "I'm not sure. Sometimes I get the feeling that Aunt Dee is watching me." She smiled. "But maybe that's because this used to be her house. Sort of like I can feel her here."

"Oh." Mabel nodded with a thoughtful expression.

"So, anyway, I'll be picking you up at school around one o'clock. That'll give us plenty of time to get to the church for the service." Daphne pulled out the note she'd written asking for Mabel to be excused early. "Are you ready to go?"

Mabel got her parka and backpack, and together they walked down the street, pausing in front of Vera's old house to observe the paint colors. "That looks pretty," Mabel said. "I think Grandma would like it."

"I do too."

"Good morning." Daniel came outside with a paintbrush in hand. "What do you think?"

"We think your mother would like it a lot."

He made a sad smile. "Yeah, I do too. I wish I'd come and done this a few years ago...so she could've enjoyed it."

"Maybe she's enjoying it now," Mabel suggested.

He patted her head. "Yeah, maybe she is."

"I made the reservation for the Fun Center," Daphne told him. "And Mabel and I finished all the party invitations yesterday."

"Yeah, we printed them on the computer. And they look really cool." Mabel began dancing around the sidewalk with excitement. "This is going to be the best birthday ever—ever—in the whole wide world—ever!"

"And remember it was your uncle's idea," Daphne said.

"Thank you so much, Uncle Daniel. It's so awesome. My friends are going to be so surprised. I can't wait to tell everyone. And Miss Simmons only lets us bring birthday invitations to school when *everyone* in the class is invited. So she'll let me give these ones out."

"Well, have fun with that. I better get back to work now. I'll see you both this afternoon...at the church."

They parted ways, and Daphne continued walking Mabel to school, just like she did every morning. The school was only five blocks from her house, and before Mabel came to live with Daphne she'd walked back and forth by herself every day. She could easily do it now, but somehow it just made Daphne feel better to accompany her. Although she'd been refraining from walking her up to the door. Now they said goodbye once the big brick building came into sight.

"Have a good day, sweetie." Daphne kissed Mabel's forehead. "I know you're excited about the invitations, but don't forget Miss Simmons' note."

As Daphne walked back, she felt concerned. Would Miss Simmons think it incongruous to have Mabel cheerfully handing out birthday invitations this morning and then soberly attending her grandmother's memorial service this afternoon? And yet, Daphne didn't regret this. Mabel had already had far more than her fair share of sadness in her life. What was wrong with adding a little sunshine whenever it was possible?

As she passed Vera's house, she thought about Daniel's words, his regret that he hadn't painted the home back when Vera could've enjoyed it. He hadn't said much about his mother or how he was dealing with her death, but Daphne suspected he felt more than he was showing. She wondered if this was a habit with him, or perhaps he simply hadn't had the opportunity to open up.

Perhaps she'd see a more emotional side of him at Vera's memorial service this afternoon. It wasn't that she wanted him to fall apart exactly. That might be weird. But it made her uncomfortable to think he was the kind of guy to bottle up all his feelings. And having been in the military—in active service where he had to have seen hard things—she wondered if he'd been trained to keep it all inside.

Chapter 8

Daphne hadn't been too surprised to find only a few people in attendance of Vera's memorial service. She knew that Vera had limited friends. About half of the people in the sanctuary were friends of Daphne's, probably there to show support for Mabel. But Pastor Andrew did a good job with the service, and Daniel, looking handsome in his dress uniform, read a nice eulogy for his mother.

Afterward, they all met in the fellowship hall for cookies and beverages that some of the women at the church had arranged. Daniel played host, thanking and greeting the guests and, all the while, remaining cool and composed. He looked slightly regal in his crisp dark uniform with the wide white belt. And the medals on his chest suggested that he'd done some important things. Mabel, obviously in awe of her uncle, was sticking to him like glue. And Daphne thought they looked so sweet together, she snagged a couple of good photos on her phone. Daniel was definitely photogenic, but his ability to maintain such a handsome smile...and to appear so upbeat—especially considering the recent losses in his—life surprised her.

"Judging by the medals, Daniel has had an impressive career," Daphne's dad said to her as they stood chatting with Karen, Jake, and Sabrina.

"Do you know what they're for?" Daphne asked quietly.

"I know they don't just hand them out like candy."

"He's got a bronze star," Sabrina said quietly. "Doesn't that mean he saved someone's life or something very heroic?"

"And he has the V for valor," Daphne's dad told them. "He's definitely been a hero."

"You should be very proud," Sabrina told Daphne.

"Why should Daphne be proud?" Karen questioned.

Sabrina's eyes twinkled with mischief. "Haven't you heard?"

"Heard what?" Daphne's dad asked with a furrowed brow.

"Nothing, Dad." Daphne rolled her eyes. "Sabrina's just slightly delusional."

"You and Daniel?" Karen asked her.

"They've been dating," Sabrina whispered.

"*Sabrina.*" Daphne shook her head. "If you'll excuse me, I want to go thank Pastor Andrew for helping put together such a nice service." As she walked away, she could just imagine what Sabrina was telling them. Well, fine, if Sabrina wanted to blow this into something it wasn't, she would be the one to sort it out when it deteriorated later. Of course, there was always the possibility that Sabrina would be the one saying *I told you so.*

As Daphne thanked Pastor Andrew, Daniel and Mabel came over to join them. "I really appreciate your help," Daniel said as he shook his hand. "I probably wouldn't have even had a service otherwise." He put his hand on Mabel's head. "But I think we all needed it. For closure."

"And, like I told you, Daniel, if you need someone to talk to, I'm here for you." Pastor Andrew smiled warmly. "Even a big tough marine can need someone to sound off to sometimes."

"I appreciate the offer, sir, but I'm fine, thanks."

They visited awhile longer, and slowly the small crowd started breaking up. Daphne went over to tell her dad and Karen goodbye. "Thanks for coming. I was glad, mostly for Mabel's sake, that the sanctuary wasn't completely empty."

"Daniel probably appreciated it too," Karen said with a suspicious expression.

"Sabrina seems pretty certain that you and Daniel were made for each other." Dad peered curiously at her.

"Oh, you know Sabrina. She's in love with love." Daphne turned to Karen. "By the way, I gave Daniel your number. He's looking for someone to list his mom's house."

"Well, thank you. I appreciate the recommendation."

"He's hoping it will sell before Christmas," Daphne said dismally. "Seems like a long shot to me."

"Don't be too sure. A lot of folks buy homes in winter these days. Especially in a desirable neighborhood like that. If we price it right, it could sell within days. Maybe even have a bidding war."

"Oh." Daphne frowned.

"You don't want him to sell it?" Dad asked.

"I, uh, I'm not sure. I guess it worries me."

"Why?" Karen asked with concern.

Daphne explained about North Carolina and how he wanted to return to the Marines. "I don't want to lose Mabel."

"Then maybe you should listen to Sabrina and hold onto both of them." Karen winked at her.

"I don't know...." Dad looked uncertain. "I'm sure you'll figure it all out, Daph. You're a smart woman."

She wanted to argue that intelligence had nothing to do with these matters of the heart, but instead she hugged them both and told them goodbye.

For the next few days, Daphne divided her time between working on the suspense novel she'd started when she moved to Appleton, planning for Saturday's birthday party—and trying to figure out her relationship with Daniel. Because of his desire to spend time with Mabel—and perhaps it was his way of spending time with Daphne—Daniel had been coming over every evening for dinner. And it wasn't as if he expected her to cook for them every night. On Tuesday he brought pizza and on Thursday, Chinese. But by Friday night, as they were eating spaghetti, it felt a whole lot like a family. And although it was sort of nice, Daphne felt uneasy.

After Mabel went to bed and Daniel went home, Daphne went to her computer. She thought she was going to get ahead on the advice column—instead she wound up writing a letter to Dear Daphne herself.

Dear Daphne,

Since I was a child, I always dreamed of growing up and having a family of my own. This was probably a byproduct of being an only child with a hardworking widower father. So I always thought

I wanted the works—a beautiful home, a loving husband, some adorable children, a couple of pets, a white picket fence and all that. But suddenly it feels as if this whole scenario has been dropped into my lap and now I'm not so sure I want it.

I don't understand why I'm not deliriously happy, but something about this setup doesn't feel quite right. I'm guessing it's me. Or maybe it's the man auditioning for "husband." He's been in the military for almost twenty years and seems a little shutdown to me. As if his emotions are suppressed, or maybe he's just very pragmatic. But it troubles me.

And then I question myself. Maybe I'm hoping for too much. Maybe I've allowed my dreams to get so big that they're unattainable. And maybe this really is my Mr. Right and he simply needs me to help him to open up. Maybe I'm so used to being disappointed that I don't know how to act when something really good comes my way. Maybe I simply need to open up my heart and my arms and accept what is standing before me.

Hoping for More on Huckleberry Lane

Dear Hoping,

It's understandable that you would carry your childhood dreams into adulthood with you. And it's not surprising that you might get cold feet in the very real plausibility that your dreams are about to come true. But it sounds like you're not quite ready for this yet. You say: "It doesn't feel quite right."

That suggests that your heart isn't fully invested yet.

Beyond that, you never say that you're in love with this military man. Are you? I suspect if you knew you loved him, you would jump into this relationship with more abandon. But if you're not in love, you would definitely be questioning yourself.

Or perhaps your uncertainty is that you're worried he's not in love with you. Is he? Until you answer those two questions, it seems unlikely you can answer the bigger question—is this really your dream scenario coming true?

Daphne

As Daphne shut down her computer, she wasn't too sure about *Dear Daphne's* advice. Was marriage always about being in love? What about marriages in the olden days when people married out of necessity? Or what about arranged marriages in other cultures nowadays? And what about that silly TV show where people married complete strangers and some of the marriages worked? Was it possible to marry for convenience and find true love along the way?

On the other hand, what about couples who married because they were "head over heels" in love, but then wound up divorced within the year? Were emotions like love completely trustworthy? Which should rule one's life—one's heart or one's head?

As Daphne turned off her office lights, she pondered these things. And she even wondered if there was any point in giving out advice to the "lovelorn." And what qualified a mixed-up person like her to dole it out? What if the readers found out that she couldn't even figure out her own love life? Of course, that took her back to Aunt Dee. She had been single her whole life, and yet her column had been faithfully read by millions of readers all across the country—it still was. Go figure!

Mabel awoke bright and early on her birthday. She was helpful and cheerful and full of high hopes and great expectations for this afternoon's birthday bash at The Big Apple Fun Center. Meanwhile Daphne felt like a huge dark cloud hung over her head. And it had nothing to do with Daniel or romance or any of life's great challenges. She was worried about the fact that they hadn't put an RSVP on the invitations. For all she knew, the birthday party might only be attended by Mabel and Lola. And although she knew the two girls would still have fun—once they got over the disappointment of no other kids—it would be a very expensive birthday celebration. And Daniel would probably be disappointed as well.

"Something troubling you?" Sabrina asked as they loaded a bag of decorations into the back of Daphne's car.

Daphne quickly explained her dilemma.

"You didn't put in an RSVP?" Sabrina looked astounded. "Really?"

"We made our own invitations and we were so excited about using the graphics and fonts and colors, we totally forgot about the RSVP."

"But you did give them the proper location and time?"

"Yes, of course." Daphne closed the trunk.

Sabrina's mouth twisted to one side. "I guess it could be like that parable."

"What parable?" Daphne looked down the street to see if Mabel and Lola were coming on their scooters.

"The one where the man has a big feast and no one comes and he eventually asks people in from the streets."

Daphne frowned. "I like that parable, but I can't imagine inviting homeless people to a little girl's birthday party."

"No, probably not."

Daphne waved at Mabel and Lola, tearing down the sidewalk toward them.

"Hey, birthday girl," Sabrina called out. "I'm driving you guys to the party." She looked at her watch. "In about an hour."

Daphne tossed her purse in the car. "And Uncle Daniel and I will already be there," she told Mabel. "Getting things ready."

"Are you going to *marry* Mabel's uncle?" Lola asked, blue eyes wide.

Daphne laughed. "Is that what Mabel's been telling you?"

Mabel wore a guilty expression.

"No one has any plans for getting married," Daphne told Lola. "How about your mom? Is she getting married?"

"No." Lola firmly shook her head. "She says she's never getting married again."

"Well, you have to watch out for that," Sabrina said lightly. "It's the ones who say no way that end up tying the knot."

Daphne waved. "I'll leave you girls to figure all that out. I need to go pick up Daniel."

At Daniel's house, he met her in the driveway then insisted she come in and have a quick look around. "Wow," she said. "I can't believe this is the same house."

"Yeah, it turned out okay."

"Okay? It looks great, Daniel. The paint colors are nice and neutral and these wood floors are gorgeous."

"All I did was remove the carpeting and hire a guy to come in here and buff it up a little."

"Nice."

"Karen was by yesterday. We're going to list it on Monday." Daphne just nodded.

"You look disappointed."

She shrugged. "Well, it's just that this seems to suggest that you really are going to North Carolina. I guess I'd sort of hoped you'd keep this house...and you and Mabel would stay in Appleton."

He frowned.

"Anyway, we better get over to the Fun Center. We've got a lot of balloons to blow up and streamers to hang."

As she drove them across town, she kept the conversation light and non-committal. But she could tell that Daniel was preoccupied. Probably by what she'd just said. She hoped she hadn't given him the wrong idea. It wasn't as if she was fishing for a marriage proposal. Or was she?

At the Fun Center, they carried a few things inside and got directions to the party room. Then Daniel made several trips to the car, bringing in the cooler and the cake and a few other things. After that, she put him to work blowing up balloons, which thankfully didn't make conversation very easy. She figured that was a relief to both of them.

"This looks really good," Daniel said as they finished with the last streamer.

"Mabel picked out the colors," Daphne told him. "At first she wanted purple and pink, but then she decided that would look too girlie and the boys might not like it. So she went with purple and red and blue—because, as she told me, red and blue make purple. I actually like it."

"Mabel should be pleased."

"I just hope Mabel and Lola aren't the only ones here."

"Why would that happen?"

Now she confessed about forgetting the RSVP.

"You're kidding." He frowned.

She shook her head. "I'm sorry, Daniel. I feel really terrible about it. I mean, you've paid for everything and it'll be a really expensive party for just two kids. If that happens, I hope you'll let me help cover the cost and—"

"No," he said gruffly. "Just forget about it."

"Okay." She glanced nervously at her watch. Daniel seemed a little grumpy. Was it because of her RSVP mistake? "The kids won't be here for another ten minutes if there's something you want—"

"Daphne." Daniel looked directly into her eyes.

"What?"

"Do you think we could make it work?"

"Make what work?" Daphne tightened up a droopy streamer.

Daniel reached for her arm, pulling her toward him. "Do you think we could make a marriage work?"

She blinked. Was this a proposal?

"I know, that sounds really abrupt. And sudden." He shook his head. "I'm obviously not good at this. I'm sorry."

"What are you saying, Daniel?"

"These past ten days with you and Mabel have been really amazing. I can't even explain it exactly, but it's almost like being home. I don't mean a home like I grew up in. I mean a real home."

She slowly nodded. "Uh huh."

"I think I love you, Daphne. I know it's probably too soon to say it. But I guess I just feel a sense of urgency. Do you think we could make it work? Would you be willing? What I'm saying, Daphne, is will you marry me?"

Daphne was speechless.

"You don't have to answer me right now. I realize it's sudden. I hadn't meant to say it like this. It's just that it was fun decorating this room with you. We have such good times together. And I got to thinking, wouldn't that be a great birthday present to Mabel? To tell her that we're getting married?"

Daphne was still speechless—trying to gather her thoughts—and hoping that Sabrina and the girls wouldn't arrive early. "Wow..." She took in a deep breath. "I'm pretty stunned by this, Daniel. I mean it's not that I haven't had similar thoughts, but—"

"You have?" Daniel's eyes lit up.

"Well, Mabel has been practically begging me to marry you." She told him about Lola's question an hour ago. "And Sabrina has been pushing it too."

"So it wasn't such a crazy idea?"

"No...not crazy. But I guess I just wasn't quite ready. I'm a little stunned."

He frowned at the brightly colored room. "I guess I could've chosen a more romantic setting too."

She laughed nervously.

He glanced over to the door then turned back to her. "And I realize we've never even kissed." She felt her heart pounding as he reached for her hands, pulling her closer. "Do you mind?"

She shook her head no—and then he kissed her. And while it was nice and slightly tingly, it wasn't exactly the fireworks she'd hoped for. But her thoughts were cut short by someone entering the room.

"Oh, my word!" Sabrina exclaimed. "Looks like we're interrupting something, girls."

Mabel and Lola burst into loud giggles as Daphne stepped away from Daniel with flushed cheeks. "You're here," Daphne said in a high pitched voice.

"Want us to leave and come back later?" Sabrina asked mischievously.

"Of course not." Daphne made a nervous smile. "So, what do you think of the decorations? Didn't Mabel pick the perfect colors?"

Mabel looked around quickly. "It's really cool!" But she turned back to Daphne and Daniel with a victorious grin. "You guys *are* getting married, aren't you? I just knew it. God answered my prayers! For my birthday!" She grabbed Lola's hands and together they did a happy jig around the room, chanting the old rhyme: *"Daniel and Daphne sitting in a tree—K-I-S-S-I-N-G! First comes love, second comes marriage, third comes a baby in a baby carriage!"*

Daphne cast Daniel a slightly exasperated glance, but he simply laughed. And Sabrina looked just like the cat that swallowed the canary, so much so that Daphne was bracing herself for the dreaded words: *I told you so.*

Chapter 9

To Daphne's relief, only one child from Mabel's class didn't show—and according to Lulu that was because Avalon was sick. Before long the party room was crawling with twenty-three second-graders. They played lots of games, opened gifts, ate cake and ice cream, received party favors, and popped balloons. By the end of the party two hours later, Daphne thought she might suffer a permanent hearing loss from the noise.

"That was the best party ever," Mabel declared from the backseat as Daniel drove the three of them home in Daphne's car.

"I've never seen so many birthday presents in one place," Daphne said in wonder. "Do you think they'll even fit in your room?"

"I want to give some away," Mabel said quietly.

"*What?*" Daniel said a bit sharply. "Don't you like them?"

"I like them," Mabel said slowly. "The gifts were all really cool."

"Then why would you give them away?" Daphne asked gently.

"I want to give them to *needy* kids."

Daphne felt her heart twist at the irony of this. Only three months ago, Mabel would've been considered a needy kid. "Oh, honey, that's so sweet and generous of you. I'm very proud of you."

"I am too," Daniel said. "You're quite a girl, Mabel Myers."

"So if you guys get married, I can still be Mabel Myers," she said in a matter-of-fact tone. "I was wondering if I'd be Mabel *Ballinger* if Aunt Daphne decided to keep me. I like that name too, but it would be easier to remember Myers since that's the name I always had. And it will be your name too, Aunt Daphne. Lola told me the woman changes her name when she gets married."

Daphne didn't know what to say to this. And so she said nothing. As they drove down Huckleberry Lane, she tried to think of some kind of distractive conversation. Anything to get them off of the marriage subject. "Oh, Mabel," she said. "You should see how Uncle Daniel has fixed up your grandma's house. You won't even recognize it."

"Can I see it?" Mabel asked eagerly.

"Sure," Daniel said as he slowed down in front of the pale yellow house.

"Go ahead and look around," Daphne told Mabel. "I'll take the party stuff home and start unloading the car."

Daniel started to protest, saying he'd come over and help her, but Daphne insisted. "I really think it would be good for Mabel to see your work—and how the house has changed." And as soon as they were out of the car, she drove on home. As soon as she got home, instead of unloading the car, she called Daniel, quickly asking if he could keep Mabel with him for a couple of hours while she ran some errands.

"And I'll leave the house unlocked if you guys want to come over here and hang," she offered. He readily agreed, and after she hung up she quickly unloaded the car, just setting everything in the foyer for Mabel and Daniel to sort out later. And then she got back into the car and drove away. She didn't even know where she was going, but she knew she needed someplace where she could clear her head and think.

She drove around town, trying to decide where to go, but eventually found herself at the Red River Coffee Company, ordering a pumpkin latte. Still feeling rattled and confused, she went over to a back table and sat down—trying to wrap her head around what had happened this afternoon. Trying to determine how she felt about it. What did she want? But instead of arriving at any answers, she was simply lining up more questions. She felt like a dog chasing its tail, going faster and faster and getting nowhere.

By the time she finished her latte, she wished she had someone to talk to. She'd noticed Olivia's car at the flower shop, which meant she was working today. So she was probably busy. And even though Sabrina would be happy to talk, Daphne knew which direction she would be headed. Daphne even considered Pastor Andrew, but he was probably preparing for the singles fellowship group by now. And Dad and Karen, well, they were still such newlyweds, she hated to impose. Closing her eyes, she took in a long deep breath, silently asking God to guide her. As she exhaled she felt herself relaxing. And then she heard footsteps.

"What's a girl like you doing in a place like this?"

"Huh?" Daphne opened her eyes to see Jake looking down at her with a curious expression and a mug of coffee in his hand.

"Sorry, that's the best line I could think of." He glanced at her empty cup. "Buy you a drink?"

"No thanks."

"This seat taken?" He nudged the chair across from her.

"Feel free."

"So what's up?" he asked as he sat down with his coffee. "You look kind of upset. Something wrong?"

She just nodded.

"Want to talk?"

She nodded again. "If you have time to listen."

"Got nothing but time. No place to go. No one to see. Spill your story, Daphne." He smiled compassionately. "I'm all ears."

And so she told him about Daniel's unexpected proposal. "I was totally dumbstruck," she admitted.

"Yeah, you still seem like you're in shock."

"I am."

"Good shock?" Jake's brow creased.

"Not exactly. Or if it is good shock, it hasn't quite registered yet." She grasped her empty coffee cup tightly. "Shouldn't a girl be ecstatic when the man of her dreams proposes?"

"Is he the man of your dreams?"

She pursed her lips, gripping the cup even tighter. "I, uh, I don't know."

"So how do you feel about him, Daphne?" His tone was slightly impartial now, almost as if interrogating someone on the witness stand.

She shrugged. "I'm not exactly sure."

"Do you love him?" Jake looked intently into her eyes, as if he might spot the true answer in there.

"Love him? You sound just like *Dear Daphne.*"

"But you are *Dear Daphne.* Remember?"

She made a half-smile, confessing how she'd written a letter asking for advice.

"I see. So what did *Dear Daphne* tell you?"

"That I needed to figure out if I was in love or not."

"And?"

"I'm not sure. And to be honest, I'm not sure it matters." Now she shared her theories about marriages of convenience and how the divorce rate probably was no different than couples who married for love. "Even strangers can learn to love each other if they have common goals and mutual respect."

"But could you be happy with that kind of relationship?" His brow creased with concern.

"I don't know. But when I consider Mabel...well, I think maybe I could."

"I see. So is this more about Mabel than it is about you?"

"It's hard to imagine losing her."

"Then maybe you should just go for it," he said in a flat tone. "Set all your personal feelings aside and marry a man you may not love in order to keep Mabel. What's stopping you?"

She frowned at him.

"Not only that, but you'll secure your inheritance. What could be easier?"

Now she glared at him.

"Sorry," he said in a much more gentle tone. "I guess I was just playing devil's advocate."

She sighed. "And I suppose I deserved that. You probably

think I'm a basket case."

"No. I think you've been put in a really tough position. A couple of tough positions. I honestly don't think I'd do any better in your shoes. Sorry for sounding so callous."

She slowly shook her head. "Don't be sorry, Jake. I actually appreciate your candor. You're just the kind of friend I needed to talk to."

"Okay, are you ready for something else?"

She blinked. "What?"

"Okay, think about this, Daphne. Mabel is seven—"

"She just turned eight."

"Right...eight. So in a short ten years Mabel will be eighteen, and she'll leave for college and a career and maybe a marriage of her own. Meanwhile, you're stuck with a man that you're not really sure you love—for another thirty to forty years, maybe more."

"You do sound like *Dear Daphne,*" she exclaimed. "Did I accidentally send those to you?"

He chuckled. "Not this time. But great minds do think alike."

"Okay, you make a good point, Jake. But you make it sound like I'd be stuck in a horrible, loveless marriage. I don't really see it that way. Daniel and I have been spending a lot of time together this past week. We're companionable. Even if I don't feel like I'm in love with him, I do like him. I respect him. I think he'd make a wonderful dad to Mabel."

Jake looked somewhat stymied now. As if she had presented the most convincing argument of this little debate. But somehow that did not bring her any satisfaction.

"Sure you don't want another coffee?" He pointed to the empty cup she was still clasping like a lifeline.

"Okay. But make it a decaf latte this time."

"You got it."

She watched as Jake went to the counter, casually chatting with the barista. As irritated as she sometimes felt for how he seemed to like to yank her chain, she also really liked and appreciated his friendship. And she trusted his advice. Aunt Dee had to have really trusted him too. And the idea of being married to Daniel, settling her estate, and seeing Jake move on from her life was a little disheartening.

"Here you go." Jake set the cup in front of her.

"Thanks," she murmured.

"So I have more questions for you. You say that Daniel would make a good dad for Mabel. And I have no doubt that you're right about that. You have good instincts. But here's my question—does he love Mabel enough to parent her as a single dad?"

"He seemed to think so. I mean, before he proposed. That was where he was headed—to raise Mabel on his own."

"Because I can attest to the fact that single parenting is a lot easier said than done. And even though my ex would never win mother of the year with co-parenting Jenna, it would've been much harder without Gwen around. I'm sure my career would've suffered too."

"So you admit a child is better off with two parents?"

"Absolutely. The second part of the single parenting question is why can't Daniel remain in Appleton and parent Mabel whether you marry him or not? Certainly he's aware that Mabel has been through a lot. Does he understand that taking her away from Appleton might not be in her best interest?"

"He's concerned for his career."

"Yes, I understand that. I had to make choices too. Appleton wasn't my first choice for setting up my law practice—although it did grow on me. But because Gwen and Jenna were here, I decided to remain here too. I don't regret it. And Daniel could find work here. He could easily live in his mom's house, which is actually pretty convenient for you. You guys could have shared custody of Mabel."

She nodded. "That does make sense."

"And that would take the pressure off of you to marry him. You'd still be able to look for a relationship that involved true love."

"True love...?" She pursed her lips. "You married for true love, didn't you?"

"I thought so at the time. But I was young and disillusioned and, as it turned out, wrong about a lot of things. It didn't take me long to figure it out, but by then there was a child involved. And, as you know, that complicates everything."

"Believe me, I know. My heart gets more pulled in each day." Daphne's eyes got misty as she told him how Mabel wanted to give some of her birthday gifts to the needy.

"She's quite a girl."

"I know. And I just can't bear to lose her."

"That brings up another question."

"What?"

"What if Daniel is still determined to rejoin the Marines? So if you did marry him—in order to keep Mabel in your life—where do you think you would live? North Carolina?"

She blinked with realization.

"Wouldn't he expect his new wife to go with him? Can you

imagine living on a Marine base, Daphne? Keeping the home-fires burning while Daniel's serving overseas somewhere?"

Daphne felt like someone had just dumped a bucket of ice water over her head.

"Or did Daniel promise to give up the military for you? Are you imagining the three of you living happily ever after in Appleton? In your sweet old house?"

She glumly nodded.

"Did you ask him about that?"

"No."

Jake reached across the table to grasp her hand. "Look, I'm not trying to make you feel bad just to be mean. And I realize I've made some stupid blunders and I've rubbed you wrong a few times. But I honestly have your best interests at heart, Daph. I really do."

"I know. I believe you do. You've been like a big brother, Jake. I'm sure Aunt Dee must've known you'd be good at helping me with this."

His eyes grew sad. "I loved Dee, but she really put me in a difficult position." He grimly shook his head as he released her hand. "Sometimes I wish she'd gone with a different attorney."

"You do?"

"Then I could simply be your friend with no one second-guessing anyone's agenda. Who knows how it would've gone without this whole crazy will business hanging over our heads. Sometimes I feel like I'm trapped, Daphne. Just as much as you are."

"But what you said about Daniel going back to the Marines, Jake. That's something I totally blocked out. You're right, I did imagine him giving it all up for me. I may be confused about some things, but I know without doubt I don't want to move away from Appleton. I love it here. The idea of giving it all up...after I've just gotten settled and made some good friends, well, it's disturbing."

"Then maybe you have your answer."

She held up a finger. "Except that I don't know that for sure. Daniel said something today. He said that spending time with Mabel and me has made him feel at home. Maybe for the first time in his life." As she said this, she was thinking about what Mabel had told her—about Daniel's bad dreams...and her own suspicion he might suffer from PTSD. Perhaps that was reason enough for him to change his career direction. But what would it be like to be married to someone with PTSD? Was that something she was ready for? She took in a slow breath. "I can only assume Daniel means he feels at home in my house, at home in Appleton. Maybe he's changed his mind about North Carolina."

"Then you better find that out. So that you can make your decision."

"Yeah." She felt somewhat clearer, like she knew what to ask Daniel now. But at the same time, she felt concerned...and confused. "Thanks, Jake, for listening to me—and for speaking the truth the way you always do. I really do appreciate our friendship."

"So do I." His lips were in a half smile, but his eyes looked sad. "Let me know how it goes. Not just because I'm your attorney, although that's reason enough. But because I'm your friend."

She promised she would and then, seeing it was nearly six o'clock and knowing Mabel and Daniel would be hungry for dinner, she thanked him again and then headed for home. On her way, she prayed again—asking God to direct her path and to give her the strength to accept his direction even if she didn't like where it was taking her.

Chapter 10

To Daphne's surprise, Daniel and Mabel were already making dinner. Not exactly what Daphne had planned to fix for Mabel's birthday dinner, but she was grateful just the same.

"We made enough for you," Daniel said as he ladled out some soup. "Just tomato soup and grilled cheese sandwiches— like my mom used to make."

"Sounds wonderful," she told him. "Thank you."

"I set the table in the dining room," Mabel said.

"It all looks perfect," Daphne told her. "And we have enough birthday cake left for dessert, if you want."

"I put the leftover ice cream in the freezer," Daniel said.

While Daniel was dishing out the food, Daphne sneaked into the dining room to put some candles and some flowers left over from Thanksgiving on the table. She was just lighting the candles as Daniel and Mabel came in.

"Another party," Mabel exclaimed.

"Well, it's still your birthday," Daphne told her.

Soon they were all seated and Mabel offered to say the

blessing, sweetly bowing her head and thanking God for all the good things that had come to her on her birthday. Daphne cringed as Mabel insinuated that she and Daniel were really getting married. Hopefully Daniel hadn't done anything to elevate her hopes any more than they already were.

As they ate their soup and sandwiches, Daphne kept the conversation light and cheerful, encouraging Mabel to replay the highlights of her day. Thankfully, Mabel had plenty of things to talk about. After the three of them finished their meals, Daphne insisted on cleaning up. "You two can go play cards or something," she suggested, eager to have some alone time as she rehearsed the questions she wanted to ask Daniel— after she was certain that Mabel was sound asleep.

It wasn't even eight o'clock when Mabel, worn out from the day's festivities, made her way to bed. By 8:30 Daphne was certain that the birthday girl had safely drifted off. She pulled the comforter up a bit and then slipped out, quietly closing the door. When she got back downstairs, Daniel was just putting another log on the fire.

"That feels nice," Daphne said as she sat down in the club chair. "Thanks."

"No problem." He sat on the sofa with a curious expression. "I'm not sure if you've had enough time to think things over, Daphne...but I thought I'd stick around just in case. If you need another day or two, I understand."

"Actually, I was hoping you'd stay." She took in a deep breath. "I did want to talk to you about, well, everything."

"All right." He sat up straight, almost as if he was at attention.

"Well, as you know I was pretty blown away by your

proposal," she began carefully. "And I needed some time to think it all over."

"Understandable."

"And I have some questions."

"Fire away."

"Well, my biggest question is regarding the Marines. I know you've expressed a desire to return to active service."

His eyes lit up. "Yes. I really feel like I'm not done yet. I'm only thirty-seven. That seems too young for retirement."

"But there are other forms of work. Just because you retire from the Marines doesn't mean you retire from work entirely."

"That's true. But the benefits I lose by retiring early...well, I've given it a lot of thought and it's just not worth it."

"So you're determined to go back then? To that base in North Carolina?"

He nodded firmly. "That's my plan, Daphne. Is that a problem for you?"

She pressed her lips tightly together, trying to put her words together as well. "I've only just returned to Appleton," she began slowly. "I came back home last May when Aunt Dee passed on. And to be honest, I never planned to stay. But then I got this house and all. And I grew to love everything about this place. And I made friends and Appleton feels like home now."

"I can understand that. I think it could feel like home to me too...in time. Maybe ten or fifteen years."

"Mabel would be grown up by then," she said quietly.

"I guess so." He nodded with a perplexed expression.

"I just wouldn't be able to do that, Daniel. I couldn't move away."

"You mean you'd want to stay here after we were married?

You and Mabel, so far away? I don't think I'd like that."

"No, I don't think that would be a good idea. When you get married, you need your wife to be willing to go where you need to go. Don't you think so?"

"Yes." He nodded eagerly. "Absolutely."

"And I can't do that." She didn't want to tell him the reason she couldn't—because she didn't love him.

He slowly stood. "Okay then."

"I'm sorry, Daniel." She stood too.

"No need to be sorry. You were honest with me." He retrieved his coat and hat, moving toward the door.

"I honestly wished that I could do that," she said gently. "And part of me could. But another part of me—well, it's just impossible."

He nodded curtly. "No need to say another word. I understand."

"Thank you," she said as he reached for the door. "And I am sorry."

"Goodnight, Daphne," he said as he went out.

As the door closed, Daphne's eyes filled with tears. Not because she had declined his proposal and not because she felt bad for hurting him—although she did—but mostly because she felt certain she had just burned the last bridge that could've kept Mabel with her. She could see the determination in Daniel's dark eyes as he was leaving. He was going to North Carolina, and Mabel was going with him. She just knew it.

The next day passed in a quiet, normal manner. Church on Sunday morning. Lunch at her parents' condo on Sunday afternoon. A quiet evening at home, going over homework with Mabel, laying out her things for school the next day. It wasn't until she was putting Mabel to bed that she brought up the subject of Daniel.

"Where was Uncle Daniel today?" Mabel asked sleepily.

"I think he was working on your grandma's house." Daphne tucked her in. "He wants to list it with Karen tomorrow. Remember Karen mentioned that at lunch today?"

"Oh, yeah. I forgot."

"And there's something I need to tell you," Daphne said gently. "I know you thought Uncle Daniel and I were going to get married. And the truth is, we talked about it. That's why you saw us kissing right before your birthday."

Mabel's sleepy eyes grew brighter.

"And I do love Daniel, Mabel. I love him as my good friend and as your uncle. But I'm not going to marry him."

Mabel's smile faded. "Why not?"

"I just don't love him like that. I thought that maybe I could. But really, I was thinking more about you than Daniel. Do you understand what I mean?"

"You mean if you married Uncle Daniel we'd all be a family?"

Daphne nodded. "And I actually wanted that."

"Then you should marry him."

Daphne sighed. "I wish it were that simple. But the other part of the problem—and this might've been the hardest part—is that Daniel wants to go back to the Marines. And that means we'd have to move far away from Appleton."

"I don't want to leave Appleton."

"I know. I don't either."

"Will Uncle Daniel take me with him when he goes back to the Marines?"

"He might." Daphne felt a lump in her throat. "And that is the reason I almost married him. I thought it was a way to keep us both here in Appleton. But I was wrong about that. And I was wrong to think that was a good reason to marry someone. It's not a good reason. I should've known better."

"Why isn't it?" Mabel was sounding sleepy again.

"Because when you get married—and I hope someday you do—it should be because you are in love with that person. You should love that person so completely that even if they wanted to go live on the moon, you'd be willing to go with them. Because you love them."

Mabel seemed to consider this. "I would go to the moon with you, Aunt Daphne."

Tears were slipping out now, but to hide them, Daphne gathered Mabel up in her arms, hugging her close. "I would go to the moon with you too, sweetie. I truly would."

After they hugged, Daphne listened to Mabel say her prayers and to her relief, when Mabel asked God to bless Uncle Daniel and Aunt Daphne, she didn't mention marriage at all.

As Daphne went downstairs, she questioned herself. If she was willing to go to the moon with Mabel, why wasn't she willing to go to North Carolina? She looked at the fireplace, which was black and dark, and wondered if perhaps she'd made a mistake. Was it really so wrong to marry someone you weren't in love with? When so much was at stake? Would she ever know the answer to that one? And, no, she had no intention of writing it to *Dear Daphne*. She already knew what the response would be.

On Monday morning, on her way back from walking Mabel to school, Daphne noticed Karen putting a for sale sign on Vera's front lawn. She stopped to say hi, and before she knew it, her new step-mother invited herself down to Daphne's house for coffee.

"I'll be about twenty more minutes," Karen told Daphne as she went back inside the house to where, Daphne assumed, Daniel was waiting.

As Daphne hurried home to make coffee, she wondered why Karen had seemed so eager to pay her a visit. It wasn't that they weren't friendly, and Daphne definitely liked Karen, but they had never really spent much time alone.

Daphne was just setting some packaged cookies on a plate when she heard the doorbell ringing and Karen calling out. "Come in," Daphne yelled back. "In the kitchen."

"Sorry to barge in on you," Karen said as she pulled out a chair.

"No problem. I'm glad you did."

"First of all, I'm so grateful to you for getting that listing with Daniel. I think I might already have a buyer lined up. If all goes well, that house could be sold by the end of the week. *Thank you.*"

"You're welcome." Daphne filled a mug with coffee.

"But we need to talk."

Daphne cringed as she set Karen's mug down. "That line always makes me uncomfortable. Is something wrong between you and Dad?"

Karen laughed. "Not in the least. We are happy as clams."

"Good." Daphne took a chair across from Karen.

"It's about Daniel."

"Oh?" Daphne picked up her coffee mug, blowing the steam.

"I know about the proposal."

"You do?" Daphne was surprised. She hadn't mentioned it to her dad yesterday. Mostly because she'd already declined it.

"Mabel let the cat out of the bag while you were in the bathroom yesterday. She told us it was a secret."

"Right..."

"But now Daniel tells me it's a no-go. What's going on?"

Daphne let out a long sigh. "It's kind of a long story."

"I'm in no hurry." She leaned back, sipping her coffee.

So Daphne went ahead and told Karen the long version, hoping that Karen would pass it on to Dad and that would be the end of it.

"Are you certain you don't want to marry him?" Karen asked when Daphne finished the story.

Daphne knew she should be prepared for this question—especially since she still hadn't broken the news to Sabrina yet. "I am positive, Karen. Would you have married my dad if you hadn't been in love with him?"

Karen just laughed. "No, of course, not."

"So there you have it."

Karen pursed her lips as if she was still not convinced. "But he seems like such a good catch, Daphne. Your dad and I both hoped he was the one."

"Well, if he'd been the one, both Mabel and I would be packing our bags to move to North Carolina. Daniel is rejoining the Marines. He doesn't plan to give it up for at least ten years. That's what really helped me to decide."

"Oh, I see. Your dad will be relieved to hear you're not going anywhere." She smiled. "Forgive me for being so intrusive. But when Daniel told me you turned him down, I thought maybe I'd heard him wrong."

"The only problem now is that I'm afraid he'll take Mabel when he goes." She sighed. "There's not much I can do about that."

"Oh, dear. He's not doing it to punish you, is he?"

"No. It was his mother's last wish that Mabel be with him."

Karen finished her coffee then frowned. "Well, if there's anything we can do to help, you just let us know." She reached over to squeeze Daphne's shoulder. "As hard as it might seem, I think you made the right choice."

"Thanks." And for some reason Daphne really appreciated Karen's words. Almost as much as if they had come from her dad. Now she only had Sabrina to tell. She was not looking forward to that. But as Daphne walked Karen out to the front porch, there was Sabrina calling out as she crossed the street with a bulging shopping bag over each arm.

"Here I am," Sabrina announced.

"Yes?" Daphne frowned at the bags.

"Did you forget that you promised me you'd let me help you decorate for Christmas today?" Sabrina set the bags on the porch with a thud.

"Oh, that's right." Daphne slapped her forehead.

"You said on the Monday after Mabel's birthday you'd get your decorations up." Sabrina jerked a thumb over her shoulder to where her house was decorated within an inch of its life. "You get to look at that beauty, but I'm stuck looking at the *black hole* over here. Everyone else in the neighborhood has gotten their Christmas lights up but you. Well, except for Daniel, but he has an excuse since his house is for sale."

Daphne reached into a bag, extracting a garland of faux greenery. "Interesting."

"I kept your request in mind," Sabrina assured her. "Everything I brought over looks pretty natural. Except that it's fake. I can't believe how many Christmas decorations I brought with me from Atlanta. I guess I thought my house would be bigger. But I really cannot use all this stuff."

"I want to get the decorations that Aunt Dee has in the attic. There's not much, but I'd like to use it anyway."

"Definitely. The more decorations, the merrier." Sabrina was already winding a green garland around the porch railing. "The lights are already in this," she explained. "You just plug it in and voila."

"Great. I'll be right back."

"We'll need a ladder and some extension cords too," Sabrina called. "And maybe a hammer and nails."

As Daphne dug out the old boxes of light strings and things, she prepared her speech for Sabrina. Hopefully she could keep it short and sweet. She came and went, gathering what they'd need to decorate the "black hole." Then, to her relief, they spent the next couple of hours focused on decorating, and topics like marriage proposals never surfaced.

"There!" Sabrina stepped back to admire their work. "We won't really know if it's right until dark, but it will definitely be an improvement."

"Thanks for your help." Daphne condensed the leftover bags and boxes together, setting them by the front door. "Mabel will be thrilled when she comes home."

"I want to see her face."

"Do you have time for a cup of tea?" Daphne asked.

Sabrina glanced at her watch. "Just let me run home to let Tootsie out for a potty break and I'll be right back."

Similar to what she'd done for Karen, Daphne put the packaged cookies out as the teakettle heated. And then, once Sabrina sat down, Daphne blurted out the news.

"Really?" Sabrina looked disappointed. "You don't love him?"

"I'm not in love with him. I thought maybe I loved him enough to..."

"To marry him for Mabel's sake," Sabrina finished. "Well, you made the right choice, Daphne. Marriage is hard enough when you think you love someone. Without love, it's just a hot mess."

Daphne smiled.

"Of course, I'm sorry we won't be planning a spring wedding. But if you're not in love...well, what can you do? I'm sure it's all for the best."

Daphne considered pointing out that Daniel taking Mabel away did not seem like it was for the best, but she didn't have the heart to have this conversation again today. Sabrina would find out about this in due time.

"How did Daniel take it?" Sabrina asked quietly.

"He was pretty stiff and formal about it. It could be his military training, but it almost seemed like he didn't even care. Except that I could see the hurt in his eyes."

"Does that make it awkward for having him around Mabel?"

"It probably will at first. And she took it a little hard, but I think she'll get past it."

"But he's still selling his house?" Sabrina said suddenly. "I assumed he was selling it because you guys would be living here. Doesn't he want to hold onto it so he can live there with Mabel? I mean, if he doesn't let you keep her."

"Daniel still plans on going back into the Marines. That hasn't changed."

"Really? I thought his interest in you meant he wanted to stay in Appleton. Goodness, that's even more reason for you to say no." Sabrina frowned. "What about Mabel."

Daphne shrugged. "He'll take her too."

Sabrina said a bad word and they both raised their brows. "Sorry," she said quickly. "I just don't like this. Not one bit."

"Nothing we can do about it." Daphne picked up their empty cups. "And now that I've frittered most of my morning, I really need to get to work."

"Getting your house decorated for Christmas isn't frittering," Sabrina declared.

Daphne put an arm around her shoulder. "No, you're right. It's not. And I thank you again. Mabel will be so pleased. And if this is going to be her first and last Christmas here, I want it to be memorable."

"He won't take her away before Christmas, will he?" Sabrina looked worried. "I mean now that you rejected his proposal."

"I sure hope not." Daphne felt a chill run through her. Was it possible she wouldn't even get that little morsel—Daniel would take Mabel away before Christmas? And what kind of Christmas would she have with Mabel gone? It was just too sad.

Chapter 11

As Daphne went to her office, she couldn't shake this depressing thought. What if Daniel relocated Mabel to North Carolina before Christmas? And the more she considered it, the more she thought it was likely. After all, what was to keep him in Appleton now? Certainly not Daphne. And he'd wrapped up his mother's memorial service. He'd gotten her house ready to sell. Plus he'd listed it today, and she knew that Karen was feeling optimistic. Besides that, he'd been here to see Mabel in the Christmas parade. He'd helped her celebrate her birthday. For all Daphne knew, Daniel was on the phone right now, talking to his Marine superiors or supervisors or whatever they were called, re-upping for his next tour of duty.

Out of desperation, and because she had promised to keep him in the loop, Daphne went to her office and called Jake. Expecting to leave a message with his assistant, she was surprised when she got put directly through.

"Well, you wanted to know how it went," she began slowly. "I told Daniel no. You were right, he wanted me to go to North

Carolina with him. It made the decision really easy."

"And Mabel?"

"I'm sure he plans to take her." Her voice broke. "In fact, I'm worried he'll take her straight away." She explained how Daniel had nothing left to keep him here. "And I really hoped she'd be here for Christmas. Her school is having a musical and the church is having a pageant and it seems so unfair to just uproot her from her life. Especially when she doesn't want to go."

"You know that for a fact?"

"Of course. She's made it clear from the start. She's happy here. For the first time in her life she's—" Daphne started to cry. "I'm sorry, Jake. But I told you this was going to be hard on me. I just love her so much. Is there anything you can do legally?" She sniffed. "I mean, you did help with Vera's legal stuff. Is there some loophole or something?"

"There's really not, Daphne. I'm sorry."

"Yeah." She reached for a tissue, dabbing her eyes. "I figured as much. But I had to ask."

"Believe me, if I knew a legal loophole I would jump through it to help you. But just like Dee's will for you, Vera's dying wish was for Mabel to be with Daniel. She obviously knew that he was a responsible person who would look after his niece when she was gone."

"But if Vera knew how badly Mabel wants to stay here—with me—I'm sure she would've changed that."

"Maybe. But that's something we'll never know."

Daphne bit her lip as she remembered the time she'd almost broached this subject with Vera. But then she waited...and it was too late. She thanked Jake, cutting the conversation short, and then she went to her room and had a good long cry.

After she'd dried her tears, she considered marching down to Daniel's house and presenting her case to him. However, she suspected that could end up in an emotional outburst that might work against her. And so she decided to do what she did best. She wrote him a letter. A heartfelt letter.

> *Dear Daniel,*
>
> *I realize that I have hurt you and although you told me not to mention it, I want to offer you a heartfelt apology. I never meant to hurt you. I actually really valued you as a friend. Both Mabel and I loved having you in my home. I enjoyed our conversations by the fireside. I know you are a good man, Daniel. And I know that should you find a good woman to be your wife, she will be a very fortunate woman.*
>
> *I also know, and you told me this very thing, you are married to your career. Your face lights up when you talk about your life in the Marines, your marine buddies, and how they are your family. But I have to question—is that a good family for a little eight-year-old girl who has been through so much pain and deprivation? A girl who has finally found her home with loved ones and friends? A girl who loves her school and wants to take ballet lessons in January?*
>
> *I'm begging you, Daniel, please consider what is best for Mabel's future. If there is some way we can arrange joint custody of her, I would be more*

than willing. I wouldn't ever want to take her away from you. She loves you, and you're an important person in her life. But she needs stability. She needs a woman's love. She needs her friends and her family. Please, don't take those from her.

I encourage you to talk to your niece, Daniel. Ask her what she wants. And ask her to be honest. She's a smart little girl, and she should have a say in this. Please, give her that chance.

Forgive me for not having this conversation face-to-face, but I know this is an emotional issue for me and I can't trust myself not to fall apart. And, if at some point in time, you wish to talk, I will do my best. But be warned, I might break down.

Sincerely,

Daphne Ballinger

Daphne felt slightly desperate as she folded the letter, slipping it into the envelope. She wanted Daniel to have it as soon as possible. But she didn't want to march down there and hand it to him.

Sabrina!

She hurried across the street, nearly jumping out of her shoes as Sabrina's life-sized singing Santa broke into "We Wish You a Merry Christmas." She pushed the doorbell, listening to the sharp barks from Tootsie until Sabrina came to the door.

"Hey, neighbor," Sabrina said cheerfully.

Daphne quickly explained her problem.

"I'd be glad to play postman with Daniel." Sabrina giggled as she took the envelope. "Well, not like that." She bent down to shove her feet into her ankle-high boots. "And you caught me just in time too—I have an appointment for a mani-pedi at one-thirty."

"Thank you. It feels urgent that he gets it now." As Sabrina pulled on her fur trimmed parka, Daphne explained how she'd just realized there wasn't much to keep Daniel in Appleton. "His house, which Karen said could sell this week, isn't very comfortable. It doesn't have a stick of furniture in it. Not very inviting for the holidays."

"That's a good point." Sabrina frowned as she pushed Tootsie back inside. "I'll be right back," she promised as she closed the door.

"Thanks," Daphne said. "And you'll make sure he actually gets it. Don't just slip it under the doormat."

"I'll plunk it in his hand," Sabrina promised.

Feeling somewhat consoled, but still concerned, Daphne returned to her own house. It was still almost two hours until school ended for Mabel, but Daphne knew she would be unable to concentrate on her novel now. Instead, she just sat in her office chair, imagining a plot where she kidnapped Mabel and together they flew to the moon and started a green cheese factory. As silly as it was, it made her feel a tiny bit better.

Finally, to calm her nerves, shortly before it was time to go get Mabel, Daphne knew she needed to pray about her dilemma again. She needed to give it to God. And that's just what she did. She not only prayed for God's will for Mabel and herself, she prayed for Daniel too. She prayed for God's best blessings for him—no matter what.

As Daphne walked down Huckleberry Lane, knowing she still had to pass Vera's old house, she considered the possibility that it might truly be God's will for Mabel to go to North Carolina with her uncle. And if that was the situation, Daphne would have to accept it. Certainly, she could remain in Mabel's life by offering her a place to visit during summers or holidays—similar to the way Aunt Dee had been for Daphne. And she could write Mabel letters and send her gifts. But she might have to let her go.

Daphne walked a little faster when she came to the pale yellow house. To her relief, Daniel wasn't out and about. She felt a little sorry for him being stuck in that empty, bleak house. The poor guy didn't even have a car. Even more reason for him to get out of town.

Daphne acted like all was perfectly normal as she met Mabel on the usual corner. She listened as Mabel gushed about the upcoming Winter Program, as the school called it, and her excitement about participating in it.

"Lulu and I get to be snow fairies," she said. "And Miss Simmons said we can make sparkly wings that look like they have frost on them. And we'll wear our tutus, but we'll pin big white snowflakes all over with lots of glitter. Doesn't it sound beautiful?"

"Yes, it really does."

Mabel paused by the pale yellow house. "Is Uncle Daniel home?"

Daphne took in a quick breath. "Well, I'm not sure. He might be home. You can go knock on the door if you like. If he's there and you want to stay, just have him give me a call so I won't worry. Otherwise, come straight home. Okay?"

"Okay."

Daphne knew it was perfectly normal for Mabel to want

to spend time with her uncle. She hadn't seen him for two days. And maybe she was worried about him. But it made Daphne uneasy just the same. It wasn't that she was jealous. Or maybe she was. She was jealous of the limited minutes she had left with Mabel. For all she knew, Daniel could be in there packing his bags. Maybe he would tell Mabel to go home and do the same.

Daphne squared her shoulders as she went into the house. If that was the way it had to be, she would handle it with grace and kindness. What else could she do? She checked to make sure her phone was on, in case Daniel was going to call, but within five minutes, Mabel was home.

"I knocked and knocked," she said with a worried look, "but he didn't answer the door."

"He must be out." Daphne helped her remove her parka. "Maybe he walked to the store for groceries."

"It made me feel sad to see the 'for sale' sign in Grandma's yard," Mabel confessed.

"Oh, yeah." Daphne nodded. "I can understand that. I'm sorry, honey. But you knew that's what was happening."

"I know, but I just hoped that Uncle Daniel would change his mind." Mabel looked up with a furrowed brow. "Is it because you won't marry him?"

Daphne made a forced smile. "No, it's because Uncle Daniel loves being a marine. It's been his life, Mabel. He's eager to get back to it. He's a very brave man who wants to keep serving his country. We should be proud of him." Daphne looked across the street, curious if Sabrina was home yet, but she didn't see her car in the driveway. "Hey, you didn't even say anything about the decorations," Daphne said suddenly.

"Huh?"

"On the house. Didn't you even see them?"

Mabel tipped her head to one side. "On this house?"

Daphne chuckled. "I'll bet you had your mind on other things." She grabbed Mabel's hand. "Come on, let's go plug in the lights and see how it looks." As they went outside, Daphne realized that Mabel must've been really distraught over Uncle Daniel to not even notice the decorations. But as she plugged them in, Mabel clapped her hands. "It's beautiful, Aunt Daphne."

Daphne went back to stand with Mabel, looking at the colorfully lit up house. Thanks to the dark clouds overhead and the dusky afternoon light, it looked pretty good. "Sabrina should be happy," Daphne said as they went inside. "She said our house looked like a black hole."

Mabel giggled. "That's silly. Our house is beautiful, Aunt Daphne. It's the most beautiful house in all of Appleton."

Somehow that did not make Daphne feel any better.

Chapter 12

Daphne didn't really expect Daniel to show up at her door with a complete change of heart regarding Mabel. But she had hoped he would call. In fact, she'd even made a dinner that she would've invited him to share with them...if he had shown the slightest bit of interest. But he didn't.

To her relief, Mabel didn't ask about Uncle Daniel, although she did remember him in her bedtime prayers. "Please help Uncle Daniel not to have bad dreams tonight," she prayed quietly. Finally she said "amen" and Daphne kissed her goodnight and turned out the light.

Daphne tried not to feel irritated at Daniel as she picked up the book she was reading. Perhaps he just needed time to think about it. Or maybe he just wanted to have this conversation with her alone. Perhaps she would hear from him tomorrow while Mabel was in school. But tomorrow came, and by noon she still hadn't heard a word from Daniel. And, she reasoned, it couldn't be because he was too busy. Really, what did he have to do?

When the phone in her office finally jingle at a little past two she eagerly grabbed it, hoping it would be him.

"Hey, Daphne," Sabrina said cheerfully. "Are you all ready for critique group tonight?"

"Critique group?" Daphne looked at her calendar, realizing that this was indeed the second Tuesday of the month. "Uh, yeah, I mean I guess I will be. To be honest, I sort of forgot."

"Need any help?"

"No, there's not much to do. I just planned to have coffee and tea and something to snack on. No big deal."

"I can bring over my famous coffee cake," Sabrina offered.

"That'd be great."

"And I've talked to a few people who thought they might want to come."

"Good." Daphne saved her work and turned off her computer, shuffling papers around and getting into a general house-cleaning mode.

"Your friend Spencer is coming, right?"

"Yes, and Mr. Renwald too."

"Good. We should have a nice group."

"Well, I better go," Daphne tossed an old newspaper into the waste basket. "I need to tidy up."

"See you at seven."

As Daphne started cleaning house, she thought about Daniel and the silent treatment he seemed to be giving her. Really, it was so childish. The best thing would be to just call him and get it over with. But just when she reached for her phone, she noticed a dark green pickup pulling into the driveway. Mick's landscaping truck was piled high with what appeared to be evergreens.

"The Christmas tree," she said aloud as she hurried to the front door.

"Special delivery for Daphne Ballinger," he called out. "Want to pick one out, or do you trust me to find you the best one?"

She laughed. "I trust you, Mick."

She watched as he poked through the trees, finally selecting a tall noble fir that he set on the ground. "How about this?"

"Perfect."

"And I got a bunch of greens for you here too." He reached for a black garbage bag, handing it over. "Want help setting this guy up?" Mick offered as he followed her up to the front porch. "I used to set Dee's up for her, and I know right where the tree stand is."

"That would be wonderful." She beamed at him. "Such service."

He leaned the tree on the porch then disappeared around to the back of the house. Meanwhile, she opened the bag of greenery, pouring the contents out onto the porch to sort out some pieces. It smelled so fresh and clean and piney. She took some of the pieces inside, using them to make an arrangement on the marble topped table in the foyer. She stepped back to admire the greens. With some glass tree ornaments, it would look even better. She hurried up to the attic to where she'd spotted a familiar old box, then came back down just as Mick was coming through with the tree.

"Dee always liked it right here by the stairway," Mick said as he placed it there.

"I know," Daphne told him. "That's where she had it when I was a little girl too."

He grinned. "Sometimes I forget that you and Dee went

back a long ways."

"That looks gorgeous," Daphne proclaimed as she stood back to admire it. "It's so pretty, it almost doesn't need decorations."

"I'll bet Mabel will have an opinion about that."

Daphne laughed. "You're right."

"This looks nice." Mick paused to watch her putting the glass balls amongst the greenery.

"And you're just in time with these things because I'm having a writers' critique group here tonight. The house will look nice and festive now."

"What's a writers' critique group?" he asked with interest.

Daphne quickly explained, and Mick scratched his chin as if he was taking it all in. "You know," he said, "I've been wanting to write a newsletter for my business. I want to let folks know I have things like Christmas trees, or when to plant tulip bulbs, or when it's time to mulch their lawns or plant peas. Do you think your writers' group would be helpful to me?"

"Sure. It's for all kinds of writers. The help comes when you read your work and get responses from the group. Then you go home and edit your work." She smiled. "Would you like to join us?"

"But I haven't written anything yet."

"That's okay. I think tonight will be more of an organizational meeting. A getting to know you sort of thing."

"That sounds great."

"It's at seven. I'd love to have you there."

"It's a date. Speaking of which, I want to invite you to my annual Christmas bash."

"Christmas bash?" She tipped her head to one side.

"I have it in the barn. Just a bunch of friends, some good

live music, and lots of Christmas cheer." He gave her a sly grin. "As I recall, you're a fairly good dancer."

"I don't know about that, but it sounds like fun."

"Great. And you make sure you save some dances for me. It's the Saturday before Christmas, and the festivities will start around seven, but probably won't get really rocking for an hour or so."

"Okay, I'll come to your Christmas bash and you'll come to my critique group."

"If my mates could see me." He laughed. "Ol' Mick Foster hanging with the literary folk."

"If you decide you don't really like us, you don't have to come back."

"More'n likely you'll send me packing."

She laughed. "Well, thanks for delivering the tree and the greens. It will make it look festive. Which reminds me, I better get busy. I still have a lot to do before seven."

After Mick left, Daphne went through the remainder of the house like a whirlwind. Not that the place was a mess, but she wanted it to look nice for their first meeting. She was just starting to put out a few more Christmas decorations when she realized it was time to meet Mabel. The afternoon air was crisp and clear as she walked past the pale yellow house. Trying not to be too obvious, she tossed a quick glance toward the big front window, but seeing no one inside, she simply hurried past.

On the way back, Mabel pointed to the kitchen window. "There's Uncle Daniel. Can I go see him?" Mabel asked eagerly.

"Of course." Daphne explained that she was hosting a writers' group tonight. "So I need to get back to get some things ready. When you're done with Uncle Daniel, come right home, okay?"

Mabel agreed, and Daphne offered to take her backpack with her before she continued on her way. She was actually relieved that Daniel hadn't come outside. The conversation she wanted to have with him wouldn't be appropriate for Mabel's ears. Besides that, a visit from Mabel might remind Daniel that he had unfinished business to take care of with Daphne. She could only hope.

Determined not to obsess over what Daniel was or wasn't doing, Daphne continued to get things ready for tonight. But seeing that an hour had passed, she grew concerned. Oh, she knew she was probably overprotective where Mabel was concerned. But in her defense, this mothering thing was still new to her. And so she called him.

"Daphne," he said. "I was just about to call you."

"I wanted to check on Mabel."

"Yeah. We were just playing cards. Mabel told me that you have some kind of writer people coming to your house tonight, and I thought she should stay with me. We could go grab a burger at the diner and get her back in time for bed."

Part of Daphne wanted to say, *No, that's not necessary*, but at the same time she realized it was ridiculous to argue this. After all, Daniel was her legal guardian. He did not have to ask for Daphne's permission. "That's a nice idea," she said stiffly. "Thank you."

"We'll pop in around eight. And I can read her a story and make sure she brushes her teeth," he offered, "if your writer friends are still there."

"Thanks. The meeting will probably go at least till nine."

And so it was settled. Daniel had Mabel for the evening.

And even though she knew she should appreciate it, she did not. In fact, it almost felt like he was drawing a line—reminding her that he was in charge. Not her.

Sabrina arrived at 6:45 with a big platter of coffee cake as well as a bag of chocolate kisses. "Well, look at you," she said as she came in, "you got your tree up and everything." She frowned at the tall tree, wearing nothing but strings of white lights. "But it looks awfully plain. Surely you don't plan to leave it like that."

"Don't worry. I plan to let Mabel help me decorate it."

"Good." She set her treats on the dining table where Daphne had set china dessert plates and beverage cups. "I'm so excited about tonight. I even wrote a whole chapter."

"A whole chapter?" Daphne was shocked.

"Well, it's only five pages and I'm sure it's just a mess, but at least I did it, right?"

"Sabrina, that's wonderful." Daphne patted her back. "I'm so proud of you."

"Well, you know what they say, *the proof is in the pudding.*" She frowned. "Although I never really understood what that meant."

The doorbell rang, and Daphne went to open it to see her old high school teacher (and neighbor) standing with a large binder in his arms. "Mr. Renwald," she exclaimed.

"If I've told you once, I've told you twice—we're not in high school anymore. Just call me Wally."

"Yes, yes. Come in, Wally."

Spencer was next to arrive. Daphne introduced him then went to the door to discover Ricardo was there. "Hello?" she said curiously.

"Didn't Sabrina tell you she invited me?" Ricardo held up a bunch of papers. "I'm working on a cookbook for men, and Sabrina thought this group would be helpful."

"Well, come on in." Daphne opened the door wider. "Who knew we had so many budding authors in Appleton." She pointed to the green pickup just parking on the street. "And there's Mick."

"Mick's a writer?" Ricardo looked surprised now.

She explained the nursery newsletter as Mick bounded up the stairs. Soon the six of them were seated in Daphne's living room and she was explaining the purpose of a writer's critique group. "Mostly it's a safe forum for writers to come and read their work. We don't come to criticize each other, per se. But to help each other. We want to learn and improve our craft." She handed out some guidelines she'd found online.

"As you can see, they are simple rules," she told them. "Mostly it's about common courtesy and kindness. One rule I want to insist upon is that every critique must begin with something positive. Not because we need to inflate our egos, but simply so we can absorb the suggestions better. It's like a spoonful of sugar helping the medicine go down."

Next, she invited everyone to tell the group a bit about their writing and their goals. She offered to begin, explaining how she was working on a novel and a bit about it. Spencer went next. "I've been writing suspense for several years, but I haven't published anything yet. I have one completed novel that I'm currently editing. I plan to read some parts of it to this group."

Sabrina talked a bit about her dream to write romance. Ricardo explained his idea for making an easy-to-use cookbook for men. "I'm glad there are several men here. That will be helpful." Mick told a bit about his newsletter plan. And Wally, sounding very much like a teacher, went on for some time about how he'd always wanted to be a naturalist and had written a number of essays about nature that he hoped to publish.

As a group they discussed some ground rules and Sabrina, offering to be secretary, wrote them down. And then Daphne suggested they break for refreshments. "And then we'll settle back in and if any brave person wants to read tonight, we'll offer critique."

They were just visiting around the dining table, munching on coffee cake, when Daphne heard the front door open. She glanced out to see Daniel and Mabel coming into the house. Daphne started to go to them, but Daniel just waved her back. "It's okay. We're fine," he called as he herded Mabel toward the staircase. And so Daphne just stayed put. But it was Daniel's expression that stayed in her mind. He looked slightly irritated—or maybe he simply had a headache. Whatever it was, he didn't seem too pleased with her. Perhaps it was the letter she'd sent. Maybe he resented her intrusion.

For the remainder of the critique group, Daphne tried to push Daniel to the back of her mind. Spencer offered to go first, and Daphne could tell that he had spent a lot of time polishing up the first pages of his novel. He was a real word smith, and she hoped it wouldn't discourage the others. But when Ricardo read, she was impressed at how compelling his introduction to the cookbook sounded. Everyone liked it. Mick took a pass, promising to read his spring newsletter next time. Wally read an essay about bald eagles that was technically correct but needed some warming up. And finally

Sabrina read the opening of her romance novel, which was surprisingly intriguing.

"You haven't read," Spencer told Daphne.

"Oh, it's late." She nodded to the mantel clock—it was nearly ten. But they all insisted she should read, and so she offered to read a few pages from the chapter she was working on most recently. She read rather quickly through three pages and then stopped, but they all begged her to read some more. And so she read a few more pages. "Now I have to stop," she said. "It's late."

"But I want to hear more," Sabrina said eagerly. "I want to read that book."

"So do I," Mick told her. "I had no idea you were so talented."

Daphne beamed as her friends all confirmed that her writing was very engaging. And even for those with words of critique (like Wally) it was minimal. Happy that their first night of critique group had been such a success, Daphne reminded them that their next meeting would be the second Tuesday of January.

"Will it be here?" Wally asked hopefully. "It's sure handy to walk."

"I'm happy to have it," Daphne told them. "And I won't need to get a babysitter for Mabel if it's here." Of course, as she said this, she realized that could be a moot point by their next meeting. But, just the same, they all agreed to meet at her house again.

After she told the last of them goodbye, she went upstairs to check on Mabel. She knew the child would be fast asleep by now, but since she'd never actually seen Daniel leaving she halfway expected to find him resting in the spare room.

And she wouldn't actually blame him either since, according to Mabel, he'd been sleeping in a sleeping bag on the floor of his mother's old house.

To her relief, he was not there. And Mabel was soundly sleeping. But as she went down, she wondered what was the reason for Daniel's grim expression when he'd brought Mabel home. Did he resent having to keep her for the evening? That seemed unreasonable since he was the one who offered. More than likely it was the letter she'd written him. She wished she'd kept a copy of it. What had she said that was so offensive? Maybe she'd never find out.

Chapter 13

Mabel seemed curiously somber at breakfast. "Did you have fun with Uncle Daniel last night?" Daphne asked as she put their dirty dishes in the sink.

"Uh huh." Mabel shoved the spelling and math papers they'd just checked into her backpack.

"Really?" Daphne helped Mabel into her parka. "That didn't sound too enthusiastic. Is something bothering you?"

"I dunno." Mabel shrugged.

Daphne pulled on her own coat. "Was it fun going out to dinner with him?"

"I guess so."

"Mabel." Daphne bent down to look into her face. "You seem a little sad to me. Really, is there something wrong?"

"Uncle Daniel said I have to go to North Carolina with him."

"Oh." Daphne took in a deep breath.

"I don't want to go, Aunt Daphne."

"Did you tell him that?"

"No...I don't want to hurt his feelings."

"Did you tell him how much you love Appleton?" Daphne wrapped Mabel's pink wooly scarf around her neck.

Mabel sadly shook her head.

As they went outside, Daphne wondered if that was even fair. Why should Mabel have to tell him these things? Shouldn't it be left to the adults to hammer these things out? Let children be children? She honestly didn't know.

"Uncle Daniel said that a lady is going to buy Grandma's house. She wants to move into it before Christmas."

"Wow—that was fast." Daphne paused on the porch steps, trying to disguise her real feelings.

"Uncle Daniel said we gotta move to North Carolina before Christmas."

"Oh...he said that?" What was he doing telling Mabel all this?

"Uh huh. He told me to start packing my stuff. He's going to bring boxes and help me pack. And we're going to fly on a big plane. I think on Saturday."

"*This* Saturday?" Daphne felt like she'd just been punched in the gut.

"Yeah. He said we have four days to get packed."

"Four days?" Daphne sat down on the porch steps, letting this news sink in.

"His friend found us a house there. Uncle Daniel showed me a picture. It's white with a blue door. And he said he's got lots of friends in North Carolina, and they've got kids and that I'm going to be really happy there."

Daphne swallowed against the big lump in her throat. "And I'm sure that's true, Mabel. I'm sure you will be."

Mabel sat down next to Daphne, reaching for her hand.

"You don't want me to go, do you?"

Daphne hugged her. "Of course not. I love you and wish you could stay here forever. But this isn't up to us."

"I don't wanna go." Mabel let out a little sob and Daphne held her tighter.

"I know, sweetie. I remember being a kid and how things happened that I didn't want to happen. It just doesn't seem fair that it's your life, but you don't really have a say in it. I know just how you feel." She hugged her awhile longer then finally let her go.

"Kids should get to say what they want too." Mabel sniffed.

Suppressing the urge to go give Daniel a piece of her mind, Daphne knew she had to take the high road. "I agree. But you know what, Mabel?"

"What?"

"I know that you are going to be happy in North Carolina. Because you are just that kind of girl. You look for the good in people. You make friends easily. You are kind and generous and fun. I know that good things are always going to follow you wherever you go."

"Really?"

"I believe that with my whole heart. You will be happy there. And, don't worry, I will still be your aunt. And I will tell Uncle Daniel that you are always welcome at my house—anytime. You can come for summer vacation or spring break or holidays or whenever. It'll be like the way I stayed with my Aunt Dee when I was a girl. And we'll write letters or email or talk on the phone. And I will always be your aunt. Okay?"

Mabel nodded with uncertainty. "Okay."

"And now we better go or you'll be late to school." Daphne

grabbed Mabel's hand, and as they walked to school, she reassured Mabel of all the things she had to look forward to in North Carolina. Did she actually believe these things herself? Some of them perhaps. But mostly, she felt like Daniel had pulled the rug out from under both of them.

On her way home, she was tempted to storm that pale yellow house and confront Daniel. But as she got closer, she thought better of it. For one thing, she was too emotional right now. She would probably put her foot in her mouth. And fighting with Daniel would not help Mabel.

As she hurried past his house on the opposite side of the street, she knew that she needed to focus her energy on winning him over. He needed to see her as his friend so that he would actually allow Mabel to come visit her. She had to convince him that she was supportive of his decision—even if she felt like throwing a fit.

But she didn't have to convince him today. For today she would go home and just let the tears flow. She needed to do her grieving in private—while Mabel was at school. And then she would get her wits about her and do whatever it took to help Mabel through this. They would sort and pack her things. They would get her ready for her "big trip."

After she recovered from her "good" cry, she called Sabrina with the dismaying news. Of course, Sabrina was livid. She hung up the phone and marched over and said all the things that Daphne had been thinking. She called Daniel every name in her polite Southern book. And finally she hugged Daphne and promised to do anything she could to help her through this crisis.

"Just knowing you understand is helpful." Daphne blew

her nose.

"I understand how broken up you are," Sabrina declared. "But I do not understand how that beastly man can force his will like this. I used to think he was a nice guy too."

"He's caught between a rock and a hard place, Sabrina."

"But that heartfelt letter you wrote to him. That I hand-delivered. And he didn't even respond to it? That's just plain rude."

Daphne sighed. "Well, we only have four days to get our little girl ready to go. It's not that she has so much to pack, but I want her heart to be ready too. She was so sad this morning, Sabrina. Almost like she wasn't the same girl."

"She's been through so much already." Sabrina scowled. "It's just wrong that she has to be put through even more."

"We don't know." Daphne walked Sabrina to the door. "I've been praying about this...maybe God has a reason for taking her away. Maybe she really will be happier there."

"Humph." Sabrina scowled. "Your faith is bigger than mine."

Daphne felt a little better after venting with Sabrina, but as she stood looking at the yet-to-be-decorated tree, she wondered how she would get through Christmas without Mabel. They had both been so looking forward to it. "Take one day at a time," she reminded herself. "With God's strength."

After school, Daphne tried to act like nothing was wrong. They spent an hour decorating the tree and, after dinner, they frosted the Christmas cookies. During these activities, Daphne made sure to have her phone ready, snagging photos here and there. Her plan was to print them out and make a small photo album for Mabel to take with her.

When it was time for Mabel's bedtime prayer, Daphne

noticed that Mabel didn't include Uncle Daniel in her "blessing" list. But Daphne didn't have the heart to mention it. After all, it was Mabel's prayer. She should have the right to pray as she wished.

While having breakfast the next morning, they decided to have their own Christmas party on Friday. "We'll invite all our family and friends," Daphne told her. "It will be just like a real Christmas."

"Will we invite Uncle Daniel too?"

"Sure, if you want to, Mabel. It's your party."

Mabel's brow was furrowed, almost as if she didn't really want Daniel at their party. Or maybe she knew that Daphne didn't. "Anyway, we need to make a to-do list." Daphne pulled out a notepad. And, as Mabel ate her oatmeal, she wrote down the names of friends and family they would invite, including Lola and Becca, Daphne's dad and Karen, Sabrina and Tootsie, Olivia and Jeff, Jake and Jenna, Ricardo and his mom, Mick, and several others. "We'll have a houseful if they all come," Daphne told Mabel. "And since it's such short notice, I'll start calling them today while you're at school."

"I'm not sure about Uncle Daniel," Mabel said. "He might not wanna come."

"Well, I'll leave that invitation up to you. Okay?"

Mabel nodded, but her eyes were sad.

After Daphne got home from walking Mabel to school, she saw the stack of flattened packing boxes on her porch. Obviously the work of Daniel. On top was a note saying to give him a call if Mabel needed help. Daphne wadded up the

note and considered texting Daniel and calling him a "chicken."
Except she knew that was childish. But it was equally childish
for him to sneak over here and drop these off. Especially since
he hadn't actually spoken to her about his decision.

Instead of obsessing over Daniel's bad manners, she went
to work calling the people on her list. Some answered and
she explained the situation, trying not to give them too much
opportunity for sympathy—which only made her feel sad. And
for others, she simply left messages, telling the reason for the
party, but trying to sound cheerful.

Then she walked to town, further distracting herself from
her sadness as she arranged for a caterer through Truman at the
Apple Basket, and ordered a Christmassy flower arrangement
from Olivia at Bernie's Blooms. She knew she was being more
extravagant than she had planned to be for Christmas, but
under the circumstances, well, she just didn't care.

In the afternoon, Daphne picked Mabel up at school in her
car. Together they went Christmas shopping at Wal-Mart.
Daphne gave Mabel the guest list as well as a budget of ten
dollars or less per person and, for a couple of delightful hours,
they both totally forgot about North Carolina. Not only that,
but Daphne took some pretty fun photos as well. Afterwards,
Daphne let Mabel choose a place for dinner. She expected
Mabel to pick a fast food place with an indoor playground,
but to her surprise, Mabel wanted to go to a "real restaurant."

"I want to remember this," Mabel said as they went into a
small Italian restaurant a few blocks from the shopping mall.

"I do too," Daphne admitted as they waited for a table.

"That was fun," Mabel said after they were seated. "I like
buying gifts for other people. I think it's even better than

getting gifts."

"I agree."

Mabel talked with enthusiasm about some of the funny things she'd picked out and Daphne pulled out her phone so they could laugh at some of the goofy photos they'd taken. All in all, dinner was a pleasant experience. And later that night, as she tucked Mabel into bed, Mabel thanked her. "And I get to wrap them tomorrow after school?" she asked Daphne.

"Yep. After you do your homework."

"I can't wait. And I can't wait to see everyone's face when they open their presents at our party." Mabel yawned sleepily.

As Mabel said her bedtime prayer, Daphne noticed again how Uncle Daniel's name was conspicuously absent. She considered reminding her, but Mabel looked half asleep already. So she just kissed her goodnight.

The next morning, shortly after Daphne walked Mabel to school, Sabrina showed up at Daphne's door, wearing her pink warm-ups and a very grim expression. "What's wrong?" Daphne asked as she led Sabrina into the house.

"Well, I have just about had it," Sabrina declared. "I am not a violent woman, but I'm about ready to commit murder."

"Sabrina Fontaine!"

"I know, I know...it's not a very Christian thing to say, but I'd like to throttle that man. Daniel Myers is a great big *so-and-so!*"

"What are you raging about? I mean, we both know Daniel is taking Mabel, but we also know it's within his legal right. I thought you'd be moving on by now."

Sabrina was pacing back and forth in the living room, clearly agitated. If she were a cartoon character she'd have steam puffing out her ears. "I hadn't planned to tell you this, Daphne, I really wanted to spare you any more stress. But I'm so enraged, I don't know what to do. I have to talk to someone!"

"What on earth is going on?"

"I staged an intervention." Sabrina looked at Daphne with two fists raised in the air. "For Daniel. I had hoped to make him see the light of day—regarding Mabel."

"*What?*" Daphne sank down onto the couch.

"It seemed like a good idea." Sabrina sat across from her with a dejected look.

"What happened?"

Sabrina explained how she'd seen Ricardo at Midge's. "He got your message about the going away Christmas party for Mabel. And he told me how he'd observed Daniel and Mabel the other night. He could see how dejected Mabel looked. But when he heard Daniel was taking her from you, he was concerned. We got to talking about it, and he said, 'Daniel needs an intervention.'" Sabrina blew out an exasperated sigh. "At the time it seemed like such a good idea. We got to talking about it and I got all excited and Ricardo put together a plan. Then I called all your closest friends and explained the problem. I invited them to join Ricardo and me for an intervention."

"You're kidding!"

"No. Ricardo suggested we have it at Midge's. After the dinner hour it gets pretty quiet in there, especially in winter. So he called Daniel, inviting him to dinner at seven. He said it would give them a chance to talk. And at seven-thirty, we all showed up. There were eight of us, Daphne. We all did our best, trying to talk Daniel into reconsidering his decision. Everyone thinks it's a mistake. Your dad tried to talk sense to him. And Jake, well, he was fabulous. I actually thought Daniel was cracking."

Daphne slowly shook her head, trying to imagine this scene. "Wow."

"Everyone said their piece," Sabrina continued. "It was actually pretty sweet. I almost wish you could've been there."

"What happened?" Daphne knew from Sabrina's demeanor this did not have a happy ending.

"Daniel stood up and thanked us for coming. Then he said that you obviously had a very full and busy life, and that you had a lot of friends, and that he still planned to take Mabel with him. And that you would get over it. And then he walked out."

"Oh." Daphne sighed. "Well, it was sweet of you guys to try."

"Maybe. But now I'm so ticked at Daniel Myers that I don't know how I'll act if I should see him. He's not coming to your party tomorrow night, is he?"

"No. I left that to Mabel and she hasn't invited him."

"Good."

Daphne felt bad. "Daniel isn't the devil, Sabrina. Honestly, if I were in his shoes, I'd be doing the same thing. Obviously. Since I want Mabel too."

"But you're able to give Mabel a home. What can Daniel offer? A single dad who could get called to active duty?"

Daphne stood up slowly, walking over to the Christmas tree and pretending to adjust a little glass elf, turning him to face out. One of the cats rubbed up against Daphne's leg, as if to comfort her, but Daphne didn't even look down. She knew Sabrina's intentions were good, but this wasn't helping Daphne to move forward.

"Thank you for attempting an intervention," Daphne said carefully. "But it's clear Daniel's mind is made up. We just need to make the best of this—for Mabel's sake. I'm trying to encourage her. Painting a positive picture for how it will be in North Carolina. And Mabel is a strong person. I'm sure she'll make the best of it."

Sabrina came over to put an arm around Daphne. "You're right. Sorry for spewing on you like that. I should've known you'd do the honorable thing. And, FYI, I won't bring any of this up again. I'll make the best of it too." She smiled brightly. "Which reminds me, I plan to make pecan pies for tomorrow night. Do you mind?"

Daphne smiled. "Are you kidding?"

Sabrina hugged her. "You hang in there, okay."

After school, Daphne told Mabel that she wanted them to spend some time packing the boxes Daniel had dropped by. "And after dinner, we'll wrap the presents you got yesterday," she said to soften the chore.

Mabel didn't protest, but they were both fairly quiet as they packed up the boxes. It took almost two hours. And Daphne could hardly bear to look at the stripped room. The only things left were what Mabel would need for the next couple of days and bedding and things that Daphne promised to pack and send on Saturday...after Mabel was gone.

"Uncle Daniel sent me a text," Daphne said as they each carried a box downstairs. "He wants us to put these on the porch in the morning. He'll pick them up and get them sent."

Daphne was glad Mabel couldn't see her face. Daphne didn't appreciate these texts from Daniel. So cold and impersonal. Polarizing.

After the boxes were all down, they had dinner. And then Daphne put on some Christmas music and set the bags full of the goofy gifts in the living room. On the coffee table, she laid out wrapping paper and tape and bows.

"Just let me know if you need help," Daphne said as she made a fire in the fireplace.

"This is gonna be fun!" Mabel unrolled some snowman paper, eagerly wielding scissors.

"It's always best to cut a little more than you think you need," Daphne suggested as she noticed that Mabel was about to cut a piece too small to wrap the gift she had ready.

"Okay."

As Mabel focused on winding paper around the box that contained a battery operated Christmas tie that she'd picked out for Daphne's dad, Daphne pulled out her phone and snapped some more photos. She planned to put Mabel's album together tomorrow—as well as one for herself. But she'd leave plenty of room for the photos she'd take at the going away Christmas party, and then she'd slip it into Mabel's suitcase before Daniel picked her up at seven o'clock Saturday morning. He had texted Daphne about that too. Informing that he would come by in a taxi and that Mabel needed to be ready to leave.

Daphne gave Mabel a few more gift-wrapping tips before she settled into the club chair to simply watch. Before long, Lucy and Ethel nestled on Daphne's lap, and for the next few moments, Daphne just tried to memorize this scene—the music, the fire, the decorations...and Mabel intently wrapping presents—using too much tape as she created strange looking packages that would probably take a long time to open. But it was all perfect. And something Daphne hoped to pull out from her memory to revisit later...on some cold, lonely winter night.

Chapter 14

Although Christmas was actually almost two weeks away, Daphne felt like this was *it* as she got the house ready for tonight's party. Her hope was to be so worn out by tomorrow that she'd have a good excuse for going back to bed after Mabel was gone. Perhaps she would stay in her pajamas throughout the weekend.

Around eleven, Jake showed up at her door. Bearing a pair of rose colored poinsettias and a sympathetic smile, he asked her if she needed any help getting things ready for the party. "I don't have much going on today."

"Thank you," she told him. "I think it's all under control. But come on in." She took one of the poinsettias from him. "These are gorgeous. I know just where I'll put them." She set it on one side of the stairway and the other on the opposite side. "Doesn't that look pretty?"

He nodded as he unbuttoned his coat. "How are you holding up?"

She shrugged. "As well as can be expected." She offered a

stiff smile. "Sabrina told me about the 'intervention.' Thanks for helping."

He frowned. "That Daniel is a hard nut to crack."

"Must be from being a marine." She nodded toward the kitchen. "I made some fresh coffee a bit ago. I was about to have a cup. Care to join me?"

"I'd love it." He removed his coat, hanging it on the hall tree.

"To be honest, I don't really want to talk about it," she admitted as she handed him a cup.

"I understand." He sat down at the kitchen table.

"Mabel is being a trooper." And, despite not wanting to talk about it, she continued to tell him of the last few days, how hard it was to pack up Mabel's room, and how vexed she was at Daniel for texting. "It's so juvenile," she declared. "Good grief, what does he think I'm going to do if he talks to me in person? Slap him?" She made a sheepish smile. "Come to think of it, I've probably wanted to a couple of times."

"It's admirable that you're holding it together for Mabel's sake. I know it's not easy."

"And you could say 'I told you so,'" she confessed. "I remember you did warn me about getting too involved with Mabel."

He reached over to put his hand on hers. "You have a big heart, Daphne. Could you really have done this any other way? And, really, do you think it hurt Mabel that you loved her so completely?"

She shook her head. "No. She needed it. I'm glad I was here for her."

"And you might not want to hear this, but maybe it was a good test for you."

"A test?" She frowned.

"A lot of women assume they want to be mothers, but when it actually happens, they realize it's harder than they thought… and maybe they don't want it as badly as they imagined."

She wasn't sure how to respond to that.

"You'd make a fabulous mom, Daphne."

"Thanks." She sighed deeply. "I guess."

"You're only thirty-four," he reminded her.

"Really? I feel like I'm about eighty-four today."

He chuckled as he squeezed her hand then reached for his coffee cup. "Well, you sure don't look like it."

"Thanks." She stared down at the kitchen table. "But the truth is I have serious doubts that I'll ever marry and have children."

He laughed. "Are you kidding?"

She looked up at him. "Not in the least. Why is that funny?"

"Because you've had various guys interested in you ever since you got to Appleton. You had at least one proposal a few months ago. And you just had another proposal—what a week or two ago? And you turned him down."

"Well, yes…." Daphne frowned. "But, really, this whole thing with Mabel has been a real eye-opener for me."

"How so?"

"Well, don't you think it's interesting how I could wholeheartedly give myself over to a child? But not to a man?"

"I think it's just because you haven't found the right man… yet."

She studied Jake, wondering if he could possibly be the right man and almost as quickly dismissing the idea. She knew from experience with him that it was best to focus on their friendship.

"And, to be fair, you've been pretty distracted with Mabel these past several months. How is there room in your life to find the right guy?"

"Maybe." She pressed her lips together. "But I'll tell you the truth, Jake. Right now I would trade Mr. Right for Mabel."

Jake looked slightly surprised.

"Of course, I would like to have them both. But I never realized how much it would hurt to lose Mabel. Do you know what I'd been thinking this morning?"

"No...."

"Don't tell anyone, but I was actually considering marching down to talk to Daniel. I imagined myself giving him an ultimatum. I would marry him if he would stay in Appleton, and I was going to tell him about my inheritance as incentive." She shook her head. "Of course, I'll admit this stupid idea came to me in the middle of the night last night, and after I'd comforted Mabel when I'd heard her crying in her bed. And, after a pretty much sleepless night, well, I'm probably not thinking straight."

"Oh, Daphne. I'm so sorry." He looked truly distressed. "Well, all I can say is the sooner this is over with, the better it will be for everyone."

"Maybe so."

"And you should probably take a nap today." He finished his coffee. "So you'll be refreshed for the party tonight."

"That's not a bad idea." She made a grateful smile. "Thanks for listening. You're a good friend, Jake."

"It's what I do." He patted her on the back. "But seriously, get some rest."

"I will. And I'll see you at seven."

"I'll be here with bells on." He chuckled. "Well, maybe not bells. But I will try to be festive."

After he left, Daphne took his advice and laid down for a nap and fell soundly asleep. When she woke up, she was alarmed to see that it was about ten minutes past the usual time she picked up Mabel from school. She leaped off the bed, calling out to see if Mabel had come home and rushing upstairs to see if she was in her room. But the house was still and quiet. Daphne pulled on her coat and dashed out the door. Of course, Mabel may have taken more time at school today. She had to gather up her school things since it was her last day. Perhaps she was just leaving the building now.

Daphne jogged down Huckleberry Lane, not even bothering to look at the pale yellow house. But she didn't see any sign of Mabel's purple parka. She continued on up to the front door of the school, glancing left and right as she went in, hoping to spot Mabel giving hugs to some of her classmates. But the school grounds were already pretty empty looking.

Daphne hurried down the hallway to Mabel's classroom where Miss Simmons was sitting at her desk, going through a stack of papers. "Is Mabel here?" Daphne asked breathlessly.

Miss Simmons jumped in surprise. "Class was let out fifteen minutes ago."

"Did Mabel stay later? To gather her things?" Daphne looked around the classroom almost like she expected to see Mabel hiding somewhere.

"Mabel left with the others." Miss Simmons stood. "In fact, she seemed to be in a hurry. I'm so sorry to see her go, Daphne. She's such a dear. She'll be missed."

"Yes." Daphne backed toward the door. "I know."

Miss Simmons frowned. "You didn't see Mabel on your way over here?"

"No. But maybe she stopped by her uncle's house. It's near here. I better go find out."

"Yes, that's probably it." Miss Simmons nodded with a concerned expression.

"Thanks." Daphne hurried out of the school, jogging back down the street to Daniel's house, her heart still thumping in fear. Of course, that had to be where Mabel was. With Daphne not there to walk her home, Daniel had probably stepped out to talk to her. They were probably sitting on the floor playing slap-jack.

She rang the doorbell and then knocked on the door. When Daniel came, with a puzzled expression, she demanded to know where Mabel was.

"She's not here." He scowled. "Did you lose her?"

"No, I did *not* lose her." She peered beyond him to where Mabel's boxes were scattered around the living room floor. With a felt pen in his hand, he appeared to be in the process of labeling them for shipping.

"Then where is she?" he asked with what seemed suspicion.

Daphne glanced around the room again. "She's really not here? Not hiding?"

"That's right," he said tersely. "Is there a reason she would be hiding from you?"

"No, of course not. It's just that I fell asleep. I usually meet her to walk home from school."

He narrowed his eyes as if questioning her fitness for parenting.

"She's probably at home," Daphne said quickly. "I must've missed her when I went to her classroom. I better go." And before he could question this, she dashed out, jogging back down to her house. This time she went from room to room, calling out for Mabel. She even checked the attic, the basement, the garage, and the backyard, her heart pounding frantically the whole while. Where could she be?

Daphne pulled out her phone, calling Becca's number. "Is Mabel at your house?" she asked desperately.

"Mabel?"

"Yes. She's missing. I think she must've gone home with Lola. Is she there?"

"I'm not even there," Becca told her. "And Lola's at Miss Kristy's. They have a dress rehearsal for tomorrow night's Christmas recital."

"Do you think Mabel went with her to Miss Kristy's?" But even as Daphne said this, she couldn't imagine Mabel doing that. Not without checking with Daphne first.

"I guess you could call to find out."

"Yes," Daphne said. "I'll do that."

"Let me know if I can be of help."

Daphne thanked her, then hung up and called Miss Kristy's, where the receptionist at the dance studio offered to look around. "Lola is here," she told Daphne. "But no one by that description or by the name of Mabel Myers is here."

"Well, if you happen to see her, can you call me?" Daphne gave her the number and hung up. Who to call? The police? Her dad?

Daphne went outside, looking up and down the street.

"What're you looking for?" Sabrina called from her front

HOME, HEARTH, AND THE HOLIDAYS

porch.

"Mabel," she yelled back. "She's missing."

"What?" Sabrina came rushing over. "What happened?"

Holding her phone and feeling close to tears, Daphne quickly explained.

"And she's not with Daniel?"

"He said he hadn't seen her. And Lola is at Miss Kristy's Dance School. Mabel's not there."

"Call the police," Sabrina insisted.

"Really?" Daphne felt uncertain.

"They say the chance of finding missing children improves the quicker you call."

"Missing children?" Daphne's voice cracked as she dialed 911. When the dispatcher answered, Daphne stumbled over her words. "My little girl—well, not mine—but that doesn't matter. Mabel Myers is missing. She left Lincoln Elementary at 2:30, she should've been going west on Huckleberry Lane. She's eight years old. She has short, dark brown hair and brown eyes and she has on a purple parka, blue jeans, and white athletic shoes that light up."

The dispatcher asked some questions, including her address, and promised to put out the information. "And a policeman will be there shortly."

Daphne's hands were shaking as she hung up. "We need to call everyone," Daphne told Sabrina. "Tell everyone to look for her."

"Let me do that," Sabrina offered. "You keep your phone line open in case Mabel calls you."

As Sabrina started calling friends, Daphne looked around the porch, curious if Mabel could've come home, found Daphne sleeping then gone out to play. But her scooter was still parked on the side of the porch. And knowing Lola was at her dress rehearsal...Daphne couldn't think of a single place Mabel would be.

As the police cruiser pulled up, Daphne felt sick. Somehow seeing the serious looking black and white car made it all seem frighteningly real. The officer introduced himself as Lieutenant Green and expressed his concern then began asking her the same questions the dispatcher had asked. Did Mabel usually wander from home? Did she have friends in the neighborhood? Trying not to be frustrated by what seemed a waste of time, she finally asked, "Why aren't you out there looking for her?"

"We are looking for her," he told her. "But your answers to these questions help us to search. Did Mabel have reason to run away? Was she mad at you about something?"

"No. She was looking forward to a Christmas party we're having tonight." Daphne explained about how she'd wrapped all the gifts and everything. "She was really looking forward to seeing her friends one last time."

"One last time?" His brows arched.

"Well, it's sort of a going away party."

"A going away party?"

"Her uncle has custody of her. He's taking her to a Marine base in North Carolina."

"You're not her mother?"

Daphne quickly explained.

"Well, that's interesting. And usually, a missing child turns out to be somewhere on the premises. Have you carefully searched your house?"

She explained where she'd looked.

"In all the closets and hiding places?"

Daphne frowned. "Not all the closets."

"Want me to help you look?"

"Sure."

As they headed for the house, Sabrina called out that she planned to drive through the neighborhood. "I'll call if I find her."

As they went inside, Daphne explained to Lieutenant Green about how she'd been late to meet Mabel after school. "I feel so badly."

"But Lincoln is just a few blocks from here."

"I know. But it's just something we always do." As he looked through the coat closet, she explained how Mabel had an uncle down the street. "I thought she might be there. But he said no."

"Did you look around his house?" He shone his flashlight into the storage space beneath the stairs.

"Well, no."

After he helped her thoroughly search her house, he asked for Daniel's name and address. "I'd like to go do a search of his house too."

"I'll stay here," Daphne told him from the porch. "In case she comes home."

As Lieutenant Green drove down to Daniel's house, Jake's SUV pulled up. "Have you found her?" he asked as he hurried over to Daphne.

"No—I have no idea where she could be. The police were just here." She felt tears coming and Jake took her in his arms. "I feel like it's my fault," she sobbed. "It's the—the only time I didn't go to walk her home from school. And now—now she's missing."

"This has to do with North Carolina," he told her.

"How do you know?" She pulled back to stare at him.

"I just know. It has to."

"Do you think Daniel took her?"

Jake frowned. "I don't know. But the timing is too coincidental. Tomorrow morning she leaves for North Carolina. Today she is missing?"

She peered down the street. "Lieutenant Green is down there now. I'm curious as to what's going on."

"Want to go find out?"

"Can you stay here?" she asked. "In case Mabel shows?"

"Sure." He held up his phone.

She took off jogging toward Daniel's house. If he had anything to do with Mabel being missing, she had a right to know! Seeing the police car in front and the door open, Daphne walked in.

"There she is," Daniel said as she came into the living room. "I'll bet you're behind this."

"What?" She walked up to him, looking him squarely in the eyes.

"You hid Mabel to keep her from going to North Carolina with me tomorrow."

"That is ridiculous." She pointed at him. "I'm guessing you've got her somewhere. Maybe even against her will. Probably because you know she doesn't want to go with you."

"You're accusing me of kidnapping my own niece? A child I have legal custody of?"

"If the shoe fits." She stuck out her chin.

"I searched the house," Lieutenant Green told her. "The child's not here."

"Nice little smokescreen," Daniel told her. "Turning me into a suspect to get the spotlight off of yourself."

"That is ludicrous. All I want is to find Mabel." She shook her finger at him. "Can you honestly tell me you don't have her? Have you hidden her somewhere away from here? A hotel room?"

"No!" he growled. "If anyone knows her whereabouts, it has to be you."

Daphne bit her lip, trying to contain her tears. "I swear to you, Daniel. I haven't seen her since this morning."

"I haven't seen her since Tuesday night."

"You swear you haven't seen her?"

He looked directly into her eyes. "As God is my witness."

Lieutenant Green turned to Daphne. "Do you think there's a chance she's run away?"

"She's not that kind of a girl. And we'd planned to have a going away party for her tonight. She was so excited about it. I can't imagine she'd run away. Even if she did run away, where would she go?"

"Family? Friends?"

"We've called everyone in town that we know. Everyone that Mabel knows."

"Classmates?"

"I checked with her best friend's mother, Becca Tyson. Her daughter Lola is at dance practice. Mabel doesn't really play with any other classmates, or go to anyone else's house. But maybe I should go talk to her teacher again. Miss Simmons might have seen her leaving the school with someone and—"

"I'd prefer you stick around home," Lieutenant Green told her. "I'll go speak to her teacher."

Daphne looked at Daniel and was relieved to see that he looked nearly as stressed as she felt. "I'm sorry I accused you," she told him as they all went outside. "I'm just so desperate to find her."

"I'm sorry too," he said quietly. "I'm going to go walk around the neighborhood—and ask around. Someone must've seen her."

"Good idea."

As Daphne walked home, she felt guilty for having misjudged Daniel. Really, it was like she'd told Sabrina—he was caught between a rock and a hard place. They both were. And poor Mabel was caught in the middle.

Chapter 15

When Daphne got home it was getting dusky, and another police car was parked in front. "What's going on?" she asked Jake as she ran up the porch steps to join him.

"This is Officer Smyth," Jake said. "He's been scouring the neighborhood for Mabel."

"Did you find anything?" she eagerly asked him.

"So far, nothing."

"Lieutenant Green went to her school to question her teacher," she told them. "Maybe she went home with someone I don't know."

"Is there any other place in the neighborhood where she spends time?"

"She goes to Sabrina's sometimes." Daphne pointed across the street. "To play with her dog and to visit. But Sabrina knows she's missing."

"Where's Sabrina?"

"Hunting for Mabel."

"Well, when she returns, I'd like to have a look around."

Now Daphne told him the names of other neighbors that Mabel was friendly with, pointing out their houses along the street. "Not that I can imagine her going to their homes."

"Well, you couldn't imagine her going missing either," the policeman said as he closed his notepad.

"That's true."

"I'll go start knocking on doors."

"How did it go with Daniel?" Jake asked after Officer Smyth left.

She told him about their blowout. "But maybe it helped clear the air," she admitted. "And I really don't think he took her now. Although I wish he had. At least we'd know where she was." She went to plug in the exterior Christmas lights. "In case she's on her way home," she told Jake, "so she'll see we're expecting her."

"Let's get you inside," he told her. "You're shivering from the cold."

As they went inside, she almost felt as if the festive Christmas decorations were taunting her. They seemed almost garish and out of place considering that Mabel was missing. "How about if I make a fire to get the chill out of here," he offered.

"Sure."

"It's sure getting cold out. I heard we really might have snow in a couple of days."

"Uh huh." She was pacing now, trying to think of where Mabel might be—if the policeman was right and she had run away. "I just can't imagine it," she said aloud.

"What?" Jake stood up from lighting the fire.

"That she would run away. It's so out of character."

"Wouldn't you rather think she'd run away...than...well, you know."

"Been abducted?"

"This is Appleton, Daphne. That kind of thing doesn't happen here. Even Officer Smyth felt certain she'd probably gone home with a little friend."

Daphne took a deep breath. "Yes, you have to be right."

"How about a cup of tea?" Jake offered. "To warm you up."

She just shrugged, but he went into the kitchen, making himself at home. It wasn't long before he emerged with two cups. "Sit down," he told her. "Try to relax. Really, the more I think about it, the more certain I feel that Mabel just went home with someone. Maybe she made a new friend at her birthday party. She wanted to enjoy playing before she had to leave. Doesn't it make sense?"

"Not really." She sipped the tea, not even tasting it. "It's not like her."

"Yoo-hoo," Sabrina called as she came into the house.

"In here," Jake called.

"Did y'all find her yet?" she asked hopefully.

"No." Jake gave her a quick update.

"The police asked to check your house," Daphne said in a flat tone.

"My house?" Sabrina frowned.

"In case she's hiding out there," Jake explained.

"Well, they're welcome to look around, but I don't know how she could've gotten in there to hide out without me seeing her." Sabrina scowled. "That is ridiculous. They should be searching the town, and airports and train stations and along the highways. It might be a human trafficker."

Daphne looked up in alarm.

"Sorry." Sabrina put her hand over her mouth. "I shouldn't let my imagination run away like that."

"Why don't you go look around your house," Jake suggested. "Just in case the police are right. That way you'll be there when they come to question you."

"All right." She went over to Daphne. "Forgive me and my big mouth."

"It's okay."

"What about the party tonight?" Sabrina looked at the clock. "It's only a couple hours now. Do you think you should cancel it?"

Daphne just nodded.

"Want me to call everyone for you?"

She nodded again. "There's a list of the guests on the fridge."

"I'll handle everything," Sabrina assured her. "And didn't you say Truman at the Apple Basket was catering?"

"Uh huh."

"I'll call him too."

"Thanks," Daphne said in a flat tone.

"And I'll stay here with Daphne," Jake told Sabrina.

"Good. I think she needs someone right now."

Daphne felt slightly numb as she sat on the sofa, staring at the flickering flames in the fireplace. "I don't know what to do," she said in a quiet voice. "I guess I should pray, but I honestly don't even know how."

"I'm not that good at it either," Jake confessed, "but I'm willing to take a stab at it."

They bowed their heads and Jake grasped her hands. And, even though Daphne still felt rather lost and numb, she appreciated how Jake prayed a very succinct and sincere prayer, asking God to get Mabel safely home to them. "Amen," he said.

"Thanks," she told him. "Sorry, I'm such a basket case."

"Understandable."

With her phone in hand, Daphne paced back and forth again. She jumped when it rang, but it was just her dad, calling to see if Mabel had come home yet, almost sounding as if Mabel had simply gone out to play and lost track of the time.

"She's still missing," she told him.

"Sabrina said you're canceling the party. Are you sure that's not premature? Maybe Mabel will show up in time and be disappointed."

Daphne looked at the mantle clock. "It's almost six, Dad. Mabel has *never* done anything like this. Not since she's been with me."

"But remember she had a whole other life before you. I suspect she was pretty independent."

"Well, that's probably true."

"I remember some times when you came home late after playing with friends."

"But not on a night when someone was having a special party for me."

"Yes. I suppose not." His voice sounded sad and tired.

"I'll let you know when she gets home," she told him. She jumped when the doorbell rang, but Jake hurried to answer it.

"It's Sabrina, and she's brought food," he announced.

"I know you probably don't think you're hungry," Sabrina said as she carried in a box. "But Ricardo insisted I bring this to you."

"Oh..."

"And I promised I'd get you to eat something." Sabrina took the box into the kitchen.

Daphne followed her, looking out the window as Sabrina busied herself with the box. "The police car is back."

"Yes. That's Officer Smyth. He looked all through my house like he thought I had Mabel bound and gagged and shoved under the bed. What a total waste of time."

The doorbell rang, making her jump again.

"It's Daniel," Jake called out.

"Don't let him in," Sabrina said quietly.

"He's not the enemy," Daphne said as she went to see.

"Sorry to intrude," Daniel told her. "Looks like you haven't heard anything either."

"No." She sighed as she wrung her hands. "I would call you if I did."

"Yeah. Me too." He looked so lost and forlorn that she actually felt sorry for him.

"Ricardo sent over food. Looks like there's enough for a small army. Want to join us?"

"No, I don't want to—"

"Come on." She grabbed his arm, pulling him into the living room. "You might as well stick around. If we're having a vigil, we should probably do it together."

Daphne went to where Sabrina was setting the dining table. "Make it for four," Daphne told her.

Sabrina narrowed her eyes. "Seriously? You're letting him eat here?"

"Sabrina." Daphne put a warning in her voice. "What would Jesus do?"

"A miracle?" Sabrina smirked.

It was nearly seven when they sat down to eat. Daphne didn't feel a bit hungry, but she tried to pretend to be eating. No one talked much. This was not like she had expected this evening to go. "Where is she?" she finally exclaimed, pushing her plate to the side. "Where on earth could she possibly be?"

"That's what I'd like to know," Daniel said glumly.

"This is *your* fault!" Sabrina shouted at Daniel.

"Sabrina!" Daphne shook her head.

"It is." Sabrina stood to gather the plates. "If Daniel wasn't forcing Mabel to go to North Carolina against her will, she would probably be here right now. I just know it."

Daphne slowly stood. "Unless she's been kidnapped," she said in a shaky voice. "What else could it be? She would never stay away this long. It's been dark for hours." And now she broke into sobs. Jake stood and, putting an arm around her, guided her to the living room, but they could still hear the voices coming from the dining room.

"Who said I'm forcing Mabel against her will?" Daniel demanded hotly. "I'm her uncle. She loves me. She *wants* to go with me."

"Ha!" This was followed by the sound of dishes clattering together. "That just shows how much you know."

"You're crazy, you know it?"

"*I'm* crazy?" Sabrina shouted. "You're the one who's flipping crazy, Daniel Myers. Mabel has been through so much!" Sabrina started listing everything. "And then Daphne comes into her life and for the first time this little girl is happy. Really happy. She's got friends and people who love her. She's got stability. And them, wham-bam-thank-you-ma'am—Uncle

Daniel comes along and blows her whole world sky high. You ought to be ashamed of yourself."

"Ashamed for taking care of my niece, the way my mother asked me to do?"

"Never mind what Mabel wants. She's just a child. She shouldn't have a say in regard to her own life. Who cares if she's happy?"

"Like I told you the other night, Mabel will like living on base. She'll have friends all around her and—"

"And what about when Uncle Daniel gets called overseas? Who takes care of Mabel then?" she demanded. "And what if Uncle Daniel gets hurt—or even killed—what happens to Mabel then? How much pain and trauma do you think a little eight-year-old girl can handle? I didn't have the nerve to say this stuff the other night, but by golly, I'm gonna say it now. You are one mean, selfish man, Daniel Myers. You might be serving your country—and I thank you for that—but you are *not* serving your family. And if Vera were alive to see what you've done to that little girl, well, I just know she'd be disappointed. Severely disappointed."

Daniel didn't respond to that. Instead he came through to the living room. "Well, I guess I should go."

"You don't need to go," Daphne told him. "Sabrina's been spoiling for a fight for a few days now. Don't leave because of her."

Jake pointed to a chair. "Have a seat."

Daniel sat down with a furrowed brow.

"A lot of what Sabrina said was true," Daphne said quietly. "But she didn't have to put it so strongly."

"I couldn't help myself," Sabrina called out from the kitchen.

"That man got my hackles up!"

"We noticed," Jake called back.

"And Sabrina raised a good question, Daniel. Did you even ask Mabel what she wants? Do you even care what she thinks?"

"She's a child."

Daphne nodded. "Do you remember when you were a child?"

"Some."

"Did you like it when the adults ran roughshod over you? You told me your home wasn't the most pleasant place—what if someone had asked you for suggestions then? Would you have had an opinion? Would you have wanted your opinion respected?"

"I guess so."

"And I doubt you ever had it as bad as Mabel has..."

"Probably not. But I wanted to give her something better."

"Better than what I wanted to give her?"

He frowned.

"Could you give her something better than what I could give her, Daniel?" Daphne waited. "And what about when you're called up to serve out of the country? What happens to her then? Have you really thought all of this through?"

Before he could answer, Daphne's phone rang. She grabbed it up, eagerly saying "Hello?"

"This is Becca, Daphne. I'm embarrassed to tell you that Lola has been harboring a fugitive in our basement."

"*Mabel?*"

"Yes, she's been here all along. I'm so sorry, Daphne. You must be worried to death."

"Not anymore." Daphne felt her spirits soar.

"Lola kept going down to the basement. Then I caught her sneaking down there with a banana after I thought she'd gone to bed. That's when I figured it out. I guess Mabel planned to stay here until her uncle flew away to North Carolina."

"Oh, my." Daphne paused to tell the others then assured Becca she would be right over to pick Mabel up. "Can you believe that?" Daphne was going for her keys.

"Why don't I go get her?" Jake offered as he joined her in the foyer. "You still seem a little shaky."

"Then I'll go with you."

He shook his head then lowered his voice. "Stay here. Keep talking to Daniel. I think you were making headway."

"Really?"

He nodded and then, to her surprise, he leaned over and kissed her on the forehead. "You're a trooper, Daphne."

She blinked then thanked him.

Chapter 16

As Daphne returned to the living room, she called out to Sabrina. "Do you mind informing the police that we found Mabel?"

"Good idea!" Sabrina yelled back. "In fact, I'll call everyone."

"Thank you!"

Daphne sat down across from Daniel. Still wearing a perplexed expression, he was nervously rubbing his hands together with a furrowed brow. "Do you know for a fact that Mabel doesn't want to go to North Carolina with me?" he asked with quiet intensity. "She's actually said those words to you?"

"She's told me *over and over*, Daniel. I asked her to share her feelings with you. I had hoped it would help you understand—if you'd heard it from her. But she was always afraid she would hurt you. She really loves you, Daniel. But she doesn't want to leave Appleton...she doesn't want to leave her home or her school or her friends."

He barely nodded. "I guess I knew that. But I convinced myself that, once we were gone, she'd adjust...and we'd be okay."

"I tried to convince myself of the same thing." She sighed. "But I still had serious doubts."

"Me too!" Sabrina echoed from the kitchen.

Ignoring her, Daphne continued. "It's not too late, Daniel... why don't you ask Mabel how she feels about moving? Listen to her—and then make your decision."

"I guess I could do that."

"Can I come out now?" Sabrina asked in a little girl voice.

"Only if you can mind your manners." Daphne shook her finger at her. "I recall you going on about Southern manners, Sabrina. What happened to yours with Daniel?"

"Oh, well, there's manners and then there's manners. I know how to make a guest at home, write a lovely thank-you note, set a perfect table. But I also know how to speak my mind." She gave them a half-smile. "And I know how to beg your pardon when my mouth runs away with me." She tipped her head to Daniel. "Please, forgive me, kind sir. I'm afraid I said too much"

He looked at her from the corner of his eye. "Guess I had it coming."

"Hello," Jake called as he and Mabel entered the house. "You'll never guess what I found in Lola's basement."

Daphne jumped up, running to the foyer where she scooped Mabel into a mama-bear hug. "Do you know how worried I was for you?"

"I'm sorry, Aunt Daphne."

Daphne hugged her close. "I love you so much, Mabel. I was sick with worry—what if something had happened to you? Please, don't ever do that again, sweetie. Not to anyone—you hear?"

"Yeah—I'm *really, really* sorry." Mabel had tears streaking down her cheeks as Daphne helped her out of her parka.

"I forgive you, darling. But you still need to explain to everyone what you did. We were all terribly worried. I think half the town has been worried."

She led Mabel into the living room.

"Why did you do that?" Daniel asked Mabel in a stern tone.

"I don't know." Mabel looked down at her shoes, clinging to Daphne's arm.

Daphne sat on the couch and, sitting Mabel next to her, she slipped a supportive arm around her. "Uncle Daniel and I were just having a very honest talk, Mabel. I shared some of the things you told me about not wanting to go to North Carolina. But he has some questions to ask too. Can you answer him honestly?"

With eyes still downcast, Mabel barely nodded.

"For starters, we'd all like to know why you hid in Lola's basement," Daphne began. "Actually, I'd like to know *how* you did it too. Wasn't Lola at Miss Kristy's?"

"Lola told me where her mom hides the key. As soon as school was out, I ran all the way to Lola's house. I went down the alley so no one would see me. I found the key under the watering can and used it to go inside. I stayed in the basement, in a closet, for a long time. Until Lola got home. It was kinda stinky in the closet, but I fell asleep, so it wasn't so bad. When I got hungry, Lola brought me some food."

"Now tell us why you did this," Daphne said gently.

"I wanted to hide in Lola's basement until Uncle Daniel went away to North Carolina."

Daphne glanced at Daniel and, seeing the pain in his face,

she continued. "But you told me you *love* Uncle Daniel, Mabel."

"I do love Uncle Daniel," Mabel declared. "But I don't want to go to North Carolina. I want to stay here—*with you.*" She looked up at Daniel with tear-filled eyes. "I'm sorry...."

"It's okay," he assured her. "I'm glad you're telling me the truth."

"I wanted to tell you before." Her voice trembled. "But you kept saying how good it would be when we got there. You said I'd be really happy." She grabbed more tightly to Daphne's arm. "But I won't be happy. Not without Daphne."

"I'm starting to understand that," he said sadly.

"Why don't you stay here in Appleton?" Mabel said hopefully. "You could get some furniture and live in Grandma's house. Tell that lady you don't want to sell it to her. We could all be happy in Appleton."

"I *could* do that." He pursed his lips. "But in the same way you know you won't be happy away from Daphne, I know I won't be happy away from the Marines."

"Oh." Mabel looked back down at her shoes.

"But if you really want to stay in Appleton, and if Daphne really wants to have you as her little girl, well, I will agree to it."

"You *will?*" Mabel jumped to her feet.

He nodded. "I'm pretty sure your grandma would've agreed to it too."

Mabel ran over to hug him. "Thank you, Uncle Daniel! *Thank you so much!*"

He hugged her back. "Thank you for being honest with me. I hope you'll always be honest with me."

"I will. And I'll write you letters too," Mabel promised him. "And I'll pray for you every night. And if you have a vacation, you can come stay here with me and Daphne." She glanced at Daphne. "Okay?"

Daphne smiled. "Very okay."

"Okay then. I should probably go do some packing." He stood up. "I have a morning flight."

"Can we give you a ride to the airport?" Daphne offered.

"Yes, yes," Mabel said. "Can we? *Please*?"

He looked reluctant but then smiled. "Yeah, that'd be nice."

"How about I give you a ride home?" Jake offered.

"It's okay. It's just a few blocks."

"I know that. But I thought we could talk about the legal part of this situation. We need to set up some kind of custody agreement between you and Daphne."

"Oh, yeah. Right." Daniel thanked him. "I'd appreciate that."

After the guys left, Mabel grabbed Daphne and Sabrina's hands and the three of them did a nice, long happy dance together—until they were all laughing so hard that they tumbled down onto the sofa in giggles.

"I'm sorry I ruined our party," Mabel said as she noticed the pile of unopened gifts under the tree.

"You didn't ruin anything," Daphne told her. "We'll still have a Christmas party. Only now it will be a real celebration."

"That's right. Instead of a going away party, it'll be more like a welcome home party," Sabrina told her.

"What about my boxes from my room? The stuff Uncle Daniel took?" Mabel's mouth twisted to one side. "Oh, I don't care. He can just keep it if he wants to. It's okay."

Daphne laughed. "No worries. I think it's still at his house. We'll get it tomorrow."

And after another good long group hug, Daphne told Mabel

to get ready for bed. Then she turned to Sabrina. "I didn't want to say it in front of Daniel, but I really did appreciate your temporary lapse in Southern manners earlier," she said quietly. "I didn't show it, but I was silently cheering you. You said all the things I'd wanted to say but didn't dare. Thanks!"

"Hey, that's what friends are for." Sabrina looked at the clock. "Speaking of friends, I better go check on poor Tootsie. He probably thinks I've abandoned him."

"You tell Tootsie I owe him a good doggie treat."

As Sabrina left, Daphne thought about the good friends she'd accumulated since coming to Appleton. Just a year ago, she never would've imagined having friends like this. People who would drop everything to come to your aid. She hadn't even realized that, other than her dad and Aunt Dee, there were people like that in this world. Now it felt like she was surrounded by them.

Chapter 17

"**I** have to admit that I'm relieved that Mabel is remaining in Appleton," Daniel told Daphne as she drove him to the airport the next morning. Mabel was wedged in the backseat next to his duffle bag and reading a book.

"I'm glad to hear that. I actually hoped that it would be a relief. Raising a child as a single person isn't easy. Especially if you work outside of the home."

"Or outside of the country."

"Yes, that was worrying me a lot."

"I just wanted to do what I thought my mom wanted," he said somberly. "But it was good talking to Jake last night. He helped me to understand some things about wills and the legal issues—and being a single dad. That Jake is a good guy."

She nodded. "He's a good friend."

"Seems to me you've got a lot of good friends, Daphne."

"That's one of the benefits in living in Appleton."

"That night when I took Mabel to dinner while you had your writing group, I was surprised when we came home at how many male friends you seem to have."

Daphne laughed. "I was surprised by how many guys want to be writers."

"Did they want to be writers or did they just want to be around you?" he said in a teasing tone.

"I don't know, but they're all pretty interested in writing."

"Well, they seem like good guys. I wouldn't be surprised if you're happily married by the time I come back to Appleton."

"Are you coming back to Appleton?" Mabel chimed in from the backseat.

"Someday, I hope so. After this visit, I actually feel like Appleton really is my home."

"It is! It is!" Mabel declared. "And I will write to you about it all the time. I'll tell you what's going on so when you come home, you won't be too surprised."

Daniel chuckled. "Well, thanks, Mabel. I appreciate that."

At the airport, they all got out of the car and Daniel picked up Mabel in a good long hug. "You be a good girl for Aunt Daphne, you hear?"

She nodded. "I promise I will."

Daphne pulled out her phone, taking some quick shots of Daniel in his fatigues with Mabel in his arms.

"And no more running away and hiding out at your friend's house," he told her.

She firmly shook her head. "I won't do that again. Not ever. I promise."

"Good." He kissed her cheek and set her back on the ground. Now he grasped Daphne's hand. "It's been a pleasure getting to know you."

"You too." She felt a lump in her throat. "Under different

circumstances...well, who knows?"

He grinned slyly. "Nah, I don't really think that was meant to be."

She laughed. "Yeah, me neither."

And now he hugged her. "Besides I'd rather have you for my little sister. And since you're going to be Mabel's legal guardian, it makes us like siblings."

"That's right." She nodded eagerly. "I always wanted a big brother."

"So you take care, sis."

"And you too, bro. You be safe, okay?"

He gave them both a solemn salute then picked up his duffle and backpack.

"I forgot something!" Daphne called out as she reached back into the car, pulling out the little photo album she'd been putting together for Mabel. "Pictures of your niece and of Appleton."

His face lit up. "Thank you. That means a lot."

She nodded, blinking back tears as she held Mabel's hand and together they watched him going into the airport.

"I feel sad," Mabel said as they drove down the highway.

"Me too," Daphne admitted. "Uncle Daniel is a good man, Mabel. You're lucky to have him for your uncle."

"I know," Mabel declared. "And I'm going to pray for him every night."

"Me too." Daphne nodded.

As they got closer to town, Mabel asked Daphne if she was going to be punished for running away yesterday.

"Oh, I don't think so," Daphne said lightly. "You were in a tough spot, Mabel. I understand why you did what you did."

"But it was wrong."

"Yes, it was definitely wrong. No question about that." Suddenly Daphne began to question her ability to parent. *Should* she punish Mabel? She sure didn't feel like it. But what if she didn't and Mabel underestimated the significance of what she'd done? What if it sent the message it was okay to do something like that?

"Well, you did promise me you'd never do that again," Daphne began.

"I will never, ever do it again."

"And I believe you mean that, at least for right now. But I suppose, well, in years to come, you might forget about that promise."

"I won't forget."

"And I don't think you enjoyed hiding out at Lola's," Daphne said. "Maybe that was punishment enough."

"I didn't like being in the stinky closet," she admitted, "but it was kind of exciting. It was kinda like being in a movie."

"Oh..." Daphne frowned as she turned into Appleton. "To be honest, I'm not really sure of the best way to handle this, Mabel. As you know, this whole parenting thing is new to me. I don't know the first thing about punishing a child."

As Daphne drove through the quiet town, which appeared to be just waking up, neither of them spoke. It wasn't until she drove down Huckleberry Lane that Mabel finally said something—in a matter of fact voice. "You should probably ground me."

Daphne blinked. "*Ground* you?"

"That's what Lola's mom does when she's naughty."

"Oh." Daphne sighed as she pulled into the garage. "Then I

suppose you are grounded."

"Okay." Daphne hopped out of the car.

As they went into the house, Daphne still wasn't sure about this punishment. "So, tell me, Mabel. When Becca grounds Lola, what exactly does that mean? And how long does it last?"

"It means she has to stay home. Except for school. And friends can't come to her house to play. And no electronics— like TV, videos, or games."

"Right." Daphne cringed to remember this was the Christmas season with a lot of fun activities going on in the next week and a half—things she'd been looking forward to doing with Mabel. "What about going to things with me?" She pointed to the calendar on the fridge. "Like Lola's recital tonight? And the school's winter program on Tuesday. And then there's the church's program next weekend. Do we have to miss all those things?"

Mabel frowned. "I don't know."

"And how long should a grounding last?" Daphne tried to conceal her dislike of this form of discipline.

"A week...maybe two weeks since what I did was really, really bad."

As Daphne started a pot of coffee, she liked this grounding idea less and less. "I'm not sure that grounding is the right punishment for you," she told Mabel.

"Why not?"

"I think hard labor might be better," Daphne said in a serious tone.

"What's that?"

"Work."

"What kind of work?"

Daphne thought. "Housework." She pointed to their breakfast dishes still in the sink. "Like you could clean up the kitchen. Load the dishwasher. Wipe the counters and sweep the floor."

"Okay," Mabel eagerly agreed.

Daphne held up the house key Daniel had given to her. "And then we'll go down and get your boxes from your grandma's house. And then you can spend the rest of the morning putting your whole room back together. *By yourself.*"

Mabel nodded. "Okay."

"After that's done. You can clean the upstairs bathroom and the powder room down here too."

"Okay."

Daphne was thinking hard, trying to come up with more hard labor.

"Should I sweep the laundry room too?" Mabel asked. "The cats spilled kitty litter again."

"Yes." Daphne nodded. "And sweep the dining room too."

"Okay."

"And the pine needles by the Christmas tree. And the porch has pine needles too." Daphne was starting to feel guilty now. "Or is that too much?"

Mabel shook her head no.

"Would you rather be grounded?"

Now she vigorously shook her head no.

Daphne suppressed a smile. "So, we agree. Today will be a day of hard labor, and when you're done, the punishment ends. Okay?"

Mabel looked surprised. "Just *one* day?"

Daphne laughed. "Yes. I think it's a fair sentence."

When Mabel looked uncertain, Daphne just hugged her. "My goodness, Mabel, it's not like I want to turn you into Cinderella."

Mabel's eyes lit up. "I *love* Cinderella."

Daphne poured a cup of coffee, leaving her little Cinderella to her "hard labor" as she went to her office to catch up with email and work on the column. But it wasn't long before Mabel was ready to put her room back together. "I can go down and bring the boxes back in the garden wagon," Mabel offered.

Daphne smiled. "That's okay. I wouldn't mind a little walk."

"But I'll do the work," Mabel assured her. "It's my hard labor."

It took two trips to get all the boxes home, and then Daphne helped her to get them upstairs and cut open the boxes. "You're on your own now," Daphne said.

Mabel just nodded, grimly looking at everything that needed to be put away.

"And I expect it to look good when you're done." Daphne feigned a stern tone. "I'll be in my office if you need me."

As Daphne returned to her office, she decided she liked her form of discipline. It was like getting two birds with one stone. Of course, she knew it wouldn't always be this simple. But hopefully, she'd have time to prepare herself for the challenges ahead by then. As she returned to answering letters for the column, she kept putting off responding to a letter from "Confused in Clarkston." Simply because it made her feel sad.

She was just about to confront this letter when the landline phone rang. Eager for a distraction, she was slightly disappointed to hear Lola on the other end, asking to talk to Mabel. Daphne carried the cordless phone upstairs, discovering that Mabel had made really good progress with her room. "It's Lola," she told her.

"Hi, Lola." Mabel paused to listen. "I can't play today." She paused again. "No, I'm not grounded. I'm doing hard labor." Daphne tried not to giggle as Mabel explained the concept to her friend. "It's really hard work, but it only lasts one day." Mabel paused to look at Daphne. "Lola wants to know if we're coming to her Christmas recital?"

Daphne nodded.

"Yes!" Mabel exclaimed. "See you later, alligator." She handed the phone back to Daphne.

"You're doing a good job in here." Daphne pointed to where Mabel had arranged her stuffed animals on the window seat. "I like that. Nice touch."

"Thanks." Mabel smiled. "I know you thought this was a good punishment, but I don't think hard labor is that bad. Next time you should probably ground me."

Daphne frowned. "*Next* time?"

"If I do something naughty."

"I'll keep that in mind," Daphne called out as she exited the bedroom. "In the meantime, keep up the good work."

Back in her office, Daphne pulled up the letter that was making her blue, reading it again—more slowly and carefully this time—as she considered her answer. This letter had hit a nerve with her. Certainly her circumstances were nothing like Confused in Clarkston's, but she could relate to this woman's concerns about an inability to love again. This was something that Daphne had dealt with before, something she had hoped to have a handle on by now. But suddenly—and perhaps it was a result of the recent emotional turbulence she'd been through—it felt very real again.

Her rational side pointed out that the situation with Daniel and Mabel had been draining. It made sense that she'd feel emotionally exhausted. So much so that the idea of getting involved with anyone sounded overwhelming. And, really, what was wrong with just settling in with Mabel for the time being? At least long enough to get them through the holidays. After the New Year, Daphne would revisit the possibility of finding her soul mate. Now was not the time. And deciding this helped her to answer the letter.

> *Dear Daphne,*
>
> *Two years ago I lost my best friend and beloved husband to pancreatic cancer. We were high school sweethearts and had been married for seventeen years. Nothing prepared me for losing him. I miss him every day. Now my friends and family are urging me to date again. But I feel stuck. My big fear is that I have already had the love of my life— he's gone, that's it, game over. My question is: Will I ever be able to love again?*
>
> *Confused in Clarkston*
>
> *Dear Confused,*
>
> *I offer you both my commiserations and my congratulations. I'm so sorry for your loss, but at the same time I commend you for seventeen happy years in a loving marriage. Not everyone gets that.*
>
> *Perhaps you've heard that a good way to forecast the future is to pay attention to the past. In your*

case, you have a solid history of a good relationship, which leads me to believe that—YES—your chances of loving again are excellent. But perhaps it's a matter of timing. Everyone grieves at a different rate. Don't let well-meaning friends and relatives push you into something you're not ready for. You'll know it when it's time to move on. And when the next Mr. Right comes along, I'm guessing you heart will be ready.

Daphne

Timing really was everything, Daphne told herself as she shut down her computer. Love should not be rushed. And the next time Sabrina tried to light a fire beneath Daphne—urging her to "find a man"—she would simply remind her of this and politely ask her to back off. If love was going to come Daphne's way, she would just need to be patient and wait.

By the end of the day, Mabel was glad that her hard labor had come to an end. But probably not as glad as Daphne. "So, let's put it behind us," Daphne told Mabel as she drove them to the middle school where the Christmas recital was being held. "Let's just focus on having an enjoyable evening."

"And next time Miss Kristy has a dance recital, I'll get to be in it," Mabel said hopefully.

"That's right," Daphne said. "I can't wait to see that." As Daphne drove through town, she realized how close they had come to losing all of this. How easily it might've all gone a different way. Right now, Mabel would've been in North Carolina. Daphne would've been sitting at home alone... missing her. As she pulled into the parking lot, Daphne said a silent thank-you prayer, knowing that both she and Mabel would have to take time to say an even better thank-you at bedtime.

Chapter 18

After the worship service was over, Daphne headed straight for Laura Berg. She was the head of the children's ministry and in charge of the upcoming Christmas program. According to the bulletin, it would be a living nativity and was just one week away—the Sunday night before Christmas. Daphne hoped it wasn't too late for Mabel to be involved.

"I know this is last minute." Daphne explained about Mabel. "We didn't sign her up because we thought she'd be gone. But she really, really wanted to participate in this." She held up the bulletin. "And I just read that you need adults to help. So I'm volunteering, as long as Mabel can be in it." She smiled hopefully.

"I *do* need help." Laura looked grateful. "And Mabel is welcome. I'm letting the latecomers be angels. I have about eight kids so far, and I'd like to put an adult with them, to give direction." Now she described the plan to stage the angels off to one side of the living nativity. "I want them to sing jubilant carols like 'Joy to the World' and 'Hark the Herald Angels

Sing.'"

"That will be a nice touch."

"So can you could take charge of that? Run herd on the angels?"

"Sure. I'd love to." Daphne didn't feel as positive as she sounded, but for Mabel's sake she was more than willing.

"Of course, you'd need to dress like an angel too."

"Okay…" Daphne was just wondering what she was getting into when Pastor Andrew joined them.

"Is Laura recruiting you for the living nativity?" he asked.

"I actually volunteered." Daphne smiled.

"She's our head angel," Laura told him.

"Great. I know some theologians would argue over a woman angel, but the Bible says there are neither male nor female in heaven, so I can't see that it matters." He laughed. "And, really, you'd think theologians could find something better to argue about."

"Or maybe they could just get along," Laura added.

He nodded. "Good point."

"Would you mind if I recruited a helper?" Daphne glanced over to where Sabrina was chatting with an older woman. "I know for a fact that Sabrina has a good singing voice. She might be a nice addition to the angels."

"Fabulous," Laura said. "I leave it in your hands, Daphne. And if you give me your email, I'll send you the names and phone numbers of your angel crew. I'd like you to have at least one dress rehearsal with them before Saturday."

Daphne gave Laura her business card then went over to tell Sabrina the news. "I hope you don't mind me volunteering you."

"Mind? I think it sounds like a hoot. And I know just what I'll wear." She described a white satiny dressing gown. "And I'll use some gold cord to belt it with."

Daphne laughed. "It just figures you'd already have an angel outfit. I still have to figure that one out."

"Don't worry. I'll help both you and Mabel with costumes. Trust me, we'll be the most stylish angels this town has ever seen."

"Hopefully we'll *sound* angelic too." Daphne explained about the singing. "If you don't mind, I'd like you to take charge of music."

Mabel couldn't have been happier to find out she was going to be an angel in the living nativity. But as they drove home, Mabel suddenly remembered about her school's winter program too. "I hope Miss Simmons will still let me be in it. I was going to be a snow fairy with Lola."

"Of course she will," Daphne assured her. "She'll be so pleased to discover you didn't move after all."

On Monday morning, it felt good to see life falling back in their old, normal routine. Except that it was icy cold outside. Daphne and Mabel bundled up, pulling on hats and gloves and scarves before they walked to school. This time Daphne went inside with Mabel, parting ways as Mabel happily headed off to surprise Miss Simmons. Meanwhile, Daphne stopped by the office to explain to Mrs. Pruitt that Mabel wasn't moving after all. "I know I asked you to send her records to North Carolina," Daphne said apologetically.

"You're in luck. I didn't have time to send them , and I

haven't even removed Mabel from enrollment yet." Mrs. Pruitt held up her hands. "Thanks to busyness of Christmas."

"That's great. And that reminds me, Mabel really wanted to be in the winter program tomorrow night. I hope it's not too late."

"I can't imagine it would be." Mrs. Pruitt shuffled some papers. "I'm sure Miss Simmons will be happy to have her participate. Do you have her costume ready yet?"

"No...she was supposed to be a snow fairy," Daphne told her. "I suppose that involves wings."

"It's been awhile since I've made wings, but as I recall, it's not too difficult. Just get some dry cleaners hangers and stretch netting around them. Add some sparkle and voila, you should have it."

Daphne thanked her and hurried back out into the cold. Before long she was scouring the fabric and craft stores, quickly gathering the necessary materials. By midday, she was in the midst of creating what she hoped would be an acceptable snow fairy costume. She was just stretching white netting around the coat hanger wire when the doorbell rang. Unwilling to set the pieces down and have to start over again, she carried the wing to the door. And, peeking out the window, she saw that it was Jake. Dressed in a navy suit and carrying a briefcase, he looked all business.

"Come in," she yelled. "My hands are full."

He let himself in, giving her a quizzical look. "What are you doing?"

"Making snow fairy wings," she explained. "What're you doing?"

He held up the briefcase. "I brought legal papers for you to sign. Guardianship for Mabel. I didn't think we should waste any time on this."

"Oh, yes!" She nodded toward the kitchen, where she'd been working. "Come on in. I was just wishing for a second set of hands. Would you mind hanging onto this clump of fabric while I sew it closed?"

"Not at all." He set down his briefcase then fumbled to hold onto the gathered netting, while she threaded a needle.

With his help, she managed to get the snow fairy wings secured. "What do you think?" Daphne fluttered them in the air like a butterfly.

"Not bad." He nodded. "Nice work."

"Well, they still need some sparkle." She pointed to the silver glitter glue and opalescent sequins she planned to use. "And I'm going to use these satin ribbons too." She held up a streamer of white and pale blue ribbons.

"Very creative."

"Really?" She set the wings down. "I hope so. I'm pretty new at this sort of thing."

"You seem to be handling it well." He looked at the messy kitchen table. "Maybe we should go to the dining room to go over these papers."

"Good idea."

It didn't take long to read and sign the papers. "I'll fax them to Daniel for his signature," he said as he slid them back in his briefcase.

As she thanked him, she could tell that he wasn't overly eager to leave. Instead, he followed her back into the kitchen, watching as she continued to assemble and decorate the snow fairy wings.

"You really do make a lovely mother," he told her.

"Well, thank you." She beamed at him. "What a nice thing to say."

"I never would've guessed that you'd be such a natural at this, Daphne, but you clearly are." He went over to check the coffee pot, which was still half full and hot. "Mind if I help myself?"

"Not at all."

With a full cup of coffee, he pulled out a kitchen chair and sat. "When I first met you, you seemed like such a city girl. Smartly dressed. Focused on your career. You even talked fast—just like a real New Yorker."

"Well, I was a New Yorker." She pressed a string of sequins into a swirl of glue. "At least I thought I was."

"I just couldn't imagine that you'd ever want to settle down in Appleton. I suspected you'd land yourself a husband—and you've obviously had your opportunities."

"Don't remind me." She rolled her eyes as she reached for the glue.

"So I figured you'd get married and secure your inheritance. And I was guessing you'd sell the house and the car—just liquidate everything into your bank account. And, call me cynical, but I thought you might even get rid of the husband. Then you'd zip back to New York. And all in a short amount of time."

"*Seriously?*" She stopped the glue bottle in midair. "You thought I was really like *that?*"

"I didn't even know you, Daphne. And hey, I wouldn't have blamed you if you had done it like that. I can't deny that Dee's will was pretty bizarre. The weirdest document I've ever drawn up. I even warned Dee that it seemed like the formula for a disaster. I told her that I thought most young women would figure a way to just take the money and run—even if it meant faking a marriage."

"I couldn't have done that."

"No. I've been pleasantly surprised. And Dee had seemed fairly certain you'd do the honorable thing."

She sighed. "Even if it means losing everything."

"May is still a ways off...."

"Yes. That's what I was just telling myself."

"Anyway, I never would've guessed you'd be such an upstanding person, Daphne. And I never dreamed you'd take in someone like Mabel and become a mother to her." He shook his head with a look of disbelief.

"Well, I couldn't be happier." She held up a wing and smiled.

"Mabel's going to love that." He took a sip of coffee. "Pretty good work for a New York journalist."

She snickered. "I wrote about *weddings*, Jake. Not exactly a journalist."

"Dee was certain you were in the wrong place."

"The wrong place?"

"In New York, working for the *Times*. She didn't think you were truly happy there. Didn't think it suited you."

"Interesting. She never said a word of that to me."

"No, of course, she wouldn't."

"She always encouraged me to follow my heart...to find my dreams."

"It wasn't her style to interfere."

"Well, until she created that ridiculous will." Daphne reached for another portion of wing, running a bead of glue along the edge. "That has been a bit of interference."

"I know it seems that way, but it wasn't her intention. She honestly felt like she was helping you by doing this."

"I know, I know...she didn't want me to end up like—like her." Daphne set down the wings then threw back her head to laugh. "But *look* at me, Jake. I am *exactly* like her."

"How so?" He made a confused frown.

"Well, besides the obvious." She waved her hand. "I live in her house. I drive her car. I care for her cats. Besides that, I write her column. And, just like she used to do, I'm writing a novel at the same time. Maybe it's not romance, but you get the picture."

He nodded. "Yeah, but you're not exactly like her."

"How about the fact that I'm a spinster who's now playing 'aunt' to a little girl who's lost her mother?" She shook her head as the irony fully registered. "Honestly, can you believe that history could repeat itself so implicitly? I mean, it's almost creepy. Except that it's kind of sweet too."

Jake chuckled. "Yeah, when you put it like that...it's a little uncanny. Not to mention amusing. But if you're going to imitate a life, I can't imagine anyone more worth imitating than Dee. She was quite a woman."

"I know."

"And she loved you dearly."

She nodded. "It's a relief to be able to talk about this stuff with you, Jake."

"Anytime."

"I mean, Sabrina can be a good sounding-board...to a point. Then she gets all focused on marrying me off. And that drives me nuts." She picked up the wings again, trying to decide where to attach the ribbons.

"Understandably so."

"Anyway, I've been thinking about something." She set the wings aside. "And I'd sort of like to hear your opinion."

"Fire away."

"This past weekend…after I knew that Daniel was giving me custody of Mabel, well, I guess it hit me. I mean, here I am signing these papers, becoming her legal parent. It's a big responsibility."

"Absolutely."

"So I started to carefully consider my future. *Our* futures— Mabel and me. And I sort of came up with a plan. A way for me to remain here even if I don't fulfill Aunt Dee's dream by getting married."

"You mean remain in *this* house?" He sounded doubtful.

"Yes." She looked eagerly at him. "I realize that, if I'm not married, the house will have to be sold by mid-May." She narrowed her eyes at him. "Unless by chance there's some clause I don't know about. Like the whole thing was a practical joke?"

He soberly shook his head.

"Right. I didn't really think so. But I'm almost done with my novel, and I think it might be pretty good. What if I contracted it before May? My advance, if it was a good one, might be enough for a down-payment. I know it's a long shot, but it could happen."

"Sure, anything can happen." Even so, he looked uncertain.

"I realize I'd still need income for house-payments and monthly living expenses. But is there any reason I can't continue writing her advice column? And doesn't that pay pretty well?"

He rubbed his chin. "Good points, Daphne."

"So I could buy this house and make a living on the column. Plus I could find a job in town. Maybe work for the newspaper, since I have experience and a journalism degree. Or maybe sell another novel. Why couldn't I remain here?"

"Maybe." He shrugged. "But you do understand that this house would need to be sold at fair market value. And that won't be cheap. This is a beautiful home and a great neighborhood. And if you didn't sell your novel, well, I can't imagine how you'd come up with a down-payment."

She felt her spirits decline. "But even if I lost this house." She looked sadly around the kitchen, knowing that Mabel might miss it as much as Daphne. "I could probably still find us a little rental. It might be a different neighborhood, but I'd make sure Mabel could still go to Lincoln."

"Uh huh." His brow creased. "So...does this mean you're giving up on love?"

"Giving up on love?" She smirked. "No, of course not. But I just don't want to keep obsessing over it. Especially now that I have Mabel—now that I'm her legal guardian. I feel like I need to step up even more. I don't really see myself dating. Certainly not like I did last summer and fall. No more blind dates or speed dates or any of that nonsense that I never liked anyway. Things I never would've done if it wasn't for friends like Sabrina...and *you* too."

He made a sheepish grin. "Hey, I already apologized for that."

"What a waste of time that was." She grimaced to remember some of her dates. "So, really, I'm done with madness. If love is out there, it will have to come looking for me. Because, from now on, I plan to be busy living my life."

Jake's eyes lit up. "Good for you, Daphne. I'm sure Dee would heartily approve."

Daphne held up the delicate white wings. They really did look lovely. Even Sabrina would be impressed. "I can't wait to see Mabel's face."

"When is the winter program, anyway?" Jake stood, pushing the chair back in.

"Tomorrow night."

"No wonder you're in a hurry to get this done. Thanks for the coffee. I won't keep you."

"Thanks again for doing that paperwork so quickly, Jake. I really do appreciate it. And I assume you'll send me a bill. I don't want Daniel to pay for it. He's already done enough by agreeing to this."

"You'll hear from my assistant."

As he left, she wondered about that. So far he hadn't billed her for anything. Not for consultations. Or for drawing up the temporary guardianship papers after Vera died. Oh, well, maybe he planned to just drop a great big bill on her after her year here was up. She looked at the calendar and sighed. Less than five months from now. Where had the time gone?

Chapter 19

On Tuesday night, Mabel looked magical in her snow fairy costume. Daphne used the leftover white netting, adorned with sequins and glitter, to wrap around Mabel's lavender tutu, which she put on over white lacy tights. After the wings were tied onto the back, Daphne safety-pinned tissue-paper snowflakes that Mabel had cut out, onto the netting and skirt. Streamers of ribbons were attached here and there.

"And now for the final touch." Daphne held up the tiara that she and Mabel had constructed last night. It was a delicate concoction of pipe-cleaners, sequins and glitter. Daphne pinned it into Mabel's dark hair.

"Oh, my!" Sabrina moved around the living room, taking more photos. "You look like a real fairy, Mabel."

"The wand," Mabel said eagerly. "Don't forget my wand."

Daphne handed her the stick that they'd wrapped in ribbon with a glittered snowflake on the tip. "Perfect."

"You will be the belle of the ball," Sabrina gushed.

"Go into my bedroom," Daphne told her. "Look in my big

mirror."

Sabrina and Daphne followed, watching with amusement as Mabel's dark eyes grew big and round. "I am like Cinderella," she said quietly.

"Cinderella?" Sabrina looked at Daphne.

Mabel pointed her wand at Daphne. "And you are my fairy godmother."

Daphne checked her watch. "And we better hurry to school before you turn into a pumpkin."

After Mabel scurried off to join Miss Simmons and her class, Daphne and Sabrina went to get seats. To Daphne's surprise, Jake was sitting up front and had two empty seats next to him. "Are these taken?" she asked hopefully.

"I saved them for you." He stood up to let them in. "I thought you might have Sabrina with you."

"This is so exciting," Daphne told him. "My first school function as a new parent."

"How did Mabel like her fairy wings?"

"She was over the moon."

"And you should see her," Sabrina told him. "Who knew Daphne was a wizard at costume making?"

Jake winked. "I suspect she's a woman of many hidden talents."

Soon the program began, starting with the first-graders wearing elf hats and pretending to make toys as they sang "Up on the Rooftop." Next came the second-graders singing "Let It Snow!" Some of the children sat around a fake fireplace while others wore winter wear and pretended to have a snowball fight. Meanwhile a boy wrapped in quilt batting was imitating a snowman as the two snow fairies danced about, waving their wands. Of course, in Daphne's opinion, the snow fairies stole the show. Although she suspected the other parents felt the same way about their children.

"Did you record it?" Daphne asked after the second-graders departed the stage.

Sabrina nodded as she put her phone away. "The whole thing."

The rest of the program continued until the fifth-graders ended the show with a romping performance of "Jingle Bell Rock." Everyone clapped enthusiastically as the house lights came on.

"That was fun," Jake said. "It's been awhile since I've been to one of these. I almost forgot how delightful they can be."

"I loved it," Daphne told them. "Better than a show on Broadway."

"Mabel was fabulous," Sabrina said. "I'm guessing that girl might have a future in entertainment."

Daphne laughed. "Well, let's not push her, okay?"

Mabel ran up to them, sharing hugs with everyone as they praised her performance.

"I know this is a school night," Jake said, "but I'd love to invite the snow fairy and her aunties out for ice cream."

"Yes-yes!" Mabel jumped up and down.

Daphne checked her watch. "I guess it's okay. We should still be able to get the snow fairy to bed by nine."

"And ice cream might help her calm her down," Jake whispered to Daphne. "It always makes me sleepy."

They met at CJ's Ice Cream Shoppe and placed their orders,

settling into a pink booth. "So, is ice cream the favorite food of snow fairies?" Jake asked Mabel in a serious tone.

"Yes." She nodded. "They usually like strawberry best."

"And what kind of weather forecast are the snow fairies making these days?"

"Snow," she proclaimed. "Definitely."

"Well, it sure feels cold enough to snow." Sabrina pulled her fur-trimmed coat more snugly around her. "I had to get poor little Tootsie a bed warmer."

"Wouldn't a white Christmas be nice?" Daphne said. "And speaking of Christmas, Mabel and I decided to have that Christmas party—the one that was postponed due to a certain missing person who shall not be named."

"Me?" Mabel paused from licking her cone.

Daphne nodded. "Anyway, we want to have it on the Friday before Christmas. And you're both invited."

"Please, come," Mabel urged them. "I have gifts for everyone. I picked them out myself, and I wrapped them too."

"That's right," Daphne confirmed. "This is going to be a double celebration. Partly for Mabel and me becoming a real family and partly for Christmas."

"Count me in," Jake assured her.

"And you know I'll be there." Sabrina winked at Mabel. "And I have a little something for you too. It just came in the mail."

Mabel's eyes lit up.

Daphne felt a small wave of concern. She really didn't want to spoil Mabel. And perhaps she and Sabrina should make New Year's resolutions together—a pact to be more cautious in their generosity with the little girl. Daphne didn't want Mabel to grow up into an entitled brat.

As they were getting up to leave, Jake asked if they were going to Mick's Christmas party.

"That's right." Daphne suddenly remembered. "It's this Saturday, isn't it?"

Sabrina's lower lip protruded. "Mick's having a Christmas party?"

"Can I go too?" Mabel asked hopefully.

"I think it's just for grownups," Daphne said as she helped her into her parka. "Besides, you already have a pretty busy schedule. Our party on Friday night. The living nativity on Sunday night. And then there's still Christmas Eve and Christmas."

"Maybe I could baby-sit for you," Sabrina offered sadly. "Since I wasn't invited."

"I think it's a pretty casual get together," Daphne said quickly. "Mick simply asked me in passing. I'm sure he'd like you to come too."

"You could come as my date," Jake told Sabrina. Then, like an afterthought, he turned to Daphne. "Both of you could."

"A girl on each arm?" Daphne asked in a teasing tone. "Seems a bit arrogant to me. Or maybe you need an entourage."

"Who will baby-sit me?" Mabel folded her arms in front with a disgruntled expression.

"How about if I ask Jenna?" Jake suggested.

"Yes!" Mabel eagerly agreed. "I like Jenna. She's so pretty and nice."

"Then it's settled," Jake declared. "I'll see if Jenna can stay with Mabel, and I'll pick up my two dates around seven. Okay?"

Sabrina still looked uncertain.

"How about if I call Mick," Daphne offered. "To make sure

he doesn't mind. Although I know he won't."

Sabrina nodded. "That would make me feel better."

Daphne turned to Jake. "And if Jenna can't baby-sit, you can simply take Sabrina as your date, and I'll happily stay home with Mabel." She slipped an arm around Mabel's shoulders as they all went outside into an arctic blast of cold air. And, although Mick's party sounded fun, she knew she wouldn't care one way or another. In the midst of all the holiday activities, a quiet evening with Mabel would be most welcome.

On Wednesday morning, to Sabrina's delight, Daphne wanted to go Christmas shopping in Fairview. "I know you're probably finished with your own shopping by now," Daphne told her, "but I thought I'd invite you anyway."

"When do we go?"

As usual, Sabrina was cheerful and energetic and helpful as they went from store to store in the Fairview Mall. Even when Daphne was ready to give up on finding the perfect present for her new stepmother, Sabrina would not let her stop until she finally bagged an attractive glass hurricane candle holder from Pottery Barn. After the packages were loaded in the car, they hit the Creative Kids toy store and finally a kids' clothing boutique.

By the time they finished, Daphne was exhausted. But Sabrina was still charged and ready to go. "How about a late lunch?" Daphne offered. "My way to thank you for all your help."

Sabrina eagerly agreed and they decided on a nearby café. But as they walked in, Daphne was surprised to see a familiar face. "That's Harrison Henshaw," Daphne whispered as they went over to a vacant table. She'd thought Harrison had seen her, but since he seemed involved in conversation with an older man, he didn't acknowledge her. And she decided to simply pretend she hadn't noticed him.

"That guy you met speed dating?" Sabrina said quietly as she pulled out a chair.

Daphne nodded, pretending to look another direction as she sat down with her back toward Harrison.

"The guy who *never* called?" Sabrina whispered.

"He called," Daphne clarified. "But we just never seemed to connect."

"He sure is good looking."

"I guess."

"Didn't you say he was the architect for the new city hall in Appleton?"

"Yeah. I actually thought our paths might cross while it was under construction. But, from what I can see, they haven't even broken ground there yet."

"I heard someone say that they'd gotten such a late start that it had to be put off until spring."

"That makes sense."

"Oh-oh." Sabrina made a pleasant smile, speaking quietly. "He's coming our way and it looks like he wants to chat."

"Daphne," Harrison exclaimed, putting his hand on Daphne's shoulder with a big smile. "Fancy meeting you here."

She smiled back. "Just doing some last minute Christmas shopping."

He grimaced. "I haven't done that yet. Hopefully there's still something left out there."

"Don't worry," Sabrina assured him.

Daphne quickly re-introduced Harrison to Sabrina then asked if he wanted to join them, fully expecting him to make some excuse not to. Instead he pulled out a chair and sat down. "How have you been?" he asked her with what seemed genuine interest.

"Well, I've had a pretty crazy month," she confessed. "But life seems to be settling down now. Well, aside from the holidays." She gave a nutshell version of getting guardianship of Mabel.

"Congratulations. You must be very happy about that."

"I am."

"I had hoped to be spending more time in Appleton," he said as he played with a napkin. "Hoped to run into you there. But you probably heard the city postponed construction until spring."

"Sabrina was just saying that."

"They just weren't able to jump on it in the fall like they'd planned. But I can't complain. I ended up getting a couple of big jobs right here in Fairview, so I've been busy."

"Good for you."

"But spring isn't too far off," he said as the waitress came over. "Maybe I'll bump into you then. If not sooner." He stood up.

"That would be nice," she told him.

"Great." He reached out to shake her hand, grasping it firmly. "I'll be looking forward to it." He turned to Sabrina. "Nice meeting you." And then he left.

Daphne tried to wrap her head around it as she placed an order for a spinach salad. After the waitress left, Sabrina giggled. "Looks like Harrison's got the hots for you," she teased.

"Oh, he was just being friendly."

"That was more than just friendly," Sabrina assured her. "That man is into you, Daphne. I could tell."

"Maybe...but he's a busy guy. I won't be holding my breath."

"But do you like him?"

"I don't know." Daphne sighed. "At one time I wanted to get to know him better. He's intelligent and interesting. But I always got the feeling his life was too full. And now I have Mabel. It just doesn't seem like it's meant to be, you know?"

"But running into him like that—and the way he looked at you, Daphne. I don't know...it might be fate."

Daphne laughed. "Well, if it *is* fate, I guess I'll find out eventually. Right?"

"I actually got goose-bumps while you two were talking," Sabrina said with enthusiasm. "Like this was meant to be."

Daphne wasn't too sure about that, but she didn't think there was any harm in letting Sabrina enjoy what felt like mostly a fantasy. However, when Sabrina started talking wedding plans, Daphne knew she had to put the kibosh on it. But instead of squelching Sabrina completely, she just changed the subject. "I just remembered a couple of items I forgot to put on my shopping list," she told her. And that was all it took.

It wasn't that Daphne had no interest in Harrison. It was more like she'd given up on him. And despite his warm words and supposed interest, Daphne would be surprised if he followed through. But if he did, she wouldn't turn him away. At least not at first.

Chapter 20

The angels' dress rehearsal was held on Friday afternoon at the church. To Daphne's relief, Sabrina was really taking the lead in this. Not only had she organized the music and printed out lyrics to a number of "angelic" carols, she took it upon herself to be the costume consultant. To this end, she'd purchased a lot of white sheets and a bunch of golden cording. She'd also found some glittery golden garland material for halos and about a gallon of gold glitter.

Sabrina assigned the wing construction to Daphne and Mabel. But instead of making fancy fairy wings, which would be a lot of work for a dozen angels, Daphne decided to use white butcher paper that she accordion pleated and decorated with lots of gold glitter that she and Mabel generously applied. They also adorned the sheets with lots of stars and swirls of glue topped with generous amounts of the gold glitter.

Wings and halos were handed out to the assortment of children—ages five to eleven—and then Sabrina and Daphne worked to combined the white pieces of clothing the children had brought with the glittered sheets. The results were not bad.

But by the time they finished their rehearsal, Daphne felt sure of two things. The children might be the most glamorous angels their church had seen, but the singing was less than angelic. Fortunately, Sabrina's clear soprano voice could be heard above the rest.

"I think you'll be our saving grace Sunday night," Daphne told Sabrina as they drove home.

"Sabrina's voice does sound like an angel," Mabel agreed. "At least that's how I think an angel's voice would sound. I've never heard one."

"You have a nice voice too," Sabrina told Mabel.

"Really?"

"With some voice lessons, you could be really good."

"How about Aunt Daphne?" Mabel asked. "Could she be really good too?"

Daphne laughed. "I'm sorry, Mabel, I'll never be a great singer. I can barely carry a tune in a bucket."

"Really?" Sabrina sounded surprised. "I just thought you were trying to sing harmony."

"I was going for the melody," Daphne confessed.

"Well, at least you sing with enthusiasm," Sabrina told her. "Now, not to change the subject, except that I want to change the subject. What are you wearing to Mick's party on Saturday night?"

"I don't know." Daphne had almost been disappointed when Jake had called to say that Jenna could baby-sit. Not only that, but he'd run into Mick and asked about Sabrina. Naturally, Mick said yes, so they were set.

"I know you said it's in a barn," Sabrina said. "So I know

it can't be formal. But I would like to dress up. After all, it's Christmas. And I have this little burgundy cocktail dress that just screams Christmas."

"What is a burgundy cocktail dress and why does it scream at you?" Mabel asked.

Daphne chuckled as Sabrina explained.

"Well, I'm going for comfort," Daphne declared as she pulled into her driveway. "Since it's in a barn, I'm thinking it'll probably be a little chilly. I do want something I can dance in if I feel like it, but I'd like something warm."

"So what are you wearing?" Sabrina asked as they got out of the car.

"I pulled out a knitted sweater dress that I've had for ages. It's got lots of cables and is sort of a rusty color. Or maybe it's persimmon. I'm not sure. But I thought I'd wear it with my brown suede boots. Maybe a little jewelry if I can find something that looks good. Just to be festive."

"How about a colorful silk scarf? I've got this gorgeous Hermes in fall tones that would be fabulous on you. Why don't you borrow it?"

"Well, I guess I could try it."

"And I'll just follow your lead and try to come up with an outfit that's comfortable and warm too." Sabrina shivered. "I'd probably freeze my behind off in that cocktail dress anyway. Maybe I'll wear it tonight. Or would that be too fancy?"

"Wear it," Mabel insisted. "It won't be too fancy."

Daphne chuckled as they hurried up the porch steps. To think Mabel had gone from a raggedy waif to a fashion expert on appropriate party garb!

"Don't you just love Christmastime?" Mabel said as they

went inside. "Everything looks so pretty, and there's so much fun stuff to do. I wish it could be Christmas forever."

"Well, I have to admit that this is the busiest Christmas I've ever had," Daphne said as she set their angel costumes down on a chair. "I've never participated in so many activities. Not even when I was a little girl."

"I never did either," Mabel said soberly. "Not even when I was a little girl too."

Daphne suppressed the urge to giggle. "And tonight is our big party." She looked at the clock. "The caterers should be here in the next hour."

"What are caterers?" Mabel frowned.

Daphne explained how she'd hired them to prepare and serve the food.

"But you know how to cook," Mabel pointed out. "And I can help. We can fix the food ourselves, can't we?"

Now Daphne explained about how she'd already hired the caterers once. She didn't go into the detail of how she'd been stressed out over the prospect of losing Mabel and hadn't felt like cooking. "And since we didn't have that party, I promised to have the caterers help with this party. Fortunately they were able to freeze a lot of the food."

Daphne collapsed into the club chair. "And I don't know about you, but I'd like a little down time before it gets really busy. I need to put my feet up."

"I do too." Mabel picked up Ethel and took her to the couch to snuggle up with.

Daphne smiled at the homey scene, pausing once again to thank God for allowing her to keep Mabel.

The caterers arrived at six, and Katy, who was in charge,

assured Daphne that it was all under control. "Your job is to just enjoy your party. Play hostess and let us do the work."

"Then I suppose I'll go get dressed," Daphne told her. "Holler if you need anything." First Daphne went to see how Mabel was doing. She was supposed to be getting into what she called her "wedding" dress—the fluffy rose colored dress that she'd worn to Daphne's dad's wedding. Daphne found Mabel on the floor trying to pull on a pair of bright red tights.

Daphne didn't like to criticize, but red and rose didn't seem too good together. "Maybe you should wear your white tights," Daphne suggested. "Or even your black ones."

"Huh?" Mabel looked up from where she was huffing and puffing.

"Let me help." Daphne reached down to tug off the tights. "That was backwards anyway. See?" She showed her the tag.

"Oh." Mabel made an embarrassed shrug.

"So what should it be? Black or white?" Daphne held up the other options.

"White. Those ones look like snowflakes and I keep praying it'll snow before Christmas."

Now Daphne reminded her how to gather up the tights and slide her foot in, helping her to pull them up.

"That was easy." Mabel reached for her dress. "I love this dress," she said. "It reminds me of Don and Karen's wedding. That was such a nice day." Her smile faded. "Well, until we found out about Grandma."

Daphne nodded as she lifted the dress over Mabel's head. "It's interesting how sad and happy memories sometimes get all mixed together, isn't it?"

"Uh huh."

Daphne buttoned the dress then spun Mabel around. "And you, my dear, look gorgeous."

"I still need my shoes."

"And I still need to change my clothes."

"Can I help you?" Mabel asked as she grabbed her shiny black Mary-Jane shoes.

"I guess so. I haven't really decided what I'm wearing yet. Maybe you can help."

"You have to wear a dress too," Mabel insisted as she followed her downstairs. "Like me and Sabrina."

Daphne had been thinking about wearing her tweed pants and her brown cashmere sweater set. "A dress?"

"Yes," Mabel declared as they went into Daphne's room. "I will pick it out."

Feeling relieved that she'd taken time to organize her closet a few days ago, Daphne opened the door. "Help yourself," she said. "Just know that I have veto power."

Mabel's eyes got big. "Veto power? Is that some kind of magic?"

Daphne laughed. "Sort of. It's the right to say no if I don't like what you pick out."

"Oh." Mabel went to the section that held dresses, going through them one by one. "This one is for summer," she said. "This one is for the party tomorrow. You wore this one with Uncle Daniel. She paused on a sage green silk dress that Daphne had gotten a few years ago in New York—and never worn. Mabel pulled the skirt, fanning it out to see better. "This is the one, Aunt Daphne. It even looks Christmassy."

Daphne pulled it out, looking closely at it. "I guess I could wear it."

"It still has the tags on it," Mabel declared. "Haven't you ever worn it?"

Daphne held the dress up in front of the mirror. "No. I always planned on returning it."

"Why?"

"Oh, I got it because I thought I was going to be invited to a party...but that didn't happen."

Mabel's smile faded. "Was that sad?"

Daphne nodded, remembering the little crush she'd had on a coworker a few years ago. He hadn't even known she existed. "Yes, it was a little sad."

"Well, you're invited to lots of parties now, aren't you?"

She smiled. "Yes, I am. We both are." She headed for her bathroom. "Now if you'll excuse me, I'd like to grab a quick shower before I get dressed. You can go out and see how the caterers are doing."

"Yes!" Mabel said eagerly. "I wanna see what they brought us."

Daphne was just slipping into a pair of black pumps when Mabel returned to her room. "Oh, Aunt Daphne, you look so pretty."

"Thank you. This dress was a good choice. Thanks for suggesting it."

"But you do need some jewelry." Mabel went over to where Daphne kept a few pieces of small fine jewelry as well as some of the bigger ones she'd saved from Aunt Dee.

Daphne prepared herself to veto anything she wouldn't feel comfortable wearing. Knowing Mabel, she'd probably pick out something big and bright. "How about this?" Mabel picked up a string of pearls that had been Aunt Dee's.

"Hmm... ." Daphne held them up and looked in the mirror. "Ooh, that looks pretty."

"Okay." Daphne went ahead and latched them. "I suppose I could wear pearl earrings too."

"Yes, yes!" Mabel clapped. "That was what I was going to say."

Daphne smiled as she slipped in the earrings. "And there, you have dressed me. How do you think you did?"

Mabel nodded with wide eyes. "I did good."

As they went into the living room the doorbell rang, and Mabel begged to get it. "I want to open the door for everyone tonight," she called out as she dashed for the door.

"Be my guest." Daphne paused to pull some of the wilted flowers from the bouquet that she'd been trying to keep fresh for the past week. It was definitely past its prime, but it looked so nice nestled in the evergreens with the ornaments about.

"It's Sabrina," Mabel yelled. "She has on a gray furry coat that feels as soft as Lucy and looks just like Ethel!"

Daphne went to see that Sabrina did indeed have on a gray fur coat. "Aren't you the glamorous one?"

"I don't really believe in wearing furs." Sabrina slipped the coat off. "But it's so cold. And that used to be my mother's."

"Heavy." Daphne held the coat.

"It's mink," Sabrina said quietly.

"I'll put it on my bed."

"Is that your cocktail dress?" Mabel asked as they went to Daphne's bedroom.

"Yes." Sabrina did a little turn. "You like it?"

"It's really pretty." Mabel went around to look at the back of her dress. "But where's the tail?"

Daphne laughed as Sabrina explained.

"I picked out Aunt Daphne's dress," Mabel told Sabrina. "And the pearls too."

"Nice work."

Just then the doorbell rang again—like a shot, Mabel took off. This time she led in Daphne's dad and Karen, followed by Becca and Lola. After greetings were exchanged, Daphne started to take their coats.

"I'll put them in the bedroom," Mabel offered. "Lola can help me. That will be our job."

"I won't know what to do with myself," Daphne told Karen and Becca. "I'm starting to feel like the queen."

Ricardo arrived next with his mother, Maria, and Wally Renwald not far behind. It seemed to be clear that Maria and Wally were a couple now. And Daphne secretly congratulated herself for bringing the two sweet older people together last summer. As more guests arrived, Mabel continued trying to greet each one, and then she and Lola would trot off with their coats.

Daphne felt certain that everyone she'd invited had shown up, which was more than two dozen people. But everyone seemed in a jovial mood as they visited cheerfully, helping themselves to the buffet table in the dining room. Sabrina seemed to be in her element, exuding sweet Southern charm as she flitted from guest to guest, looking stunning in her sparkling burgundy cocktail dress. She truly was the life of the party. And unless Daphne was mistaken, the guys were paying close attention. At one point, Sabrina had Mick, Ricardo, and Jake all circled around her, listening as she told them a funny story about her daddy teaching her to shoot a shotgun. Daphne knew she should probably take social lessons from her amiable neighbor, but short of a lobotomy it would probably be useless.

"Doesn't Aunt Daphne look beautiful?" Mabel whispered to Jenna as she and Jake chatted with Daphne.

Jake grinned at Mabel. "You both look lovely."

"I picked out Aunt Daphne's dress and everything," Mabel told Jenna.

"You should become a stylist," Jenna told her.

"What's that?"

Jenna gave a quick explanation and Mabel agreed that she'd probably be good at that. "Have you seen *Frozen?*" Mabel asked Jenna with hopeful eyes.

"I actually haven't seen it yet," Jenna admitted.

"Really?" Lola looked shocked.

"I think I may be the only girl on the planet who hasn't," Jenna told them.

"I have the video," Mabel said with excitement. "When you come to baby-sit me tomorrow, we can watch it. Okay?"

Jenna smiled. "I can't wait."

At 8:00, Mabel eagerly asked Daphne if it was "time" yet. "It's your party," Daphne told her. "Do *you* think it's time?"

Mabel nodded vigorously, so Daphne rang a fork against a glass to get everyone's attention. "I have an announcement," she said formally. "This gathering is partly to commemorate Christmas and partly to celebrate that Mabel is now a permanent part of my life." She put an arm around Mabel. "I'm very thankful for her. And to celebrate this, Mabel has chosen special gifts for each of you. She wrapped them herself and she would like to present you all with them now."

Mabel hurried over to the pile under the tree, gathering

an armful.

"Feel free to keep visiting," Daphne said, "while Mabel passes them around. And then if you don't mind, Mabel wants to join you as you open your gifts."

After the rather unique gifts were disbursed and opened, one by one, amidst peals of laughter and lots of thank-yous, Jake asked if he could make a toast. Holding up his glass, he looked at Mabel. "We're all so happy that you're a fulltime resident of Appleton," he told her. "We welcome you into our community and into our lives. And someday, when you're a rich and famous actress in Hollywood or serving as Madame President in the White House—we'll all say that we knew Mabel Myers back when."

Everyone chimed in "hear, hear" and a couple more sweet toasts were made. Daphne could tell that Mabel was enjoying this, basking in the love and admiration of her friends and family. Daphne just hoped it wasn't too much. The last thing she wanted was for this to go to Mabel's head.

But when it was time to go, Mabel was still sweet Mabel. She and Lola helped gather people's coats. And Mabel politely thanked them for coming. Jake and Jenna were the last ones to leave because Jenna had started gathering dishes and glasses from the living room and taking them to the kitchen. The catering crew was long gone by now, and Daphne had planned to clean the mess up later. But when Mabel noticed what Jenna was doing, she scurried off to help her.

"Your Jenna is a jewel," Daphne told Jake as they stood by the Christmas tree.

"So is Mabel." Jake loosened his dark tie a bit. "This was a lovely evening, Daphne. Thanks for including us—once again.

You make us feel almost like family."

"That's because you are like family." She smiled warmly. "You've been so helpful, Jake. Especially through these recent trials over Mabel's custody. I'll never be able to fully repay you."

"I don't want you to repay me." He seemed to be studying her intently. So much so that she felt a bit uncomfortable.

"So we're all set for tomorrow?" she said lightly. "You'll bring Jenna to stay with Mabel and then you'll attend Mick's bash with a woman on each arm?" She smirked at him.

His brow creased. "Just to be clear, that's not really my style. I rarely have *one* woman on my arm, let alone *two*. I hope I'm not expected to dance with both of you at the same time." He put on an uneasy smile.

"Well, Mick did ask me to save him some dances," she said teasingly, "And I'm sure Sabrina can rope some unsuspecting guy into dancing with her. Hopefully you won't feel overly tied down by the two of us."

"All done," Jenna announced as she and Mabel joined them.

"Thank you so much," Daphne told Jenna. "I was just telling your dad what a prize you are."

Jenna shrugged as she pulled on her coat. But as they walked them to the door, Daphne decided she'd give the helpful teen an extra tip for baby-sitting tomorrow.

"See ya tomorrow night," Jenna told Mabel. "Looking forward to *Frozen.*"

Mabel danced happily around the foyer. "Me too!"

After they left, Daphne informed Mabel it was time to get ready for bed. "I realize you're probably still wound up." She placed a hand on her head. "I'm going to let the kitties out of the laundry-room, then get into my PJs, and then I'll come up to read you a story to help you settle down. Don't forget to brush your teeth."

Mabel happily galloped up the stairs, but by the time Daphne got into her own pajamas and went up to her room, Mabel was sound asleep. "Goodnight and God bless." Daphne kissed her forehead and turned off the light. "Sweet dreams."

As Daphne went back downstairs, she felt bothered by the way her conversation with Jake had ended. It was as if it had left a bad taste in her mouth, and she suspected it was her own fault. Although she'd turned most of the lights off, the fireplace still glowed and the Christmas tree lights still shone. And so she sat down in the club chair, soon accompanied by the cats, and she replayed that last encounter with Jake.

At first it had seemed so congenial and, unless she was imagining things, slightly romantic. Come to think of it, Jake had seemed friendlier than usual of late. Unless she was simply delusional. And she didn't think she was. But when she made those comments about having a woman on each arm—their conversation had seemed to take a dive.

When he'd said that "it wasn't his style," she had felt slightly chastened, as if he regretted including her. After all, it had been his idea to take Sabrina as his date. But then he'd gotten stuck with Daphne too. Which was why she'd made that silly comment about Mick. To cover her own insecurity. Sure, it was true Mick had asked her to save dances for him, but had she needed to say it like that? To sort of throw it in Jake's face? What was wrong with her?

As usual, Daphne felt somewhat clueless when it came to relationships with men. She had such a knack for saying or doing the wrong thing. No wonder she was still single—and probably would continue to be single. Despite her ability to counsel others through the *Dear Daphne* column, her own skills were sadly lacking. She seemed to have a habit of either over-thinking a relationship, or obliviously letting it float right over her head. Would she ever learn?

Chapter 21

Daphne was glad she'd dressed warmly as they entered Mick's barn. Despite a welcoming bonfire outside the door and the kerosene heaters burning inside, it was definitely on the chilly side. Still, the place was so festive—decorated with dozens of strings of lights and Christmas greenery and interesting garden things—that she felt a warmth despite the cold temperature.

"Oh, Mick," she said, "This place looks magical."

He nodded over to where Julianne was chatting with some other guests. "That was mostly Julianne's doing. She's a clever girl, all right."

"She really is." Daphne nodded.

"I'll bet Julianne could open up her own decorating business if she wanted," Sabrina said.

"Bite your tongue." Mick grimaced. "She'll be hitting me up for a raise if she hears you talking like that."

"Better hang onto that girl," Sabrina warned.

Mick shook Jake's hand with a wry grin. "So, Jake old man,

I see you brought two dates tonight. What's the story?"

Jake shrugged. "What can I say?"

"The band already warmed up," Mick explained. "They'll be back in about ten minutes. Check out the eats—or just *mingle*, as Julianne says." He waved toward the door. "If you'll excuse me, I need to go play host."

Sabrina nudged Daphne with her elbow. "Am I imagining things, or is that your friend Harrison coming in right now?"

Daphne watched as Mick went to the door, greeting a tall, attractive man who did indeed look very much like Harrison Henshaw. But what would he be doing here?

"Someone you know?" Jake asked curiously.

Daphne nodded. It was definitely Harrison.

"It must be fate," Sabrina said dramatically. "Go tell him hello, Daphne." She gave her a gentle shove.

"Okay." Daphne agreed. But as she went over to where Mick and Harrison were chatting away like old friends, she felt a little uneasy—and she wasn't even sure why.

"Hey, Daphne," Mick said solicitously, "I'd like you to meet—"

"We've already had the pleasure," Harrison told Mick as he grasped Daphne's hand. "So we meet again." He grinned. "That's twice in one week. What do you suppose it means?"

"How do you know each other?" Mick asked with interest.

"It's a long story." Harrison winked at Daphne. "One we don't particularly like to tell."

"I want to know how *you two* know each other," Daphne said to Mick.

"Harrison accepted my bid," Mick said proudly. "Picked me as the landscape designer for the new city hall building."

"Well, congratulations." She patted his back. "That's fabulous news." She turned back to Harrison. "Mick has done wonders at my house. I highly recommend him to everyone."

Now the band was starting to play, and Mick excused himself to greet some new guests just coming in. "Care to dance?" Harrison asked Daphne.

"I, uh, I don't know." She winced at the empty dance floor area.

"Sorry. I should've asked if you came with someone."

"Not exactly. I mean I came with a couple of friends." She gave him a sheepish smile. "It's just that I'm not a great dancer and being the first ones on the dance floor, well, it feels a little intimidating."

He laughed. "I hear you. How about if we check out the refreshments and wait for a few others to break the ice."

"Perfect," she said in relief. They went to the festive looking table, joining others who were now filling small paper plates and getting drinks. Daphne introduced Harrison to several friends, including Olivia and Jeff and Ricardo. Then as the others filled their plates, Harrison led Daphne over to a nearby pub table where they continued to visit and eat.

"I'm beginning to see why you're so enamored with Appleton," he said as he sipped his drink. "A lot of great people in this little town."

"There really are." She told him about a few of the other guests and the various roles they played in Appleton. "I'm so glad I moved back here."

"I'm looking forward to spending more time here in the spring—once the building commences."

As they were finishing their refreshments, the music grew

merrier and the dance floor started filling up. "Isn't that your friend Sabrina out there?" Harrison pointed.

Daphne scanned the couples. "Yes. She's dancing with Jake McPheeters. He's an attorney." She felt an unexpected and unwanted twinge of jealousy. Was it possible that Jake truly was interested in Sabrina? That inviting her to come tonight was more than just a fluke? And certainly, Sabrina was pretty and witty and fun, but they seemed like such polar opposites. Daphne never would've imagined them as a couple before, but suddenly she wasn't so sure. And she wasn't sure how she'd feel about it if they were. And why was she even thinking about such things?

"Ready to dance yet?" Harrison asked.

She forced a nervous smile. "Sure."

As it turned out, Harrison was an excellent dancer. So good, in fact, that he actually made her look good. And he made dancing enjoyable too. Daphne was having so much fun that after the second dance, she happily peeled off her coat, tossing it onto the growing heap on a hay bale against the wall.

By her third dance with Harrison, Daphne noticed Sabrina had changed partners. She was now dancing with Ricardo. For some reason, this made Daphne feel relieved.

"Want to take a break and get a drink?" Harrison asked as another fast song began to play.

"Yes," she said breathlessly. "I can't believe I'm not cold anymore." She fluffed the scarf that Sabrina had talked her into wearing. "In fact, I'm almost hot."

Harrison grinned. "I'd say you *are* hot."

She laughed. "Thanks—I think."

As they were having a drink, Sabrina joined them, pointing

a finger at Harrison. "I've noticed you on the dance floor," she said in a slightly flirtatious tone. "You've got some pretty good moves, and I'm hoping Daphne doesn't plan to keep you all to herself tonight."

Harrison just chuckled.

"Harrison is free to dance with anyone he pleases," Daphne assured her.

"You done with that?" Sabrina pointed to his nearly empty drink cup.

Harrison chugged it down. "I am now." Then, tossing Daphne an apologetic look, he allowed Sabrina to lead him out to the dance floor.

"There's my favorite redhead," Ricardo said as he joined Daphne. "Care to cut the rug?"

She laughed. "I don't see a rug, but I'd love to dance with you."

As they danced to a slower song, Ricardo asked her about Harrison. She filled him in about city hall and how he'd chosen Mick as the landscaper.

"According to Sabrina, you guys are meant for each other." Ricardo's dark brows arched with curiosity.

"You're kidding? Sabrina said that?"

"She seems certain of it. Says that it's fate."

"That Sabrina. As much as I love her, she can aggravate me." As the song ended, they stepped to the sidelines but continued talking. "Just when I'm ready to read Sabrina the riot act for interfering in my life, she'll give me that sweet little smile of hers, and then she'll beg my pardon in her honey-coated Southern drawl." Daphne held up her hands. "And, well, what can I do? I have to forgive her."

Ricardo chuckled. "She's one of a kind, that's for sure. At first I thought she was just a charmer, you know, all about the surface—but the more I get to know her, the more I realize there's more going on underneath."

Daphne nodded as she watched Sabrina dancing with Harrison. "Sabrina's got a big heart. Even though I haven't known her all that long, I've noticed lots of great qualities in her."

"Such as?" Ricardo leaned in to listen.

"Well, Sabrina is extremely loyal. And she's very caring, and sometimes she's generous to a fault." Daphne laughed. "She keeps getting stuff for Mabel. But she loves Mabel dearly. I understand."

Ricardo nodded with a thoughtful expression. "Yeah...I've been thinking I should get to know Sabrina better."

Suddenly Daphne felt very curious. "Are you interested in Sabrina?" she asked as the song ended.

Ricardo looked slightly embarrassed, but shrugged. "She seems like the real deal."

"Ricardo." Daphne grinned at him. "You really *do* like her, don't you?"

"Maybe." His smile was crooked.

"Time to switch partners," Daphne said as she led him back to the dance floor. As the next song began, Daphne grabbed Sabrina by the hand, gracefully exchanging Ricardo for Harrison and all of them began to dance again.

Sabrina giggled as she tossed Daphne an *I told you so* look. As if she thought Daphne snagged Harrison for other reasons.

"Nice to be such a sought after dance partner," Harrison said as they danced to the slower music.

"Sorry to be so pushy." Daphne explained her surprising discovery about Ricardo's interest in Sabrina. "I never would've imagined him and Sabrina together. Some people in town think of Ricardo as a confirmed bachelor. But that's only because the love of his life passed away." She explained about Olivia's older sister, Bernadette, and how she started the florist shop that Olivia now owned.

"So do you know *everyone* in this town?" he asked as the song ended.

Daphne grinned. "Not yet." Her eyes skimmed over the crowded barn, suddenly curious as to Jake's whereabouts. She'd only observed him on the dance floor a couple of times. Once with Sabrina and once with the beautiful Julianne, who was now dancing with Mick. And, judging by Julianne's expression, she was still in love with Mick. And, really, they made a gorgeous couple—not to mention their similar interests in landscape and design.

Not seeing Jake anywhere made Daphne feel concerned. Was it possible that the man with two dates had gone home? Would he do that without telling them? Seeing that Sabrina was dancing with Ricardo again, Daphne decided it was time to investigate.

"If you'll excuse me, I think I should go check on my friend," Daphne told Harrison. "The other one that Sabrina and I came with." For some reason she wasn't eager to tell Harrison that they'd come with Jake. Not because she was Jake's date—because she wasn't—but simply because she didn't want to explain it.

Daphne wandered around the crowded barn, peering around at dark corners and various groups gathered around the pub tables. But after she'd circled the perimeter without seeing Jake anywhere, she noticed the barn door cracked opened, and the crackling bonfire outside. She slipped outside and there, by himself in front of the leaping flames and warming his hands, stood Jake. He had his overcoat on, and unless she was imagining it, it looked like he was ready to call it a night.

"So what're you doing out here by your own little lonesome?" Daphne asked as she joined him.

He looked surprised. "Just enjoying the evening air." He tipped his head upward. "It's a clear, starry night."

She looked up and nodded.

"There's Orion's Belt."

As her eyes adjusted to the dark sky, she realized how bright the stars overhead really were. "Where is it?"

He stood beside her, guiding her focus as he pointed upward. "See those three bright stars lined up there, and the one below?"

"Yeah." She nodded. "So that's Orion's Belt?"

"That's right." He continued standing close to her.

"So you're just out here star-gazing?" she asked quietly.

"Uh huh."

"But it's cold out here." She wanted to move even closer to him—and not just for the warmth either.

"You should go back inside." Jake stooped over to toss another piece of wood onto the bonfire.

"I will when I'm ready." She held her hands over the fire. "I was actually getting a little too warm in there."

"Dancing will do that." His tone sounded slightly stiff.

"Yes. And Harrison is such a good dancer too. I was so surprised to see him here tonight. I had no idea he was a friend of Mick's."

"According to Sabrina, he's a friend of yours too."

"Yes." She turned around to warm her backside. Was she imagining it, or was Jake fishing for information?

"Are you having a good time?" he asked pointedly.

"Sure. It's fun." She turned to look at him. "How about you?"

He frowned. "The truth is I've never been a real social butterfly."

"*Really?* I never would've guessed that, Jake. You always seem like a pretty socially accomplished sort of fellow to me. Well-spoken and good manners. Comfortable in any social situation."

"Then you're deluded. The truth is I'm not a real party kind of guy. Never have been. Don't ever plan to be."

She frowned. "Do you want to go home?"

"No, no, of course not. I just needed a break. Some fresh air."

Daphne wondered if that was all. Unless she was mistaken, Jake was unhappy about something. "I saw you dancing with Sabrina. You guys seemed to be having fun. And you looked good together."

He gave a half smile. "That probably has more to do with Sabrina than me."

"Is that why you're out here?" she asked suddenly. "Because Sabrina is dancing with Ricardo? I know you sort of asked her to be your date tonight, Jake, but I think she thought that you were just being nice, trying to include her."

He laughed. "I *was* just being nice. And, no, I'm relieved Sabrina is dancing with other guys." He lowered his voice. "And if you ask me, Ricardo is putting the move on our little Southern friend."

"Putting *the move* on her?" Daphne was amused by his choice of words.

"Seriously, Daphne. I noticed it last night. Ricardo was really into her. I think he might have a thing for Sabrina."

"As it just so happens, I completely agree with you." Now she confided about Ricardo's earlier admission. "I can actually imagine the two of them together," she said. "But I have no idea how Sabrina feels about Ricardo."

"Perhaps more importantly, how does Ricardo feel about *Tootsie?*"

Daphne laughed loudly. "Good point!"

"There you are." Harrison emerged from the barn, coming over to join them. "I thought you'd vanished, Daphne."

"Sorry." She introduced him to Jake, explaining how he'd brought her and Sabrina to the party. "Jake's lovely teenage daughter, Jenna, is babysitting Mabel for me tonight—so I couldn't very well lose him."

Harrison shook Jake's hand. "Pleased to meet you, Jake. I hear you're an attorney."

"Appleton's *best* attorney." Daphne made an involuntary shiver as the icy cold night air seeped through her sweater dress.

"You're cold," Harrison said with concern. Before she could respond, he removed his leather blazer and slipped it over her shoulders. "How's that?"

"Warm," she admitted.

"I heard we may have snow before Christmas," Harrison said as he warmed his hands over the fire.

"Mabel has been praying for snow." Daphne told him about the snow fairy costume. "She even gets out her wand and goes around trying to make it snow."

"If anyone could do it, I'd put my money on Mabel," Jake said and, sounding almost paternal, he told Harrison even more about Mabel. "And tomorrow night, she's playing an angel at their church's living nativity." Jake was taking on a slightly proprietary tone. "She told me all about it last night. Mabel, Sabrina, and Daphne, all playing angels tomorrow." He chuckled. "Can't wait to see that."

"Interesting." Harrison nodded. "Maybe I'll have to check it out too."

Daphne felt slightly flabbergasted as the two guys continued in an odd sort of bantering. As crazy as it seemed, she suspected that they were both vying for her attention. Or maybe she was just reading too much into it. Or on some kind of ego trip. But if they really were attempting to show their interest in her, how was she supposed to react? It actually made her feel uncomfortable, not to mention a bit confused. And she was tempted to just excuse herself and walk away. She wondered how *Dear Daphne* would advise her.

Chapter 22

Daphne was still scratching her head over Jake and Harrison the next day. Fortunately with Christmas just a few days away and the living nativity that evening, there was plenty to keep herself distracted from fretting over the men in her life.

"Jenna said she's coming to our living nativity," Mabel announced as Sabrina drove them to the church.

"Did you have fun with Jenna last night?" Sabrina asked.

Mabel went into a happy blow-by-blow of everything they did, finally concluding that Jenna was the coolest teenager in the world.

"She's a very sweet girl," Daphne agreed.

"I told Jenna she could be an angel with us tonight," Mabel said, "but she just wants to come watch us instead."

As Sabrina turned onto Main Street, she launched into "Hark the Herald Angels Sing," and Daphne and Mabel joined in. They had just finished stumbling through the first verse, with Mabel getting about half the words right and Daphne controlling her laughter when she didn't, as Sabrina pulled into the church parking lot.

"I'm glad you printed out the lyrics to the carols," Daphne told Sabrina.

Before long, they were gathered in the fellowship hall, helping the other angels with their rather glamorous and glistening angel-attire. "I hope you all wore your long johns," Daphne said as she handed out the music sheets and the mini flashlights that she and Mabel had wrapped in gold paper to look like star wands. "I heard it might snow tonight."

"Let's start singing as we go outside," Sabrina said. "To warm up our vocal chords." Parading out of the church, Sabrina led them in "Joy to the World," and Daphne led them to the section of parking strip assigned to the angels. Other members of the living nativity entourage were still getting into place, including several slightly confused wooly sheep, a reluctant donkey, and even a cow that was being enticed to the rear of the stable with a handful of hay.

During the setting up time, Sabrina did a fabulous job of keeping the angels enthused over singing, and Daphne played guardian angel by making sure none of the children stepped over the curb and into the street. At six o'clock, the living nativity was all set—and surprisingly realistic. It wasn't long before the first cars and pedestrians began to stream by. The nativity was arranged for viewers to pass by the angel section first—where they were supposed to be welcomed by angelic singing. Then the viewers continued to where the shepherds outnumbered the sheep (four to one) and on to the three wise men sans camels, and finally to the wooden stable, where the donkey and cow were now securely tethered in place. The spotlight, literally, was on Joseph and Mary and Jesus (played by 'Mary's' actual baby). It was really quite lovely.

Although Daphne stayed in angel-character, she was happy to see that Jenna and Jake were among the strolling viewers. They took their time and even snapped some pictures on their phones. They had just gone over to the refreshment area, where complimentary hot drinks and cookies were being served, when Daphne noticed Harrison walking by. Again, she stayed in angel-character. Even though Sabrina nudged her with an elbow. But Daphne nudged Sabrina back when Ricardo ambled along. And, unless Daphne was imagining things, Ricardo's eyes were glued on Sabrina as she sang the solo part for "O Holy Night."

Daphne supervised shift changes as various angels needed bathroom, refreshment, or warm-up breaks. But as the night wore on and the viewers thinned out, she could tell that some of the angels were getting weary and cold. And noticing that the shepherds' numbers were steadily shrinking, and with parents nearby, Daphne quietly let the younger angels know that they were free to go home with their parents if they wanted. She even told Mabel that she could go inside the church if she wanted, but Mabel firmly shook her head as she continued singing.

During the last half hour of the living nativity, with their numbers significantly decreased and the real baby replaced with a lifelike doll, snowflakes began to fall. Illuminated in the various spotlights, the snowflakes resembled stars as they gracefully floated downward, frosting everything with a sparkling beauty.

It was only Sabrina, Daphne, and Mabel now, quietly singing

their greetings, as the last stragglers came to view the nativity. But to Daphne's surprise, Jake was back. By himself this time, he quietly strolled down the sidewalk, walking past the whole scene before he came back to simply gaze upon the angels. He had a hot drink in his hands as he stood on the sidewalk, just listening to them singing—Sabrina leading the carol in her strong soprano, Mabel trailing along in her sweet little girl voice, and Daphne singing an unintentional harmony in a slightly hoarse tone.

Daphne couldn't help but smile as she looked into Jake's eyes. It was sweet of him to come back by on such a cold night—almost as if he wanted to encourage them at the end of a long evening. She would have to remember to thank him later.

The next day, while Mabel and Lola were playing up in Mabel's room—after a couple of hours of rollicking in the nearly six inches of fresh snow—Daphne and Sabrina drank coffee in the kitchen.

"Did I tell you that Mabel invited Jenna to spend Christmas Eve with us?" Daphne said absently. "The funny thing is that I hadn't planned to do anything special for Christmas Eve. I thought we'd just crash in on Dad and Karen. I hadn't planned to entertain here."

"That Mabel is turning into a real party animal." Sabrina laughed. "So what did Jenna say to the invite?"

"She said yes. Apparently she'd told Mabel that it was just going to be her and her dad on Christmas Eve. She'll spend Christmas Day with her mom and their family, but since Jake's relatives will be gone during the holidays, it was just going to be the two of them."

"So you and Mabel are having Jake and Jenna..." Sabrina made a sad little frown. "That's nice that you have someone."

"Would you like to join us?" Daphne offered.

Sabrina brightened. "I'd love to. Thank you very much. And I'll bring some goodies. I love to cook holiday food." She told Daphne about some new recipes she'd just found.

"I wonder if there are any other lonely single folks that would appreciate an invitation." Daphne watched Sabrina closely. "Like Ricardo, perhaps."

Sabrina's pale brows arched slightly. "Oh, he'll probably be with his mother. And maybe Wally too. You know, Marie and Wally are getting to be quite the couple."

"Maybe we should invite all of them."

"Yes!" Sabrina eagerly agreed. "That would be fun."

"Do you want to handle that?" Daphne asked cautiously. As much as she wanted to encourage Sabrina regarding Ricardo, she did not want to intrude. If they were really meant to be, it would happen without any prodding or pushing. The same way Daphne wanted any romantic interests to blossom in her own life—without being forced.

"Gladly."

"And if you know anyone else who's single and feeling left out," Daphne added, "feel free to ask them." She nodded to the sounds of the girls' voices as they clomped down the stairs. "I think I'll invite Lola and Becca too. They might have plans, but I know Mabel would enjoy having Lola around."

With Daphne's help, they eventually put together a list of about a dozen guests, along with a menu that didn't look like too much work for either of them. "And if you don't mind, I'd like to give Mabel an early Christmas present," Sabrina said as she was leaving.

"But you already got her the ballet—"

"It's just that sweet little lavender dress I ordered from HSN," Sabrina said quickly. "I wouldn't want her to outgrow it."

Daphne rolled her eyes. "All right."

"Besides, she might want to wear it to your party—or perhaps on Christmas Day."

Daphne pointed her finger at Sabrina as she opened the front door. "But you and I must make a New Year's resolution. We must both promise to refrain from spoiling Mabel. Deal?"

Sabrina shook her hand. "Deal."

On Christmas Eve day, Mabel was Daphne's right-hand gal. She started by tending to the cats, then she decorated cookies and eventually moved on to dusting and a number of other small but necessary chores. By five o'clock there was nothing left to do but get dressed. And since 'Auntie' Sabrina was bringing Mabel's dress, Daphne told her she'd have to wait. "But I think I'll grab a quick shower and get changed." Daphne looked down at her grungy house-cleaning clothes.

"There she is," Mabel called out as she ran for the door.

Sabrina entered the house with a puff of cold air and an armful of packages. "Ho, ho, ho," she said merrily. Before long, Mabel held up the sweet princess dress. "And this is for you." Sabrina handed a shiny bag to Daphne.

"But I—"

"No arguing." Sabrina held up her hand. "It's very bad manners to refuse a gift."

"But you—"

"Come on." Sabrina peeled off her furry coat to reveal a glistening emerald green dress. "It's time to be merry." She pointed to the clock above the mantel. "And you girls only have about forty minutes to get ready for the party. I suggest you get a move on." She tapped the bag in Daphne's arms. "Please, go try that on. I won't insist you wear it tonight, but if you don't I will be severely disappointed and hurt." She made a pouty face.

"But I—"

"While you get into that dress, I'll go help Mabel get ready," Sabrina said.

Realizing it was useless to argue or point out that she had planned to wear her sage green silk dress again, Daphne went to her bedroom and, preparing herself for something flashy and blingy and over the top, she pulled the tissue from the bag and lifted out what felt like a luxurious garment. It was a soft velvety fabric in a dark purple shade. She held it up in wonder. Other than being much more elegant than what she was used to, it was actually rather nice. The only "bling" was shiny beadwork on the collar and cuffs, but even this was tasteful and elegant. The rest of the dress was simple and classic and as she held it up before the mirror, surprisingly attractive. That Sabrina!

Daphne took a quick shower, spent a few minutes on her hair and makeup, then slipped into the luxurious dress, which she hoped would fit okay. Thanks to the stretch in the fabric, it was just fine. She was just checking it out in the mirror when Sabrina and Mabel came into the room.

"You look like a beautiful queen," Mabel said happily.

"It's just perfect," Sabrina said as she came over to see. "I knew it. I knew it."

"Knew what?" Daphne asked.

"As soon as I saw it on HSN, I knew that dress was made for you. It was just screaming 'Daphne.'" Sabrina moved Mabel next to Daphne. "And look how beautiful you two look together. I have to get some photos."

"Let me get my shoes on first," Daphne told her.

After their photo session, Daphne gratefully hugged Sabrina. "You're like our fairy godmother. Thanks so much!"

When it was almost six, Daphne went around lighting the various candles she'd placed about the house. It had always been a dream to have a Christmas Eve by candlelight, but she'd never had a house or an opportunity before. Daphne felt happily anxious as she lit the hurricane candles on the coffee table in the living room. The idea of spending Christmas Eve with Jake filled her with hopeful delight. Certainly, they'd had lots of ups and downs this past year, but something seemed to have changed of late. Their relationship—unless she was imagining it—had gotten more depth to it.

She was just lighting the last candles in the foyer when the doorbell rang and Mabel, followed by Sabrina, raced to answer it.

"Harrison!" Sabrina exclaimed. "Welcome, welcome. You're our first official guest. Here, let me take your coat."

Daphne turned around in shock. Harrison was here? She tossed a questioning look at Sabrina as she went over to greet him, introducing him to Mabel.

"I thought that was Mabel last night," he told her as he removed an overcoat. "Pleased to make your acquaintance, my lady," he shook Mabel's hand, and she giggled.

Daphne controlled her expression from showing surprise as she walked him into the living room.

"Everything looks beautiful," he told her. "Including you."

"Thank you." She gave him an uncomfortable smile.

"You know, I've always wanted to see more of your house." His gaze swept the room. "Such interesting architectural details in these old Victorians. Mind if I look around?"

The doorbell was ringing again, but before Daphne could respond, Sabrina spoke up. "You go give Harrison the full tour while Mabel and I greet the other guests." She gave Daphne a gentle push, winking slyly as if she had this all planned out.

Daphne felt slightly speechless as she led Harrison through her house, listening as he described the various styles of crown molding and cornices and stair railings. He obviously knew his stuff. And it was actually somewhat interesting. But this was not what she'd planned for her evening. Not at all.

They were just coming down the stairs, when Harrison reached for her hand. "Your home is almost as delightful and charming as you," he said warmly.

"Thank you," she said a bit crisply, trying to think of a graceful way to extract her hand from his.

"Daphne," Jake said from the bottom of the stairs. "Harrison," he added in a stiffer sounding voice. "Good to see you both. Merry Christmas."

Slipping her hand away from Harrison, she hurried down to greet Jake. Taking him by the arm, she led him into the living room. "I'm so glad you guys could come," she said quickly. "You know that you and Jenna were the impetus behind this party." She nervously went on to explain Mabel's idea. But it seemed her words fell on deaf ears. And as soon as Jake got the chance, he broke away from her and went over to visit with Ricardo and Wally in the dining room.

And such was the evening...while Harrison remained politely attentive and interested and charming...Jake coolly ignored her. It wasn't until the party started to wind down that they exchanged words again. Naturally, Jake and Jenna were the first ones to call it a night.

"Thanks for coming," she told Jake and Jenna. "Merry Christmas to you both."

"You too," Jenna said warmly. "Thanks for everything." Then Jake crisply thanked her and they made a quick exit.

By now Daphne knew that Sabrina had invited Harrison. After all, Daphne had told her to invite anyone who was single or lonely tonight. Sabrina had simply done that. And, judging by Sabrina's victorious smile, after the last of them had left and Mabel had been tucked into bed, she truly believed she'd done the right thing.

"Harrison couldn't take his eyes off you tonight." Sabrina grinned as she pulled on her furry coat. "And I could tell he wanted to get you under the mistletoe too."

Daphne had to bite her tongue—reminding herself that this was Christmas Eve, a time of peace on earth, good will toward men...and women. She could straighten out Sabrina later. "Merry Christmas." She hugged Sabrina tightly. "And thanks for the dress. It's lovely."

"It looks amazing on you."

"And, for the record, Ricardo couldn't take his eyes off *you* tonight." Daphne opened the door, allowing a whoosh of cold air inside.

"Oh, you're just saying that." Sabrina giggled as she pulled up her collar.

"Not at all." Daphne shook her head. "Trust me, Ricardo is getting serious about you. If you're not interested, you should probably send him some clear signals. I'd hate to see him get his heart broken."

Sabrina blinked. "Well, he doesn't need to worry about that with me, Daphne. Not one bit. The only signal I have for him is a green light."

Daphne smiled. "I'm happy for you then. Merry Christmas."

"And I'll come by in the morning," Sabrina called out. "For opening gifts?"

"Absolutely," Daphne called back. "Be careful. It looks slick out there." And standing in the cold, she watched, making sure her neighbor safely made it home. But as Daphne closed the front door, she couldn't help but feel slightly annoyed. Why had Sabrina invited Harrison tonight? Why? Why? Why?

Chapter 23

As planned, Sabrina joined Daphne and Mabel for the opening of gifts on Christmas morning. Keeping in the spirit of Christmas, Daphne controlled herself from expressing her disappointment over Harrison's unexpected arrival last night. Instead she focused all her energy on oohing and awing over the various gifts—mostly for Mabel.

And when Mabel presented Daphne with a school picture that she'd made a special frame for, Daphne cried happily, hugging Mabel tightly as she thanked her.

"Here's another one for you," Mabel announced as she brought a small narrow box to her, waiting while Daphne examined the tag.

"It's from Jake," Daphne said woodenly.

"Open it!" Mabel exclaimed.

"It looks like jewelry," Sabrina said with wide eyes. "Do you think Jake would give you jewelry?"

"No...I don't think so." Although Daphne had to agree with Sabrina as she peeled the paper away from the heavy box.

She opened the lid, preparing herself for either a necklace or bracelet. But it was a pen.

"What is it?" Mabel leaned in to see.

"A silver writing pen." Daphne removed it, holding it up and trying to disguise the tears in her eyes. "Because I'm a writer."

Dad and Karen eagerly welcomed Daphne and Mabel into their condo. Although Daphne knew her dad was happy and loved his new wife, it still felt strange not to be in their old house—particularly at Christmas. But she kept her feelings in check and, after gifts were opened and Mabel was overwhelmed again with too many things, Daphne went into the kitchen to help Karen with the midday meal she was preparing.

"You seem quieter than usual," Karen said as she closed the oven.

"I think I'm tired of all the festivities." Daphne sighed as she peeled a carrot. "To be honest, I'll be glad when the holidays are over and we get back to a regular routine. It feels like it's been a long time."

Karen laughed. "Welcome to motherhood. It must be somewhat shocking to you though. Getting it all foisted into your lap so instantly."

"Yes, that's occurred to me."

"Well, your father is sure thrilled about playing grandpa." Karen rinsed a mixing bowl in the sink. "And listen to those two out there trying that new video game. It's like two little kids."

"He makes a wonderful grandpa." Daphne sighed.

"You're not having second thoughts are you?" Karen frowned curiously at her.

"What?" Daphne set down the carrot. "Second thoughts?"
"About Mabel?"

Daphne shook her head. "No, not at all. I couldn't be happier with her."

"But you're having some kind of second thoughts?"

Daphne bit her lip as she picked up another carrot.

"What's wrong, Daph?" Karen went over to look in her eyes. "You can trust me, sweetheart. I know I'm not your mother, but I'd like to think I'm your friend. I can be a good friend, if you let me."

Daphne studied her. "I guess I'm just sad because it feels like I keep blowing something. I mean, I'm not always the one to blow it. But it's like we get so close, and I get my hopes up—and then wham-bam, thank you ma'am—it all falls apart."

Karen nodded. "With a guy?"

"Yeah."

"Is it Jake?"

Daphne blinked. "What makes you think it's Jake?"

Karen shrugged. "I've seen you together before. I thought I saw some chemistry." She chuckled. "Although your dad keeps holding out for Ricardo. If he could arrange your marriage with someone, he'd pick Ricardo."

Now, partly to change the subject and partly to give her dad a head's up, she told Karen about Ricardo's interest in Sabrina. "She's interested in him too. And I couldn't be happier for both of them. But I don't think you should probably repeat this."

Karen made a zipper motion over her lips. "You can trust me."

"And same thing over what I said about Jake." Daphne shook her head. "I keep telling myself if it's meant to be...it'll happen. And the fact that it keeps getting torn apart...well, it makes me wonder. Maybe it's not meant to be."

Karen just shrugged. "Time will tell."

To Daphne's relief, the days following Christmas fell into a nice, calm, peaceful pattern. Even though Mabel wasn't in school, they created their own sort of norm by sleeping in a little, having slow, lazy breakfasts, shoveling snow, and just taking whatever life brought their way, which, thankfully, wasn't much.

But after several days, Sabrina came over and insisted upon taking them to lunch. "You need to get out," she declared. "I thought we could all walk to town. Tootsie can come too. I'll put on his boots and down coat."

"Let me guess where we're going," Daphne teased. "Midge's by any chance?"

Sabrina wrinkled her nose. "You have twenty minutes to get ready."

Before long, the four of them were bundled up and walking to town together. Tootsie looked like an alien in his yellow rubber boots and lime green puffy jacket, but Mabel was proud to hold his leash, walking up ahead while Daphne and Sabrina followed.

"Have you seen Ricardo since Christmas Day?" Daphne asked curiously. She knew that Sabrina had been invited to Marie's that day but hadn't heard anything new since then.

"Not exactly." Sabrina adjusted her hot pink scarf. "I'm trying really hard to have self-control, Daphne. I don't want to rush things. Don't want to scare him."

"But your reason for going to lunch at Midge's?"

"Just to see him." Sabrina shrugged. "And I'm tired of my own cooking. And you and Mabel have been hermits."

"We've been enjoying some down time."

"So...have you heard from Harrison?" Sabrina questioned.

"He called the other day."

"And...?"

"And we chatted."

"And...?"

"And he asked me out."

"And...?" Sabrina looked hopefully at her.

"And I told him I was enjoying my down time with Mabel right now."

"What?" Sabrina sounded shocked.

"I just didn't feel like going out with him."

"But he's such a great guy. And I could tell he was pretty smitten with you at your party. Why wouldn't you go out with him?"

"I'm just not that into him," she said quietly.

"Why not?"

Daphne could tell that Mabel had slowed down some. "Little pitchers have big ears," she said.

"What does that mean?" Sabrina made a harrumph sound. "My grandma used to say the same thing and I never got it. Pitchers don't even have ears."

Daphne laughed. "I never got it either. But it's a handy expression. And someday I'll try to explain the whole Harrison thing to you, Sabrina. Just not today. Okay?"

Sabrina agreed, and since they were at Midge's she was distracted anyway. Before long they were seated and, although

Kellie came to take their order, it was Ricardo who delivered their drinks, taking a moment to chat congenially with them. But as he visited, Daphne could see that his eyes were mainly on Sabrina. His ears seemed finely tuned to her words. And it was sweet. Daphne tried not to feel jealous. Maybe she would have that someday too. Maybe... .

"So you girls heard the latest scuttlebutt, didn't you?"

"What's scuttlebutt?" Mabel asked.

"It's like gossip," Sabrina told her.

"But isn't gossip bad?" Mabel frowned.

"Sorry, this isn't really scuttlebutt or gossip," Ricardo clarified. "It's the truth. I heard it from the horse's mouth."

"What horse?" Mabel asked with wide eyed interest.

Ricardo laughed, sliding in next to Sabrina. "I heard this bit of news from Mick. He stopped by here yesterday. I'm surprised you girls didn't hear it already."

"What is it?" Sabrina asked eagerly.

"Mick and Julianne got engaged."

"You're kidding!" Daphne felt shocked. "Mick is getting married?"

"That's wonderful," Sabrina gushed. "I'm so happy for them. What a gorgeous couple they make."

"I can't believe it." Daphne shook her head. "Mick engaged?"

"Aren't you happy for him?" Sabrina asked.

"Well, yes, of course. And I've always thought that Mick and Julianne were a good match. But he always treated her like an employee. And he always acts like such a confirmed bachelor. I'm just a little stunned."

Sabrina giggled. "It's probably my fault."

"Your fault?" Ricardo frowned.

"I told Mick he should give Julianne a raise—just to make sure she didn't go find another job. She's so talented at design and décor. I wasn't sure Mick realized what a prize she was."

"Apparently he does now." Ricardo smiled at Sabrina. "But maybe your words registered with him. Julianne should be grateful. She's been after Mick for ages."

"Hopefully they'll invite me to their wedding." Sabrina sighed. "What a beautiful affair that will be. I hope they have it in their barn."

"A wedding in a barn?" Mabel frowned.

"Not just any barn," Daphne explained. "They would fix it up really nice. It'd be pretty special." She looked at Ricardo. "But I'm still trying to wrap my head around it. Mick engaged. Go figure."

"I know," he said. "I never really imagined Mick getting hitched."

Daphne pointed at Ricardo. "Says one confirmed bachelor about another. Maybe he's trying to drop a hint—jump in, the water's fine."

Ricardo laughed as he stood. "On that note, I better get back to work. You girls enjoy your lunch."

"Wait a minute, Ricardo." Sabrina chirped at him. "I almost forgot something."

"What?" He looked hopefully at her.

"I know it's short notice, but I'm having a little New Year's Eve celebration. There's not really time to send out proper invitations, but I'd been meaning to invite you." She smiled brightly. "Seven o'clock on New Year's Eve. Can you make it, do you think?"

"Sure." He nodded. "Sounds great."

After he left, Daphne tossed Sabrina a puzzled look. "You never mentioned your little shindig before. Just the two of you?"

"No, of course not." Sabrina grinned mischievously. "I want y'all to come too. I'll invite lots of folks to my little shindig."

"What's a shindig?" Mabel asked.

Sabrina and Daphne both laughed. "It's just a funny, old-fashioned word for a party," Daphne explained. "Sabrina's having a New Year's Eve party."

"Can we go?" Mabel asked eagerly.

"Sure." Daphne nodded. "But we might not be able to stay until midnight."

When Sabrina told Daphne that she planned to invite "the regular suspects," Daphne played nonchalant. She assumed that Jake would be invited but didn't want to inquire, didn't want to draw attention to her interest. That is, if she had interest. She wasn't totally sure. But when Sabrina suggested that Daphne secure Jenna as a babysitter for that night, just in case Daphne wanted to stay later and Mabel needed to go to bed, it seemed a good opportunity to check on Jake. And, of course, when Mabel got wind of a possible evening with Jenna, she suggested that she and Lola could have their own "party" and just stay home.

Daphne briefly considered calling Jake as a pretense to reach Jenna—and to assure herself he'd be at Sabrina New Year's party. But, knowing he'd see right through her thin pretenses, she simply called Jenna herself.

"I realize you might already have plans," Daphne told Jenna.

"Maybe you and your dad are—"

"No, I'm not doing anything."

"Great." Now Daphne explained how Becca needed a sitter too. "So you'll get double pay," she told her.

"Cool."

"Do you, uh, need a ride?"

"I'll check to see," she said. "Maybe."

"Just let me know."

As it turned out, Jenna did need a ride and wanted to be picked up at her dad's house. Naturally, this was disappointing to Daphne because it suggested that Jake wasn't attending Sabrina's party after all. And the fact that Jenna needed transportation suggested he must be going to someone else's party. Or going out with someone else. Not that she planned to obsess over it. Not much anyway.

As Daphne and Mabel drove Jenna to their house, Daphne couldn't help but feel disappointed. But, just like she'd been trying to convince herself—if it was meant to be, it would happen naturally. If it wasn't meant to be, it wouldn't. And she didn't plan to push it. Or to question Jenna on her father's whereabouts.

"You girls have fun, but *be good*," she told Lola and Mabel. "You know where I am if you need me," she quietly told Jenna and, knowing the party was already in full swing and that she was late, she hurried across the street.

Despite Sabrina's suggestion that this was a dress-up occasion, Daphne had decided to keep it casual with black pants and a print silk tunic. And unless she was having a fabulous time, Daphne had given herself permission to leave early as well. Of course, as fate—and Sabrina—would have it,

Harrison was there.

Daphne was barely in the door when he rushed over to eagerly greet her, quickly bringing her up to speed—both on his life and regarding some of the guests there. "Can you believe old Mick got engaged?" he told her as he led her to the food table.

"Yeah, I was pretty surprised too," she admitted as she loaded a small plate with appetizers.

"There's a spot to sit over there." Harrison pointed to a loveseat in front of the French doors. As they sat down together, she knew that she was probably sending the wrong message to anyone paying attention. Not that anyone was, and not that it mattered much since she knew people would believe whatever they wanted. Sabrina, for instance.

Besides, she told herself as they chatted and ate, maybe she hadn't really given Harrison a fair chance yet. What if he truly was *the one* but she'd been so busy looking over her shoulder that she had totally missed it? Wouldn't that be a travesty!

And so, letting her proverbial hair down, Daphne decided to simply enjoy herself for a change. Quit second guessing everyone and everything. Just be in the moment. So when Sabrina organized some goofy games like Pictionary and, later on, charades, Daphne jumped in with both feet. And it was actually fun! As she and Harrison laughed and exchanged clues, she remembered how Jake had confessed how he wasn't a real party person. In all likelihood, he wouldn't even enjoy this. She wanted that to make her feel better, but it wasn't quite working. She still felt a bit out of sorts. As if she'd messed up somehow—or forgotten something...or someone.

But blocking these intrusive feelings, she laughed and joked and played games, and for brief moments she almost imagined she was the life of the party. Harrison certainly seemed to enjoy himself with her. Whenever partners were required, they always paired up. And to her surprise, he brought out a competitive side to her that she had nearly forgotten was there. Together they were formidable.

Finally, it was nearly midnight and Sabrina turned on her flat-screen TV so everyone could watch the big crystal ball being lowered in Times Square, counting down loudly together. And suddenly it was midnight and they were all pulling poppers and blowing shrill paper horns and tossing streamers—like an old fashioned movie. Before she knew what was happening, Harrison swooped her up into a big hug, landing a solid kiss onto her un-expectant lips.

Wanting to be fully present and part of the New Year's celebration, and longing for real romance that would lead to a lifetime of true love that would last forever and possibly solve most of her problems, Daphne gave in to the kiss. Relaxing, she allowed it to sink in. But when they stepped apart, she felt slightly disappointed. As if something was missing.

Instead of revealing her real feelings, she gave him a big smile as she wished him "Happy New Year!" And feeling like a great big phony, she made some excuses about needing to get her sitter home, then thanked Sabrina and told everyone goodnight. Before Harrison could stop her, she slipped out the door and raced home. With silly tears streaming down her cheeks, she hurried into her house and was just locking the front door when she remembered she still needed to get Jenna home.

Chapter 24

Jenna met Daphne in the foyer. "What's wrong?" she asked, her dark eyes concerned.

"Oh, nothing." Daphne gave her a shaky smile as she wiped her cheek. "Just silly me."

"You're really upset." Jenna put a comforting arm around Daphne's shoulders. "I can tell. What happened over there?"

Daphne took in a deep breath, trying not to crumble beneath Jenna's unexpected sympathy. "Oh, I don't know. I'm just being overly emotional. It's nothing really."

"Come sit down," Jenna said kindly. "You can tell me. I'm a good listener."

Daphne sighed as Jenna led her to the couch. "Oh, it's really dumb. I was actually having a really good time tonight. We played games and just acted like kids. It was fun. Then it was midnight and, uh, this guy kissed me and, well, it was just *all wrong.*" To her embarrassment, Daphne felt her eyes filling again. "And it's so childish to feel like this. It's just ridiculous. But I was disappointed, you know? I hadn't wanted that guy to kiss me. If I was going to have the perfect New Year's kiss, I wanted it to be from someone else. You know?"

Jenna nodded with wide eyes. "Yeah, totally. I get it."

"You do?"

"Sure. I've had a crush on Noah Hadley since eighth grade, but he still doesn't know I'm alive."

Daphne shook her head. "And you're such a beautiful girl, Jenna. And so good and kind and smart and industrious. Noah obviously does not know what he's missing."

Jenna smiled. "Yeah, that's what Dad tells me too." Her smile faded now. "That guy—the one who kissed you when you didn't want it—it wasn't Dad, was it? I mean, I know he was invited to Sabrina's, but he told me he wasn't going."

"Oh, no," Daphne said quickly. "He wasn't there at all."

"Oh, good." Jenna looked relieved.

"Speaking of your dad." Daphne frowned. "If he's out tonight—at a party or on a date—do you think he'd mind stopping to pick you up?"

"As far as I know, he's at home."

"At home?"

"Yeah. He had some invites, but he doesn't really like parties that much. I mean, he likes some parties, like if he knows everyone. But he's not really a party guy. Plus he was feeling a little down."

Daphne nodded, wondering why Jake was feeling down and wishing it was somehow related to her. "Anyway, I can give you a ride if you don't mind waiting a bit. Sabrina offered to come over to sit with the girls while I run you home."

"That's okay. Dad said he'd come get me." Jenna picked up her phone. "I'll just let him know I'm ready now."

While Jenna called Jake, Daphne ducked into the bathroom to erase all remnants of her tears. What had she been thinking to confide in a fifteen-year-old girl like that? And then to hear Jenna's relief that it wasn't Jake who'd kissed her. Naturally, Jenna would feel protective of her dad. She probably didn't want him kissing anyone. That's exactly how Daphne would've felt at Jenna's age.

"He's coming," Jenna said as Daphne emerged.

"Thanks. Although I'm sorry to drag him out so late."

"Don't worry. He was awake." Jenna frowned. "Did Dad tell you about my mom?"

"Your mom?" Daphne felt puzzled.

"Yeah. Mom got married tonight."

"You're kidding?" Daphne blinked in shock. "She got married *tonight?*"

"Yeah. In Vegas. I know, it sounded crazy to me too. But she and Frank Danson flew down there yesterday. I just got a text saying they tied the knot before midnight."

"Wow." Daphne didn't even know what to say.

"Frank wanted it to be legal before midnight. For tax purposes, you know." Jenna just shook her head.

Daphne suddenly felt embarrassed for her own little pity party. To think poor Jenna was dealing with something like this. "Are you okay with that?" Daphne asked with deep concern.

Jenna shrugged. "I guess so. I mean Vegas doesn't sound too romantic to me, but it was what Mom and Frank wanted."

"So how do you feel about the marriage? Are you okay with your new step-dad?"

Jenna shrugged again. "I'm okay. I knew it was going to

happen eventually. And, really, Frank's all right. He's actually pretty cool. And Mom's really glad that he's got money. That's important to her."

"And to you?"

Jenna smiled. "I'm not that into money. I'm just not very materialistic."

Daphne couldn't help but hug her. "You don't need to be materialistic, Jenna. You're like a wonderful treasure all in yourself."

Jenna gave her an embarrassed smile. "Thanks."

"And even though you're not *into money.*" Daphne went for her purse. "I still need to pay you for tonight." She fished out the cash and handed it to Jenna.

Jenna grinned as she shoved her pay into a back pocket. "Just because I'm not into money doesn't mean I don't know what to do with it."

Daphne laughed. "I know just what you mean."

"Anyway, Dad's kind of having a hard time with it…I think."

Daphne paused to consider this—was Jake still in love with his ex? He'd never made it seem that way. "You mean with your mom remarrying?"

Jenna nodded. "I think that's the real reason he stayed home tonight."

"That's understandable. I'm sure he has some regrets."

"Yeah. Not so much over Mom marrying Frank. More for how stuff went down a long time ago—when I was pretty little." She sighed. "But I get it. Those two never should've got married in the first place. It was a huge mistake. For as long as I can remember, they've been fighting."

"Maybe it will get better for them with Frank in the picture."

Daphne wasn't even sure how this could be, but she wanted to say something encouraging.

"Yeah, maybe." Jenna pointed out the front window. "Well, there he is. Thanks, Daphne."

"Thank *you*," Daphne called as Jenna headed for the door. "Happy New Year."

Jenna echoed the words back as she hurried outside. Daphne watched her running out to the SUV and suddenly wished she'd asked Jenna to keep what she'd just confessed about the disappointing New Year's Eve kiss confidential, but maybe it didn't matter. Jake and Jenna were probably preoccupied over Gwen and Frank's elopement. Daphne had met both of them before. And, although she wasn't a big fan of Gwen's perfection and pretension, she thought Frank seemed like a pretty nice guy. Hopefully it would be a good match. But Vegas, really?

The big news of the New Year—at least in Appleton—seemed to be that Ricardo and Sabrina were officially dating. Of course, there were other bits of interesting news, like Mick and Julianne's engagement, and Gwen McPheeters's elopement with Frank Danson. But, because everyone knew and loved Ricardo and because Sabrina was a relative newcomer, their news seemed to be the talk of the town. And Daphne wasn't a bit surprised when she heard that Kellie had quit her job at Midge's Diner. She suspected almost everyone was glad about that.

"Have you heard from Harrison yet?" Sabrina asked a week after the New Year's party.

"He asked me out for Saturday," Daphne told her without

much enthusiasm.

"That's fabulous." Sabrina patted her on the back. "I honestly thought you might've lost him when you pulled your little disappearing act on New Year's Eve." She chuckled as she sat down at the kitchen table. "Honestly, Daph, when it comes to scaring off men, you could probably win a trophy."

"Thanks." Daphne handed Sabrina a cup of coffee.

"Seriously, since I've known you, how many guys have you sent packing?"

"I don't actually keep count." Daphne filled her own cup.

"Well, at least you're giving Harrison another chance." Sabrina frowned. "Because, like I already told you, it's not fair to make a judgment call on any fellow's first kiss. First kisses are highly deceiving. My first kiss with my ex-husband was total loser-ville, but after a few tries, we had real success."

"Well, except for the tiny little fact that your marriage failed," Daphne pointed out.

Sabrina chuckled. "Well, yes, there was that. But it didn't fail over bad kissing. And you really shouldn't throw out the baby with the bathwater, Daphne. Just one little nervous kiss on New Year's Eve is no way to judge a man. I'm very relieved to hear you're not giving up on Harrison. He's a good guy. And not just in the looks department, although he's nothing to complain about, but he's smart and fun, and I happen to think you two make a great pair."

Daphne wondered what that meant—what exactly constituted a "great pair"? Was it something visible? Or something you just felt? And why wasn't Daphne feeling it?

Mabel was glad that Daphne was going out with Harrison too. Not so much because she liked Harrison but, Daphne suspected, because that meant Jenna was babysitting again. To Daphne's relief, she picked Jenna up at her mom's house the next time. Rather, she picked her up at their "new" house since Jenna and Gwen had moved into Frank Danson's hilltop mansion.

"Your house is really big," Mabel said when Jenna got into Daphne's car. "Is it like a castle or something?"

"Not exactly," Jenna told her. "But you're right, it is big. It takes some getting used to living there."

"Do you feel like a princess in it?" Mabel asked.

Jenna laughed. "No. But it does have a nice swimming pool. Maybe I can bring you over to see it next summer."

Of course, that sent Mabel right over the moon, and she asked Jenna a dozen more questions as Daphne drove them back to the house. By now Jenna knew the routine and since she and Mabel were already perusing the DVDs for tonight's movie selection, Daphne decided to spend a little more time on taming her hair. The recent damp weather had been playing havoc with her auburn curls.

But by the time Harrison arrived, she hadn't really made much progress. She told the girls goodbye and went out to his car with him. Even though she was fairly well acquainted with him, she suddenly felt nervous. As if this was their first date. When she asked herself why, she realized it was because the stakes felt higher.

To her relief, Harrison seemed relaxed and in good spirits. And midway through the date, she realized she was relaxed too. And having a good time. It wasn't until he was taking her home that she began to feel nervous again. She knew she had to say something. "I've been wanting to apologize for dashing off like that on New Year's Eve," she began. "I realize we weren't on a date or anything, but I know it must've seemed rather abrupt and rude."

"Yeah, it did leave me scratching my head. Like maybe I should've doubled up on the mouthwash or something." He laughed.

She smiled. "No, that wasn't it. I think the problem was that I just wasn't ready."

"Oh...I had wondered about that. And in that case, I should apologize, Daphne. I didn't mean to rush you. I just got swept away in the moment."

"I thought so." She sighed. "And, you see, I really did want to get to know you better, Harrison, but I was worried if we moved straight into kissing—and the physical side of things, well, it could be a distraction to our friendship."

"Our friendship?"

"Yes," she said firmly. "I've always believed that any good relationship—I mean a romantic relationship—should be built on friendship."

"Interesting."

"I think a solid friendship is foundational to a lasting relationship." She glanced at him. "How about you?"

He slowly nodded. "That makes sense."

"So, you'll understand if I want to hold off on the physical side of things for a while. I mean if we're going to continue going out." She felt her cheeks warming now. Was she asking him to go out again? And if so, did she really want that?

"I'm good with that. In fact, it actually makes sense. I've

been in other relationships with women where things moved too fast and, well, it ended up in the ditch, if you know what I mean."

She didn't completely know what he meant, but maybe that didn't matter. "I'm so glad you understand," she said as he pulled up to her house. "Communication is important to me. It's a relief to know we're on the same page."

"Can I walk you to your door?" He grinned. "If I promise not to kiss you goodnight?"

She laughed nervously. "Yes, of course."

At the door, true to his word, he simply grasped her hand and thanked her for a delightful evening. "Thank you," she said back to him. "I thoroughly enjoyed it."

"Same time next week?" he asked hopefully.

"Okay," she agreed, but even as she said this, she felt unsure. What was she getting into? Did she really want this to become a regular thing? And if not, why not? But she simply told him goodnight and slipped into the house.

"Did you have fun?" Jenna asked as she picked up her jacket, slipping her phone into a pocket.

"Yes. It was nice."

"When I saw Harrison's car in front, I went ahead and called Dad to come get me."

"I thought you were at your mom's house this weekend," Daphne said.

"That was just because Dad was on a business trip and didn't get back until a couple hours ago. I'll spend the rest of the weekend at his place."

"Oh...right." Daphne hung her coat in the hall closet. "Does that ever get confusing to you, Jenna? Like you can't remember where you are when you wake up?"

Jenna laughed. "I guess so. And living at Frank's house takes some getting used to. But it's not too bad." She pointed out the window. "There's Dad."

Daphne peered out to see Jake in his SUV peering toward the house. She wasn't sure if he could see her or not, but waved anyway. He didn't respond, not until he spotted Jenna running through the rain toward him. Then he waved—at Jenna. As Daphne closed the drapes, she felt a wave of sadness coming over her. The words she'd said to Harrison tonight were absolutely true. She did believe that any good and lasting romantic relationship should be built on friendship. Similar to the friendship she'd felt she and Jake had been building. And yet their relationship always seemed like it was two steps forward and one step back. Or sometimes two steps back...or three. But it had been built on friendship.

Her next date with Harrison was much like the previous one. As they talked and laughed and bantered, it hit her—the reason she didn't feeling that connected to him was because most of their conversation only seemed to scratch the surface. Certainly he was charming and could talk comfortably on a variety of interesting topics, but it never went deep. At least that's how it seemed to her.

Tonight when he drove her home, he brought up some of the plans for the new city hall building. "We hope to break ground in early February, weather permitting."

"That's wonderful," she said as he pulled in front of her house. "I'd love to see the plans for it."

"I'll bring them next week." He grinned. "If we're still on for next week."

She didn't know what to say and so she just nodded. "Sure. Of course." But as he walked her to the house, she wanted to retract those words. She wanted to tell him that although he was a nice guy, he just wasn't right for her. And yet she couldn't bring herself to say it. Once again, he grasped her hand, thanked her for the date and, without even attempting a kiss, he told her goodnight.

As she went into the house, she felt confused and frustrated. What was wrong with her? Why did she allow herself to agree to something she didn't even want? Was she just a coward? Or simply that desperate? Whatever it was, she didn't like it.

"Did you have fun?" Jenna asked as she pulled out her phone.

"I'm not sure." Daphne frowned as she removed her coat and scarf.

Jenna peered curiously at her. "You seem unhappy."

"I'm okay." Daphne's smile felt stiff though. "Probably just tired." She pointed to the phone in Jenna's hand. "Is your dad coming?"

"I didn't call him yet."

"Thanks once again." Daphne handed Jenna her babysitting payment. "I always feel so comfortable knowing Mabel is with you."

"But do you need to talk, Daphne? Remember, I'm a good listener."

Daphne's smile loosened up. "I know you are, sweetie, but you're only fifteen. I can't go dumping my silly old problems on you. I'll be fine."

"It's okay." Jenna grabbed her hand, pulling her into the living room. "I'm interested in your problems. Don't forget that we're both writers—I think we should understand each other."

Jenna looked so hopeful that Daphne gave in, sitting down with her on the sofa. "It's no big deal. I guess I'm just second-guessing myself on some things."

"Harrison?"

Daphne sighed. "I don't think I want to keep going out with Harrison."

"So, what's wrong with that?" Jenna said brightly. "Just dump him."

"Except that I just stupidly agreed to go out with him again next week."

Jenna frowned. "That's awkward."

"As soon as I agreed, I regretted it. But I didn't know how to take it back. I felt stuck. And that's ridiculous. Good grief, I'm a grown woman—I should know better."

"Just text him and say you made a mistake," Jenna suggested. "No big deal."

Daphne chuckled at the teenager's solution. "Tempting... only I'm not sure a text is a good idea. But I get what you're saying. I should just tell him the truth. Be honest."

"Exactly." Jenna nodded. "But texting is easy and efficient."

"Maybe. But it feels a little cowardly to me. I think Harrison deserves a phone call from me."

Jenna seemed to consider this. "Yeah, you're probably right. A phone call is more personal."

"Speaking of phone calls, you should probably call your dad. It's getting late." As Jenna called Jake, Daphne considered calling Harrison, but then she realized he'd be driving right now. And even though it would make her feel better, it was probably selfish. Better to wait a day or two...let him down gently. And, really, who would've thought it—Dear Daphne taking advice from a teenager!

Chapter 25

Daphne waited until Tuesday afternoon to call Harrison. And, although she could hear the surprised disappointment in his voice, he didn't question her or try to talk her out of her decision. She expressed appreciation for the times they had shared, but let him know in no uncertain words that she was not ready for a dating relationship. And, even if it wasn't the complete truth, she used Mabel as a partial excuse. "Being a fulltime mother is still relatively new to me, and I'm just not ready to keep taking that much time away from her." So they parted, she hoped, as friends.

But on the following morning, when she told Sabrina about her decision, she felt certain that half the neighborhood must've heard her friend's loud shrieks of protest. Hopefully no one was calling 9-1-1 right now.

"*No, no, no!*" Sabrina declared after she'd calmed down a bit. "This is all wrong! Are you insane, Daphne?"

"I'm quite sane, thank you very much."

"You cannot keep doing this. It's like you're on a path to self-destruct and, as your good friend, I cannot allow it to go on." Sabrina held out her phone. "You call that man right back. Call him right now and tell him that you were wrong. Tell him that you're sorry and that you still want to go out with him on Saturday."

"I will do no such thing." Daphne pushed Sabrina's phone back at her.

"Daphne Ballinger, do you realize you have less than four months to get married? And you finally get a live one on the hook—and you let him go?"

"I'm sure Harrison would appreciate being considered a 'live one,'" Daphne said dryly.

"You know what I mean. You guys were dating regularly. You were making good progress. Honestly, Daphne, you probably could've gotten a proposal out of him by Valentine's Day. Even by then, there's only three months to plan your wedding."

"You've obviously given this a lot of thought." Daphne sipped her coffee.

"*Three months*! Do you understand that is barely enough time to get out wedding invitations with time for RSVPs?"

Daphne just shrugged.

"Are you even listening to me?" Sabrina shook a fist in the air.

"It's hard not to, dearest."

"Can you give me one good reason why you gave Harrison his walking papers?" Sabrina's brow creased as she pounded her fist onto the table, making their coffee cups jump. "Seriously, Daphne. I'm worried about you. And, all right,

I understood the problem with Daniel. That meant moving away. I get that. And I totally understood why you rejected that horrid old skunk of a boyfriend who just wanted to marry you for your money."

"My *aunt's* money."

"Yes. He needed to be given the boot. And the other various guys, the ones you gave up on before it got serious, well, maybe they just weren't terribly interesting, or y'all didn't have good chemistry, or whatever. I get that. But *Harrison*?" Sabrina's blue eyes got big. "What on earth is wrong with that handsome man? I saw you two together. You had fun with him at Mick's party. And I know for a fact, he's a darn good dancer. And at my party, you guys had a fabulous time. And he was good at playing games. And he's smart and funny and charming and—most importantly—he *likes* you!"

Suddenly Daphne felt worried. Everything Sabrina said was absolutely true. Harrison was a great guy. What was wrong with her?

"Honestly, Daph, you could do worse." Sabrina sighed. "Trust me, I know."

"I won't argue that Harrison is a great guy."

"That's right! And you still haven't given me one good reason why you gave up on him." Sabrina folded her arms in front and scowled. "I'm *waiting.*"

Daphne thought hard. "It just didn't *feel* right."

"Did you guys kiss again?" Sabrina demanded. "Was that it? Was there just absolutely no chemistry—no electricity? Because, although I find it hard to believe, I could maybe understand it."

"No...we didn't kiss again. But that wasn't it."

"I swear, I do not understand you." Sabrina carried her empty coffee cup to the sink, putting it down with a loud clank. She shook her finger at the kitchen clock. "Time is running out, my friend. The clock is ticking."

"I know." Daphne slowly stood. "If it makes you feel any better, I'm starting to question myself right now. I honestly don't know what my problem is."

"Maybe you're just scared—did you get cold feet?"

"I don't know...I suppose that's possible."

Sabrina eagerly grabbed Daphne's arm. "Maybe it's not too late. You could still call Harrison. Just tell him you made a big mistake. And, who knows, it could work out for the best. Sometimes a guy needs a gentle boost—if he feels like he's lost you, it could make him want you more than ever. You really could be engaged by Valentine's Day."

Daphne set her own cup in the sink.

"You can't give up, Daphne. If you can't do it for yourself, you could at least think about Mabel. Do you know how hard it will be on her when you guys have to move away from this house? Maybe even leave Appleton?" Sabrina peered into her eyes. "It'll be hard on me too. And what about Olivia? I just saw her yesterday. Her baby's due in a month, and I know she wants you to be around to play auntie. Can't you at least try it awhile longer with Harrison? What if you just gave up too soon?"

Daphne let out a long sigh. "Fine, I'll think about it. Okay?"

Sabrina gave her a relieved smile as she crossed her fingers. "Okay. But think about the *whole tamale*, Daphne. Not only Harrison, but your whole life—and Mabel's too. Think about how quickly the next few months will fly by—and they will.

And when it's suddenly May and there are no husband prospects waiting in the wings, what will you do? *Where will you be?*" Sabrina hugged her by the front door. "I don't want to look across the street and see someone else living here. That would be unbearably sad."

Promising to really give Sabrina's lecture some thought, Daphne was glad to close the door behind her. Oh, she knew Sabrina meant well and some of the things she'd said were true. But Sabrina did not know the real reason Daphne had cut things off with Harrison. She just couldn't shake off the feeling that there could possibly be something between her and Jake.

She went to her office, fully planning to work, but instead she leaned back in her chair and thought about Jake. Replaying all their ups and downs of friendship, the times she'd gotten her hopes up then felt let down, the times he'd seemed interested in her but she was with someone else. She also replayed all the times that Jake had come to her side, given her his friendship and advice, just when she needed it.

And then she thought about Harrison. Her time with him had been much more limited. And yet it had been thoroughly enjoyable. Sure, it might've seemed a bit more superficial, but was that her fault? Had she held him off at arm's length to make sure things didn't move too quickly or get deeper? Was that fair to him?

Suddenly Daphne remembered a letter she'd read for the column yesterday—one she hadn't answered yet. She pulled it out and read it again.

Dear Daphne,
I find myself in an awkward position. I think I

am in love with two men at the same time, and I don't know what to do. I've been dating 'Mark' for the last three years and he is absolutely great. We're like best friends. And I have actually been expecting a proposal from him for more than a year now. But I recently met 'Simon' and, although he is the exact opposite of Mark, I find myself strangely drawn to him. Where Mark is very open and easy going, Simon is mysterious and independent. As different as these two men are, I feel equally pulled toward both of them. But at the same time, I feel guilty for my duplicity. And I'm worried it could ruin my chances with both of them. What should I do? How can I make up my mind?

Double-minded in Detroit

Daphne reread the letter, trying to find that thread of ironic truth that she usually looked for—the way she felt that most of the people writing for advice already knew their answers. But for some reason this one was tricky. And it didn't help matters that Daphne could almost relate. But then an idea came to her—and she quickly wrote her response.

Dear Double-minded,

First of all, I want to point out that being double-minded in the area of romance will probably trickle over into other areas of your life. So unless you like this feeling of instability, you should probably make a decision. That said, I have an exercise for you to perform.

Flip a coin. Heads for Mark. Tails for Simon.
Now, I realize this advice sounds a bit crazy, but I'm
guessing that when you see which side of the coin is
on top, you will know your answer. You will either
feel relieved—or you will feel uneasy, like you want
to toss the coin again. If you're relieved, you should
go with whoever won the toss. If you're uneasy, go
with whoever "lost" the toss.
Daphne

Daphne wasn't certain she would really send that letter, but just for fun, she pulled out a quarter. Heads for Harrison, tails for Jake. She flipped it high, letting it land on the carpet in her office. Stooping down, she saw that it was heads. Harrison. Feeling disappointed, she picked up the quarter, refraining from giving it another toss. She had her answer.

Suddenly Daphne remembered the real reason Sabrina had popped in this morning, the reason that had gotten buried in their frustrating conversation over Harrison. Sabrina had been shopping in Bernie's Blooms yesterday afternoon, and Olivia had hinted about a baby shower. "I think y'all should talk about it," Sabrina had said with concern. "Because Olivia has expectations."

Daphne had slapped her forehead as the realization hit her. Of course, Daphne should have a baby shower for Olivia. What had she been thinking? Obviously, she'd been focused on her own life. Too busy to keep up with Olivia and her pregnancy. What kind of friend was she anyway? Determined to make it up to Olivia, Daphne pulled on her coat and headed for town.

Chapter 26

Olivia acted a little chilly at first, but at least she agreed to let Daphne take her to lunch. And after a bowl of delicious seafood chowder at Midge's Diner, Olivia finally let down her hair. "I'm so tired all the time," she admitted. "I thought it was just because of the holidays. Too much to do. But now that's behind us, and I'm still exhausted."

"I'm sure it must be normal to get tired when you're pregnant." Daphne pointed at Olivia's midsection. "Just looking at you makes me tired."

Olivia almost smiled. "It feels like I never get a break. I realize I've got to keep working. I can't afford to hire another employee. And Jeff has been so busy with his work, he's not much help."

"It must be hard." Daphne frowned. "I'm sorry."

"And you've been so wrapped up with your life." Olivia set her spoon down. "I feel like I barely know you anymore. We were so close last summer...before I found out I was pregnant."

"I'm sorry I've been so distracted," Daphne said. Sometimes

she wished Olivia was privy to the details of Aunt Dee's will, like Sabrina. But she also knew it was supposed to be secret—Sabrina's discovery had been a complete fluke. "I know I haven't been a very good friend these past few months. So much has been going on."

"Well, you've had a lot on your plate too. Good grief, who knew you'd beat me to motherhood." Olivia ran her hands over her rounded belly. "Although you did it the easy way."

Daphne frowned. "I suppose it looked easy."

"Sorry, I didn't mean to sound snarky." Olivia let out a sigh, pushing a strand of dark brown hair away from her eyes. "They say being pregnant diminishes brain cells. I'm not sure if that's true, but it sure feels like it sometimes."

"Well, I really am sorry I haven't been as available to you as I'd like to have been. And the reason I wanted to meet with you today was to ask if I could host a baby shower for you."

"You want to do that?" Olivia's eyes got misty. "Really?"

"Absolutely. And Mabel will love helping me. I know you're having a girl, but have you picked out a name?"

"I want to name her for my sister."

Daphne thought about Olivia's older sister, a dear woman who died too young. "That would be a lovely way to honor her. And Bernadette is a beautiful name."

"And when she's old enough, she can help me with the flower shop. Maybe she'll run it someday." Olivia sighed. "The sooner the better."

"I have an idea," Daphne said suddenly. "I love your shop. What if I volunteer to work a few hours a day for you, you know, several days a week. I could do it through the end of your pregnancy and for several weeks afterward."

"Oh, Daphne, that would be fabulous." Olivia started to cry now. "My emotions are going nuts on me." She reached for a paper napkin, blowing her nose. "You would really do that for me?"

"It'd be fun. And if it was just two or three hours a day, I'd still have enough time to work on my novel. Or, if it was slow in the shop, maybe I could write on my laptop and even put in a few more hours."

"Absolutely! You could write as much as you want to. It's pretty slow most of the time—especially mid-morning and mid-afternoon. But someone needs to be there just the same. And you wouldn't even have to do floral arrangements. You could just take orders and I'd fulfill them later."

They chatted awhile and soon got it settled, even agreeing on a schedule and that, starting tomorrow morning, Daphne would come in at ten and work until two.

"You really are my best friend," Olivia said as they were leaving. "And I know you've gotten to be buddies with Sabrina, and I like her, but I have to admit I was getting jealous too. Jeff told me it was silly to be jealous—because I have him." She laughed. "And you guys are both single and needed each other. But here's the truth—there are times I'd gladly trade Jeff for a good girlfriend. Just temporarily."

Daphne laughed. "You don't have to do that."

"Speaking of Jeff," Olivia lowered her voice as they crossed the street. "I'm afraid he's going to be pretty much worthless when I go into labor."

"What do you mean?"

"I mean, he's been taking Lamaze classes with me, and I can tell he's not comfortable with it. Also, he's been known to faint at the sight of blood."

Daphne laughed to think of Olivia's big macho husband fainting. "Well, you know what they say—the bigger they are, the harder they fall."

"That's what I'm afraid of." Olivia stopped in front of the flower shop, grabbing Daphne's hand. "Would you want to be my birth coach?"

Daphne sucked in a quick breath. "Well, I don't know."

"You're not squeamish, are you?"

"No, I don't think so."

"Oh, it's too much to ask." Olivia was digging through her purse, but her eyes were getting moist again. "I'm sorry."

"No," Daphne said firmly. "I would be honored to be your birthing coach. I'm just not sure what that means exactly?"

"Well, you'd have to come to Lamaze class with me. It's mostly about breathing and relaxing. And then when I go into labor, you'd be the one beside me, helping me to manage the pain so that I don't need anesthesia too soon. That's not good for the baby. But I don't plan to go totally natural. Just as much as I can take. You know?" Olivia produced a big key ring, slipping it into the door.

"Okay." Daphne nodded, although she knew she was in over her head.

"I'll email the Lamaze information to you." Olivia opened the door, flipping the 'I'll Be Back' sign over before she hugged Daphne. "You don't know how much this means to me, Daphne. You coming here today is like a breath of fresh air. I think I might actually be able to get through this thing now." She smiled as she led them inside. "Thanks so much."

"I'm happy to help however I can. And Mabel and I will have

fun planning for Bernadette's shower. You email me any places where you've registered for gifts or anything like that. And names of people I might not know, like out-of-town relatives."

"How about if I show you around the shop a little," Olivia offered as she stashed her purse beneath the counter. "It's really pretty simple, and I have some stuff written down." They spent nearly an hour going through the shop and learning how the cash register worked. "And you can call me if you need to," Olivia assured her.

Daphne could tell that it really was pretty simple, and it would probably even be fun. A way to help Olivia and get some writing done. It seemed like a win-win.

Although Sabrina was disappointed that her pep talk regarding Harrison had fallen on deaf ears, she was somewhat heartened to be invited to help with Olivia's baby shower. Not only that, she was getting so swept away with her own dating life with Ricardo that she almost seemed to forget about Daphne's lack of one. Daphne wasn't sure whether she should be relieved or worried.

But between planning the baby shower, volunteering at Bernie's Blooms in the midday, going to Lamaze classes on Monday nights—which meant Sabrina came over to stay with Mabel—hosting the critique group, attending a neighborhood association meeting, and just the general responsibilities of life, Daphne's schedule for the duration of January seemed pretty well packed. No time for regrets over Harrison. No time to wonder what might've been with Jake.

Daphne and Mabel, assisted by Sabrina, hosted a fabulous

over-the-top baby shower for Olivia later in the month. More than thirty local women attended, as well as several out-of-town relatives, and it was a truly delightful time. Olivia couldn't have been more thrilled—and grateful. And when it was all done, Mabel turned to Daphne and asked if they would ever get to have a baby.

"You and me?" Daphne suppressed laughter as she looked at Mabel. "A baby?"

"Yeah. I could be the big sister and you could be the mommy. Maybe we could have a boy."

Daphne smiled. "Well, miracles happen. And a year ago, I never would've dreamed that I'd be living here with you for my little girl. So who knows?" Oh, she knew she was simply placating Mabel. But the truth was, she was too tired to go into all the details of the birds and the bees. Besides, Mabel was only eight. Surely that conversation could wait awhile.

As Daphne worked at Bernie's Blooms, she began to entertain the idea of finding a part-time job like this, where she could both write and make a little money. Perhaps it wasn't unreasonable to think she could manage to support Mabel and herself. Lots of single moms did it. Becca for instance. Although Daphne knew that Lola was left to her own devices a lot. And, according to some of Lola's stories, like the time she cooked an egg and forgot to turn the stove off, it wasn't exactly safe. However, Lola had assured Mabel and Daphne that her cooking privileges had been suspended until she was ten. That was a relief. Still, the idea of Mabel being left on her own made Daphne sad. As did the thought of leaving Aunt Dee's sweet home behind.

The winter weather didn't let up in January. As a result,

Bernie's Blooms, as well as most of the downtown establishments, experienced a real lull in business. The upside was that Daphne got lots of writing done while she worked at Bernie's. The downside was that Olivia wasn't making much. But at least Daphne's labor was free.

As January rolled into February, the weather warmed up for a few days but then turned chilly again—similar to business at Bernie's Blooms. When the sun came out, the customers came in. But mostly it was slow. As Daphne dusted shelves, swept the floor, and did a general straightening, she hoped this slump wasn't too disappointing to Olivia. Although Olivia had already reassured her it had nothing to do with Daphne's saleswoman expertise.

So Daphne decided to simply make the most of it and, seeing as it was the beginning of February, she was determined to see how much of her column she could complete before the end of the week. But when she was about halfway done, one letter stopped her cold. It took all her self-control not to just trash the stupid letter. After all, who would know or care? When it came to the *Dear Daphne* column, it was up to her discretion to decide what to use and what to lose. Why torture herself with this one?

But being Sabrina had just gotten on her case this morning, pointing out the date on the calendar and the dire situation facing Daphne in just a few months, she decided this might be a good day for torture. And so she read it again, more slowly this time.

> *Dear Daphne,*
> *I recently read that a 'never-been-married woman*

over the age of thirty-five has a better chance of getting killed by a terrorist than getting wed.' Is this true? The reason I want to know is because I turn thirty-six next month and I am feeling very hopeless and borderline depressed. And I am not unattractive. In fact, some people say I'm quite good looking. And I have a college degree and a good job. I am kind to animals and children. I have many interests and lots of friends. In other words, it's not like I'm the cat lady who lives by herself and knits six-foot-long scarves while watching the home and garden channel. Tell me the truth, Daphne, do you think it's really too late for me?

Frightened in Florida

The reason Daphne found this letter so unsettling was because she would be turning *thirty-five* in just one week. She'd heard this ridiculous quote before, long ago when she was too young to take it seriously. But suddenly, in light of her upcoming milestone birthday and this disturbing letter, it felt scary real. It felt like thirty-five was looming over her like the guillotine that would chop her life in two—her marrying, pre-thirty-five years behind her, her post-thirty-five spinsterhood years ahead. It was truly frightening.

She pulled out her smart phone and googled the stupid terrorist quote, which of course was considered bogus by reliable reference sites. However, there was another quote that popped up along with the terrorist one. And although she wasn't sure it was true, although it did sound like the result of real research, it was equally daunting. She stared at the bold words: *Only five percent of never-married women over age 35 get married.*

What if it really was true? *Only five percent?* And if that stat was true, she certainly couldn't share that news with *Frightened in Florida.* Good grief, she couldn't bear to repeat it to herself. And certainly, she realized, it had proved true in Aunt Dee's case. She never married. As for sitting home with cats and watching home and garden TV, Daphne could actually relate. And as a New Year's resolution, she and Mabel had taken up knitting! *Egad!*

Chapter 27

Unable to answer *Frightened in Florida's* letter, Daphne had simply put it in the "later" file, but it felt like a fermenting monster that was hidden away in the dark, waiting to explode and wreak havoc. Fortunately, Daphne had plenty to keep herself busy and distracted. Between helping at Bernie's Blooms, going to Lamaze classes with Olivia, and being a mom to Mabel, she had little time to lament over her upcoming doomsday birthday and that gloomy statistic, which probably wasn't even legit.

As a child Daphne had always loved having a birthday that fell just four days before Valentine's Day. It was like a double-dip ice cream cone. But now it felt like a bad omen. The sooner she got past these dates the better.

It didn't help matters that Sabrina was obsessed with Valentine's Day and romance. And, Daphne couldn't disagree that despite the wintry weather, love seemed to be in the air. Sabrina knew for a fact that Wally planned to propose to Marie, because he had asked Sabrina to help him pick a ring.

And everyone knew that Mick and Julianna had set a date for a mid-April wedding. "Because that's when the spring flowers will be at their prime," Mick had told Daphne a few days ago when they bumped into each other. And even this morning, Sabrina had been giddily dancing around Daphne's kitchen, almost certain that Ricardo was going to "pop the question" to her on V-Day too.

Daphne didn't want to sound like the Valentine's Day scrooge, especially since Mabel was so excited about making Valentines for her entire class. But Daphne was literally counting the days until it would be past her. Less than a week to her birthday and then four more days until Valentine's was over with. She could hardly wait. And so far, no one except for Dad, who usually forgot anyway, and Olivia, who was sworn to silence, knew Daphne had a birthday coming up. And the only reason Olivia seemed aware of Daphne's birthday was because she was hoping Bernadette would come early and be born on that day. Not even Sabrina or Mabel knew it was this week, and that was exactly how Daphne planned to keep it.

But Daphne was trying to keep these troublesome thoughts at bay as she rewound a roll of red florist ribbon that had been pulled too quickly. Olivia would probably be going through a lot of this when Valentine's Day started up in a few days. But for now, the shop was relatively slow.

"You seem deep in thought."

Daphne looked up from the ribbon bolt to see Jake gazing at her. "Sorry." She continued winding the slippery ribbon around, wondering if she should've checked her teeth after the spinach salad she'd had for lunch. "Can I help you?"

He made a crooked smile that sent an unexpected tingle

down her spine. "It's just me, Daphne. You don't need to be so formal."

"Sorry. I'm still kind of new at this." She set the bolt down and smiled. "So what can I help you with?"

"It's my mother's birthday this weekend. I nearly forgot. But I'd like to send her something."

"This weekend?" Daphne's birthday was Saturday. "What day?"

"Saturday."

Daphne simply nodded.

"And she'll be sixty, which is kind of a milestone. I wanted something beyond the traditional card and bouquet of flowers."

"Your mother is only sixty?" Daphne was surprised, since her dad was in his seventies and she knew Jake was her senior by a few years, but mostly she was trying to wrap her head around the fact that she and Jake's mother shared a birthday. How weird!

"Mom was pretty young when I was born," he explained.

"Right. So do you have anything specific in mind for her?"

"Not really. It's not as if she needs anything. I just figured I'd look around and if I don't find something that seems fitting, I can always just do flowers. They'd make it to Chicago by Saturday, wouldn't they?"

"Absolutely. I don't usually arrange the flowers myself, for which you can be grateful." She chuckled to remember the tulips and irises she'd fussed over yesterday when a gentleman felt certain he couldn't wait for Olivia. "I've made a couple of attempts, but I don't quite have Olivia's magic touch. But if you go with flowers, I can take your order and Olivia will get it assembled and sent out before closing this afternoon. I mean, if you don't find something else for her."

"Perfect. I heard you're volunteering for Olivia...to help her through her pregnancy. That's very generous of you, Daphne."

"Olivia is an old friend. I'm happy to help. And, hey, this is a pretty cool place to work. Plus I get to write on my novel when there aren't customers, which is actually most of the time."

"Great setup."

Daphne led Jake over to the gardening section. "These gift baskets for gardeners just came in for spring. I think they're pretty nice." She held one up that she liked. "Does your mom garden?"

"Not particularly. She has *people* who do that for her." He made a slight smirk, almost like he didn't quite approve of having "people," and she suddenly remembered him saying how his mom had married a very wealthy man when he was young.

"Right. We have these decorative plates and platters." She picked up a bright colored plate. "If your mom likes a more modern sort of décor."

He shook his head. "She's pretty traditional."

She showed him several other options, then stopped by the candle section. "We have some lovely scented candles that just came in. Nice springy colors." She selected a large pale green column. "This is verbena, which I don't usually like, but this one has a nice fresh fragrance."

He sniffed. "Not bad."

"And the candle holder selection is pretty good too." She set the candle in a glass and metal candle holder. "You could put decorative rocks on the bottom to secure it. And I'd pack it carefully to make sure it doesn't break."

He nodded with actual interest now. "That's a really good idea, Daphne."

"And I can wrap it up really nicely. Olivia's got fabulous gift wrap to choose from. And even if it doesn't go out until tomorrow morning, it should easily make Chicago by Friday."

"I think you've solved my problem."

"Great." She picked up the candle and candle holder, carrying it back to the counter. "I'll just write this up then get it ready. Do you want me to add the rocks I told you about? I think they'd look pretty."

"I trust your judgment, Daphne."

"Thanks." She felt a warm rush as she began to write down the purchases on the small pad like she'd been taught to do.

"Jenna has been missing you." Jake selected a birthday card from the rack on the counter, laying it down beside the candle and things.

She looked up. "You know, I was just thinking the same thing last weekend. I've been missing her. In fact, Mabel went through a bit of Jenna withdrawal a couple of weeks ago."

"So you're really not going out with Harrison anymore?" His brow was slightly creased.

"No." She looked back down. "I haven't seen him for more than two weeks. It's over."

"I'm sorry. And he seemed like such a nice guy too."

"He is a nice guy." She looked back up. "But please don't be sorry on my behalf, Jake. I'm the one who broke it off." She slowly shook her head. "Sabrina just about disowned me for a while. She was so mad that I'd let one get away. But, honestly, I just couldn't see the point."

"See the point?" He looked puzzled.

"In dating someone I knew I couldn't marry."

"So you knew that for certain? That you *didn't* want to marry him?"

"Why else would I break it off?" She controlled herself from rolling her eyes. And before he could respond, the bell on the door jingled, signaling there was another customer in the shop. The afternoon rush.

"Good afternoon," she called out cheerfully. "Let me know if I can help you with anything." Turning back to Jake she smiled stiffly. "How would you like to pay for this, Mr. McPheeters?"

"Oh." He reached for his wallet, handing her a card. "Thanks."

"And if you write down your mother's address here," she slipped a card across the counter, "we can have it shipped out this afternoon. You don't even need to stand around and wait."

"What service."

As he filled out the address, she rang up his purchases then waited as he signed the receipt. "That should take care of it. Anything else I can get for you today?" She smiled brightly, wondering why she was acting so oddly around him. Why was she nervous? Perhaps because she felt her heart leaning forward...once again...and it made her uneasy.

"Yes." He nodded. "*Coffee.*"

She tilted her head to one side. "You know, serving coffee to customers is not a bad idea. I'll mention that to Olivia."

"No. I mean coffee *with me.*"

She tried to appear nonchalant, although her heart rate was increasing. "Are you asking me to coffee?"

He nodded. "I am."

She twisted her mouth to one side, glancing at the elderly woman examining the kitchen linens. "Are you asking to meet me for business? As your client? Or are you asking me on a date?" Okay, she knew this was very bold on her part, but she wasn't sure she cared. She was so tired of this cat and mouse game that they'd been playing for months.

"I am asking you on a coffee date," he said evenly. "Nothing to do with business."

The elderly woman looked their way, clearly interested in this conversation.

"Oh...when, uh, were you thinking?"

"Today."

She took in a slow breath. "I get off work at two. But Mabel gets out of school at 2:45 and I usually walk to meet her."

"Maybe Auntie Sabrina would like to meet Mabel today. They both might enjoy that."

"That's true."

"So, is that a yes?"

She smiled. "I guess so—well, depending on Sabrina."

"I'll be planning on it unless I hear differently from you. So Red River at two-ish?"

She simply nodded, then he tipped his head and left.

Daphne wasn't quite sure what to think as she texted Sabrina about Mabel. Had she just pressured Jake for a date? Or had he asked her?

"That Jake McPheeters is a nice gentleman," the elderly customer said as she placed some kitchen towels on the counter. "And a fine lawyer too. I highly recommend him to anyone who asks."

"Yes, so do I." Daphne rang the towels up, took the woman's cash, and counted out change. "May I ask you a question?"

"Certainly." The woman beamed at her.

"Did Mr. McPheeters ask *me* out on a date? Or did I ask *him*?"

The woman laughed. "He asked you out, dear. How could you miss that?"

Daphne giggled as she wrapped the linens in tissue paper. "Oh, I don't know. I think perhaps I miss a lot of things."

"Well, if I were thirty years younger and Jake McPheeters was asking me out, I would *run not walk* down to the coffee shop."

Daphne handed her the bag.

"Good luck, honey."

Daphne thanked her then went back to preparing the package for Jake's mother. As she carefully padded the items in the box, she was tempted to slip in a note saying that they were birthday partners but knew that was pushing it. Next she wrapped the box in the most luxurious paper, a rich floral pattern in spring colors, tying it with a rose colored satin ribbon and bow, tucking in some sprigs of rosemary and lavender like she'd seen Olivia do. As she carefully secured Jake's card, she knew it looked beautiful. Even the woman who had everything would be impressed. Next, she packed it into another box, making sure that the packing peanuts were evenly distributed and finally, she put on the UPS label.

Sabrina texted back to confirm she was happy to get Mabel. And then, seeing it was nearly two and the shop was void of customers, Daphne made a quick dash into the employee restroom, checking her teeth and smoothing her hair and retouching her lip gloss. She was dressed somewhat casually in jeans and boots, but at least she had on her sage green cashmere sweater and a pretty scarf.

As she emerged from the restroom, Olivia arrived, looking more rested than she'd appeared this morning. "I feel guilty," she told Daphne. "About all I did was sleep today. But when I consider how many times I got up last night, I think I needed it."

Daphne laughed. "Hey, you should probably enjoy getting some down time. In a couple more weeks you won't be able to nap whenever you want."

"They say new moms should sleep when their baby sleeps. I plan to cash in on that." Olivia moved the UPS package to the end of the counter. "You seem happy."

Daphne shrugged, suppressing the urge to giggle like a school girl.

"What's up?"

So Daphne told her about Jake's coffee invitation. "I'm trying not to get too excited. But for so long, Jake and I have been like ships in the night. You know? It will almost seem like we're connecting, like our relationship is about to go somewhere, and the next thing I know something derails us."

"What's derailed you?"

"A bit of everything." Daphne thought. "A boyfriend from my past. Some crazy blind dates. Mabel—and then her uncle Daniel. Lately it had been Harrison. But, like I told you, that's over and done with."

"You've been a busy girl."

Daphne rolled her eyes. "Tell me about it." She sighed. "I just wonder if this could finally be our chance."

"That'd be amazing, Daphne. Jake's such a great guy. I can imagine you two together."

"I feel like I've learned a lot about dating and men this past year. Ever since moving back to Appleton." She almost mentioned Aunt Dee's motivation, but stopped herself. "Anyway, I think I'm tired of some of the games. I feel like I'm ready to be more honest about my feelings. I'm ready to get serious. You know?"

"Good for you." Olivia patted Daphne's back. "Go get 'em, girl."

Daphne thanked her and, holding her head high, headed out. But as she walked down Main Street, she said a silent, simple prayer. *If this is meant to be, let it be. If it is not meant to be, please, nip it in the bud! Amen.*

Chapter 28

A s Daphne passed the various businesses, waving to people she recognized along the way, she felt both surprisingly determined and a little bit nervous. If she was really going on a date, she wanted to behave like this was a date. No more playing like she thought Jake was really her "big brother" or her "legal advisor" or even "just a friend." No more keeping him at a cool arm's length. No more skirting around the big issues—like she didn't care one whit that he was representing Aunt Dee's will. She knew Jake well enough to know he would never marry someone for money. Besides, from what she could see, he had enough money. And besides that, she trusted him. To be honest, she always had. And, perhaps more importantly, so had Aunt Dee.

Certainly, she didn't want to push Jake into something he wasn't ready for. She didn't want to pressure him into a deeper relationship, if he only wanted to be friends. But like the nice woman had confirmed, Jake had asked her out. And, based on that, Daphne intended to behave if she were on a real date.

She glanced up at the gray, cloudy sky, feeling the heaviness of impending rain in the air, which meant that her hair was probably already getting wavy. Nothing she could do about that. Besides, Jake had seen her wild hair before. Hadn't seemed to bother him. She felt amused at her insecurities. Shouldn't a woman of almost thirty-five have more confidence? And yet she knew that she had much more confidence than she'd had when she first moved to Appleton. The uptight, insecure New Yorker almost seemed like a stranger to her now. And she liked who she'd become during this past year...she looked forward to who she was becoming. In fact, she'd never felt so comfortable in her own skin before.

As she pushed open the door to Red River, the warmth and the aroma of freshly ground coffee enveloped her. Unbuttoning her trench coat, she spied Jake coming toward her.

"I hope you don't mind that I ordered for you," Jake closed the door behind her, nodding to the line of customers at the counter. "I just got your usual latte, but I can still change it."

"Perfect," she told him.

"I didn't want to be presumptuous, but I wanted to beat the crowd. Plus I wasn't sure how much time you'd have."

"Sabrina was glad to get Mabel." She removed her coat, slinging it over her arm. "So I'm not on a real deadline."

"I got us a table." He pointed to where his jacket and briefcase held a table in back. "I'll just pick up our order and meet you."

As she walked to the somewhat private table, she thought that this really was feeling like a date. She hadn't been delusional after all. She watched as Jake came to the table with a tray. He looked so handsome and, unless she was imagining it, *hopeful*.

"I got you a lemon square." He set the plate in front of her, laying a fork and napkin next to it. "I remember you used to like those."

She smiled. "Thank you. I still do."

"Or if you're craving chocolate, feel free." He set a rich looking brownie with nuts down, followed by the coffees.

"Tempting. Thanks."

Jake sat down and then just gazed at her. "So how are you, Daphne? What, besides breaking up with Harrison and helping out Olivia, have you been up to these last few weeks?"

She gave him a quick lowdown on her life, the ordinary goings-on at home with Mabel, attending Lamaze classes with Olivia, and how she longed for some real spring weather. "Although the daffodils are coming up at my house. Their sunny yellow faces feel so spring-like. And hopefully the tulips won't be far behind. As I recall they usually bloom right around my—my... ." She stopped herself.

"Your what?" He looked curious.

She waved her hand, feeling embarrassed. "Oh, nothing."

He frowned slightly. "Do you know how much it frustrates me when you do that?"

"Do what?"

"Hold back something."

She felt a wave of guilt and realization. "Do I do that?"

He nodded. "Oh, yeah...you sometimes do."

She considered this, remembering her new resolve not to play games and to be honest. "I'm sorry, Jake." She sighed. "It's a bad habit I have—especially when I'm feeling a little insecure or like I'm on shaky ground."

"Is that how I make you feel?" His brow creased.

"No. Not really. I mean I don't think *you* make me feel that way. I think *I* make me feel that way. I suppose it's because I think so highly of you, Jake." She looked into his eyes. "It makes me a little nervous."

"You think highly of me?" He seemed slightly blindsided by this. "Really?"

She smiled and nodded. "I always have."

"Well, that makes me feel better. Sometimes I'm worried that you just see me as a great big pain in the neck."

"If I act like that, I don't mean to."

"And it's understandable. I have interfered in your life...a lot."

"You've helped me a lot too."

"Thanks." He sighed. "That's a relief you see it that way."

"And when I walked down here today, I was determined to be more forthcoming with you. I mean, it's not like I'm hiding anything. But I do sometimes feel guarded around you. Afraid I'll say the wrong thing. You know?"

"I can understand that. To be honest, I probably feel that way around you sometimes too."

She blinked. "Really? You always seem so self-assured."

He laughed. "Well, I learned long ago that's the best way to cover up my own insecurities. But sometimes I probably take it too far. And when it comes to you, I'm afraid I've stuck my foot in my mouth more than a few times."

"Not that we're counting. And my biggest regret is giving you the wrong impression a few times." She explained about the Christmas Eve party when Sabrina had caught Daphne by surprise when she'd invited Harrison. "And he seemed to think he was my personal date for the night," Daphne said with regret. "And you and Jenna left early and I felt like I'd lost another chance with you."

"I'll admit I got the wind knocked out of me when I saw you and Harrison coming down the stairs. You looked so beautiful in that purple dress. And Harrison was holding your hand. Well, I guess you could say it got my goat." He took a sip of coffee. "I'm afraid it affected my manners. Sorry."

"No need to apologize. I felt terrible about it that night. Like I'd blown my last chance with you." She felt herself being pulled into his espresso brown eyes.

"Really? You felt like that?" He set down his mug. "I just figured that Harrison had the inside track. And, really, it made sense. As your attorney, I knew I should be happy for you. But at the same time, well...as Jenna would say, I was pretty bummed."

Daphne slowly shook her head, resisting the urge to pinch herself. Was this really happening? Were she and Jake really having this conversation? Or was she just daydreaming? Spinning a tale in her writer's brain?

"Do you know what a relief it is to have this conversation?" Jake asked.

"Yes." She held up her coffee mug. "Here's to us having a more open and honest relationship."

"Hear, hear." He clicked her mug. "So what was it you were about to say about the tulips blooming around your—*your what?*"

She laughed. "My birthday. There, I said it. For some reason I've been dreading my birthday this year. I wanted to pretend like I wasn't turning a year older."

"When's your birthday?"

She wrinkled her nose. "Same day as your mother's."

"Seriously?"

She nodded. "Yep."

"But why are you dreading it?"

She grimaced. "Really? The truth?"

"Didn't we just toast to that?"

She couldn't help but smile as she imagined him cross-examining a witness. "You know, Jake, you'd make a good lawyer."

"So I've been told. But why are you dreading your birthday, Daphne?"

So she explained about the *Dear Daphne* letter and the quote about thirty-five-year-olds and terrorists. Of course, he just laughed, dismissing it as nonsense.

"Oh, I know it sounds silly—especially when I say it out loud. But considering my situation and, as Sabrina pointed out this morning, *that I go through men like Kleenex*—those were *her* words. Well, that dumb quote combined with my upcoming birthday...it's a little disturbing. As a result, I've been keeping news of my birthday under wraps. I'd appreciate it if you did too."

"I think it's sad to conceal your birthday, but your secret's safe with me. And I want to go on record stating that I think that thirty-five-year-old business is ludicrous. Especially in your case, Daphne. Ever since I've known you, you've had men flocking about. And how many proposals have you had? You've been such a hot commodity that I've given up on you several times."

She couldn't help but laugh. "You know what's totally weird

is that all those years in New York—straight out of college until last year—besides my pathetic relationship with Ryan, I probably had three dates. And not one proposal."

"See what I'm saying?" He forked into the brownie. "I'm guessing you hadn't even hit your prime yet. If you ask me, you're the kind of woman who will get better with age."

Daphne didn't know how to respond, but she was so touched that she felt slightly teary. "Thanks," she mumbled. "That means a lot."

For a moment, they just sat there, looking at each other. But it was one of those moments in time—the kind that Daphne never wanted to see end. As she swallowed a bite of lemon square, she felt so happy that she couldn't help but just smile.

"So, tell me, what's Miss Mabel up to these days? Jenna isn't the only one missing that little girl."

Relieved to talk about something other than themselves and their feelings, Daphne filled him in on the valentines she and Mabel had started to painstakingly create last night. "Mabel wasn't content to get the kind of cards that you just sign and stuff in an envelope. She wanted to cut out hearts and use doilies and glitter and stickers and all sorts of things. It's good that we got an early start. At this rate, I hope we can get done in time for Valentine's Day next week."

They continued visiting, catching up with lots of things, and before long it was nearly five. Daphne didn't even know where the time had gone. As much as she hated to bring it to an end, she knew it was time to say goodbye.

"I need to get home to Mabel," she told him. "But I've had a really lovely time."

"And you wouldn't mind doing it again?"

"I'd *love* to do it again."

"Have you made any plans for Saturday night yet?" His eyes twinkled with merriment.

"You mean for my...?"

"Your birthday," he finished for her.

"No, no plans."

"Can I take you out then? To celebrate that you're coming into your prime of womanhood?"

She laughed. "That sounds fabulous. Thanks, Jake."

"It's a date then." He reached for her hand, giving it a squeeze that sent warm tingles down her spine as he helped her into her coat.

As they walked through the coffee shop, a man in a business suit greeted Jake, asking if he had time to chat. "In a minute," Jake told him as he escorted her to the door. "I'm really looking forward to Saturday night," he whispered into her ear, sending even more shivers down her spine. "Thanks for seeing me today."

"Thank you." She smiled happily. "I enjoyed it immensely."

As Daphne strolled home, she felt impervious to the dark clouds still gathering overhead. In fact, she almost felt like she was walking on clouds. And the cool breeze didn't bother her at all, because an electric sort of warmth was rushing through her.

It seemed like life was about to change for her. Indeed, it had already changed. Just like that—in the twinkling of an eye—she had gone from feeling a terrorist attack more likely than marriage to finding true love. Because, as she turned down Huckleberry Lane, she felt almost certain that Jake was the one. Like he'd always been the one. But she'd either been too busy or too distracted or just too darn insecure to know it.

Better yet, it seemed as if Jake realized it too. At least she hoped so.

As she reached the old Victorian house that she and Aunt Dee, and now Mabel, had loved and called home, she observed the raindrops pelting the sturdy yellow daffodils. She hadn't even noticed it was raining! But she paused to admire them, realizing that she and Aunt Dee had planted those bulbs many years ago.

She looked over to where the tulips had come up last week, with their thick, bright green leaves stretching optimistically toward the sky, even though cold weather still loomed ahead. Their tightly closed, oblong buds bobbed in the rain, as if to say, "It's not time yet." She smiled to realize that she had helped to plant those bulbs too, back at a time when she never could've imagined how her life would be decades later.

And then she noticed that one of the tulips, a tall sturdy one that was planted near the sidewalk, was just starting to open up. She knelt down to study the brave flower, seeing that its petals were a luscious shade of coral, and that it promised to yield a beautiful bloom in a day or two. Or perhaps just in time for her birthday. And as she stood, she thought she could hear Aunt Dee speaking to her, saying those old familiar words that she hadn't heard in years. *"Well done, dear girl, well done!"*